A satirical smile curved his lips. "Being alone with me is a problem? Now why is that, I wonder? Could it be you don't trust yourself, Miss Gower?"

His arms went around her, pulling her against him. "You know you love me, and I love you," he said in a husky voice. "Marry me."

The breath caught in her throat as his head descended till his lips were just brushing hers. His lips firmed in a ruthless kiss that set her head reeling. She pushed him away and stood panting.

"No, Dick. We must rescue Pronto first."

"You're right. But after we settled this business, Deirdre—"

"I haven't definitely said yes."

"You said 'not here'—that implies—"

"That implies uncertainty," she pointed out, and before he could say more, she walked away.

Also by Joan Smith
Published by Fawcett Books:

BABE
AURORA
LACE FOR MILADY
VALERIE
THE BLUE DIAMOND
REPRISE
WILES OF A STRANGER
LOVER'S VOWS
RELUCTANT BRIDE
LADY MADELINE'S FOLLY
LOVE BADE ME WELCOME
MIDNIGHT MASQUERADE
ROYAL REVELS
THE DEVIOUS DUCHESS
TRUE LADY
BATH BELLES
STRANGE CAPERS
A COUNTRY WOOING
LOVE'S HARBINGER
LETTERS TO A LADY
COUNTRY FLIRT

LARCENOUS LADY

Joan Smith

FAWCETT CREST • NEW YORK

A Fawcett Crest Book
Published by Ballantine Books
Copyright ● 1987 by Joan Smith

Library of Congress Catalog Card Number: 87-91024

ISBN 0-449-21261-0

Manufactured in the United States of America

First Edition: January 1988

Chapter One

Deirdre Gower sat at the window, staring with glazed eyes at the frozen landscape beyond. She looked frozen herself as she sat, immobile. Her sullen gray eyes mirrored the gray skies glowering down on the meadow, where tufts of yellowed grass pushed through the remains of snow. Where had all the snow gone? There had been a foot of it last week, and no thaw or sun to evaporate it. She was struck with the fancy that Belami had taken the sun away with him. Belami. A wan smile tugged at her lips, completing the picture of dejection. With her black hair bound in a bun and her pale face silhouetted against the wall, Deirdre looked like a delicate cameo. But inside that still facade, a storm of passion brewed.

Tall, dark, dashing, intelligent, *impatient* Lord Belami. It seemed a miracle she had won the affection of the most dashing bachelor in all of England, but somehow she had. And now she had lost him forever. One could hardly blame him for leaving. She had promised to marry him right away. Was it her fault that Aunt Charney had developed pneumonia? You couldn't desert a sick aunt who had raised you as her own daughter. And Dick had wanted to run off to Italy for the honeymoon besides. She would have married him if he'd agreed to remain at Fernvale till Aunt Charney recovered.

The temperature in the room hovered in the high fifties,

but Deirdre's cheeks were warm at the memory of their parting. "A honeymoon in this house?" he had asked, as though she were an imbecile to suggest it. "I'd rather honeymoon in Hades! Charney would have her nose at the keyhole—providing she ever condescended to leave us alone at all."

"Dick, I can't desert her. You must see that."

"It's only a head cold. You have dozens of relatives who could stay with her. My own mother would be happy to do it. You've put the wedding off three times already. You *promised* me, Deirdre. This is it. It's now—or never."

The memory of those black eyes burning into her still turned Deirdre to crystal. She felt as if she would shatter at a touch when Dick mounted his high horse and turned imperious. She should have agreed, but she knew that if he were in front of her now, making his impossible demand, she'd say no again. She'd done the right thing, but it was hard to know that while she paid for her rectitude in the frozen loneliness of Fernvale, Dick was in London celebrating his freedom with a string of flirtations.

Abovestairs in her canopied bed, the dowager duchess of Charney hollered for another blanket. She was feeling remarkably better after a month's respite from that noble guttersnipe, Lord Belami. Her chest no longer felt as though Saint Paul's were resting on it. She secretly rose from her bed every day now and walked around her room for half an hour to strengthen her legs. The major deterrent to her recovery was concern for her niece, who came like a ghost to the room each afternoon to read in a sepulchral voice. Outside of herself, the one person in the world for whom the duchess harbored a feeling softer than hatred was her niece. Deirdre had toed the line nicely in the matter of Belami, and she must be rewarded, before she went off her looks entirely and dwindled to a spinster.

She noticed Deirdre always read books about Italy, where she and Belami had planned to jaunt off on their honeymoon. It sounded like a place of some interest. The warm temperature would heal her lungs, the accommodations were not at all expensive, and wine—her own weakness—must be virtually free. There would, of course, be a bunch of foreigners speaking some incomprehensible mumbo jumbo but one need have nothing to do with the local riffraff. Best of all, Belami would not be there. One heard quite shocking stories of his carrying on in London. To take Deirdre to London for the spring season would be hell for the girl.

The duchess regularly enlivened her dull days by creating little schemes and mysteries. On this occasion, she decided to make the travel arrangements in secret. Many letters were sent off to a travel agent in London and replies received. "I am corresponding with an expert on pneumonia," she told her niece, who believed it. The girl hadn't the gumption to steam open the letters and see what was really going on. Obviously it would be a crime to hand such an innocent over to a rake like Belami.

Not till the day of departure was near did the duchess rise up from her deathbed like Lazarus and announce, "I have decided to take you to Italy, Deirdre. We shall be leaving on Monday. Pray tell Haskins to pack up our trunks."

The secrecy was worth it. The girl nearly swallowed her tongue in shock. It was better than a raree-show to see her stare and stammer. If a tear moistened the old lady's eyes when Deirdre pitched herself into her arms, it was blinked away too swiftly to be detected. How Fernvale rang with merry laughter then. Especially belowstairs, where the servants felt they had been released from Newgate.

"Well, is it to be Covent Garden or Lady Fiona's ball or the Addisons' rout?" Pronto Pilgrim asked his companion as they sat together in Belami's elegant saloon. "And don't say all three, Dick, for I'm worn to a shadow trotting so hard. Take a look at this jacket," he demanded, and pulled his black jacket out in front of him. It was true his ungainly stomach had shrunk an inch. He was now only stout, not fat. He straightened his narrow shoulders and puffed.

It bothered Pronto to see his friend so deranged. "We're going to have the time of our lives," the poor old sprout had promised when they went pelting off to London after the wedding was called off—again. Looked like they meant it this time. A month had passed since Deirdre jilted him. But if Dick called running around to every party in town a good time, Pronto did not. One party a night was what he called a good time. Meet up with a couple of the bucks, find a nice quiet corner where the hostess didn't plague you to stand up with all the ugly leftover girls, have a few hands of cards and a couple of wets.

"None of them," Dick answered.

"Eh?" Pronto demanded, and leaped like a gaffed fish. "Does that mean you've got a case?" he asked hopefully.

Dick was a famous hand for solving other people's mysteries, with a little help from Pronto. Murder, robbery, blackmail—all in a day's work to the team of Pilgrim and Belami, gentlemen investigators. Pronto went on staring and deducing. A case wouldn't leave Dick's face hanging so lax. No, sir, when he had a case in hand, he was like a squirrel, scurrying around for clues to deduce from. Or like a dog chasing his tail.

"Dreamer! Don't I wish I had a case," Belami said. "No, I've done some deep thinking, and I've decided I'm a jackass."

Pronto made a puffing noise of disagreement. "Only natural. Bowled for a duck three times hand running. Must feel a bit like a discarded boot, I daresay, but not a jackass."

"Yes, I am," Belami insisted. "In a short while Charney will bring Deirdre to London again. I meant to be engaged when they arrived, and get married within a week. I'm still letting that curst woman lead me."

4

"Charney could lead devils in hell."

"I meant the other curst woman. Why should I marry to spite Deirdre Gower?"

"Marry?" Pronto asked. "You haven't given yourself time to say 'Good day,' let alone 'Will you marry me?' We're in and out of all the parties like a pair of darts."

"I wanted to see all the women," Belami explained. "I wanted to be engaged to *the* most beautiful woman in town, but the fact is, I don't want to get married at all."

"Wise choice," Pronto said, and raised the bottle of wine. "Does that mean we get to stay home?" he asked hopefully.

Belami lifted his head and smiled. There was a peculiar charm in Belami's smile. One mobile brow lifted in an arch and his dark eyes flashed. Demmed handsome rascal when all was said and done, Pronto thought. A regular Adonis, with that tall build and the best-cut jackets in London. He was curst with a broken nose himself. His frame stood five feet, six inches in height, slightly less in width. Nice hair though, he modestly allowed. A deep chestnut brown, luxuriantly waved.

"Stay home? No, my friend. It means we go to Italy as I had planned all along. I had the itinerary arranged for Deirdre and myself. Why should I abandon the trip?"

Pronto nodded pensively. "I'd been looking forward to it. Not that you invited me," he mentioned, but between them, it was pretty well acknowledged that he'd tag along. "Italy, eh? Daresay the place is overrun with Italians and Roman ruins. Other than that, I haven't a word to say against it. At least there won't be any snow. Réal won't care for that," he warned. "Always talking about the snow mountains in Canada."

"Réal will love it. As long as there are extremes of one sort or another for him to ignore, my groom will be in his element. I'll get the brochures and maps."

Belami went to his office. Pronto noticed he didn't drag his heels this time. He wasn't at all sure he wanted to go

5

to Italy, but Dick needed a change. Clever as Dick was, he didn't realize he'd gone into a decline. If Charney brought Deirdre to town, the two of them would get together again. Another bust-up, and another period of depression that tried to masquerade as gaiety. He was glad to see Belami was beginning to recover. He couldn't take much more fun.

At Dover, the duchess was the first person on the ship leaving for Calais, and Lord Belami was the last. While she derided her private apartment and ordered a bottle of wine, Belami stopped to buy a newspaper from the paper wagon and nearly missed the ship entirely. He hopped aboard just as the gangplank was being drawn up. A stiff wind made the deck unpleasant, so Belami and Pronto went below.

"A hot coffee would hit the spot," Pronto suggested, and ordered a pot.

Belami opened the newspaper and perused it while they drank. "Listen to this, Pronto," he said. "We should have come down to Dover a few days early. The Jalbert gang was here, but got away."

"Jalbert gang?" Pronto asked, frowning. "Is that the bunch of smashers I've been hearing about?"

"That's right. They're counterfeiters—gold coin, not bills. They have such excellent dies you can't tell to look at the money that it's fake. They make guineas with an iron slug inside, covered with gold so that the surface isn't slippery. Counterfeit coins usually feel greasy—if they're made from an alloy, I mean. The color is a little off as well."

"How would you know you'd got one?" Pronto asked, and rooted in his pockets for coins.

"The weight would be short. Iron's lighter than gold—it has a density of about eight, whereas gold is high, around nineteen. In a small coin, however, you mightn't notice the difference if you weren't paying much attention."

"Have I got one of the phonies?" Pronto asked, handing Belami three coins.

Belami hefted them, bounced them on the table, where they appeared to ring true. "They seem genuine to me," he said, and emptied his own pockets of coin. He had only one guinea, and bounced it on the table. A quick frown creased his brow. It had a less ringing sound than Pronto's money. He picked up one of Pronto's guineas and his own, hefting one in either hand. "By God, I've got one of the fakes," he exclaimed. "Mine's lighter than yours."

It seemed odd to Pronto that this should bring a smile to his friend's face. "Daresay you can pass it off in Italy, where they ain't so used to English coinage. The agent said they take any coin, so long as it's gold or silver."

"I'll keep it for a souvenir of my gullibility. I wonder where I picked that coin up," Belami said, thinking back over the past few days. "I believe it was at the inn at Dover. I paid the reckoning with a five-pound note this morning, and got this in change. I even saw the man who gave it to the clerk. You remember the old fellow with the pipe?"

"Nope. The Jalbert gang must have been at the inn."

"Not necessarily," Belami said. "They'd be more likely to pass the counterfeits off at some place other than where they were staying. I almost regret having left. The Jalbert gang got away, you know."

"Then you can catch them when we come back," Pronto decided. "Meanwhile, keep the coin for a good-luck piece."

"It would only bring counterfeit good luck," Belami said, and laughed. "Of course till the coin's subjected to the Trial of the Pyx, I'm only guessing it's a fake."

"Picks?" Pronto asked suspiciously. "What the deuce have picks got to do with it?"

"Not the digging tools," Belami corrected. "I mean p-y-x."

7

"Ain't that something in the Roman church?" Pronto asked.

"It holds the consecrated host, but the word only means box. At the Royal Mint, it's the box that holds the specimen gold and silver coins for testing. The Goldsmiths' Company carry out tests for purity and weight of the coins."

Pronto was aware of his friend's propensity to deliver a lecture at the drop of a hat and swiftly changed the subject. "This coffee's making me sick," he complained. Even as he spoke, he noticed Belami was rocking to and fro in his chair. "Stand still," he said, scowling.

"It's the ship that's rolling," Belami replied. "Rather heavy weather. I feared we wouldn't be leaving today at all."

Pronto's pink face blanched to white, and he wobbled to his feet. "Believe I'll just have a lie-down. Lucky if I don't flash the hash." He left and Belami strolled to the common room to see if anyone else was still up and about. He took his newspaper with him in case he was destined to be alone.

The room was thin of company, but one elderly gentleman sat at a table smoking a meerschaum pipe and having a brandy as he perused some newspapers. Belami recognized the man he had just mentioned to Pronto and went to greet him.

"Good day, sir. May I join you?" Belami asked.

"I'd be delighted for the company," the man answered.

Belami glanced at him and wondered who he might be. A stocky man in his early sixties with gray hair and a ruddy complexion. He was obviously a gentleman, and obviously not a gentleman of the first stare. The nap was worn from his jacket, and his linens were the worse for wear. A bachelor, probably.

"Are you traveling alone?" Belami asked, as he took up a seat.

"Aye, I'm traveling through life alone. The name's Captain Styger, late of His Majesty's Navy."

"Belami," Lord Belami said, and offered his hand. "That accounts for your sea legs. Does a brandy help?"

"A brandy never hurt anyone, at sea or ashore. Allow me to treat you."

Styger called for another brandy for himself and one for his companion. They fell into conversation. "I'm off to see the world," Captain Styger said. "Thus far I've only seen ports and shores. Now I mean to land and walk on foreign grounds."

"Where were you during the Napoleon campaign?" Belami said.

"I'm afraid I captained a desk at Plymouth during those crucial days," Captain Styger admitted sadly. "I took a ball in the leg during the early French blockade and they locked me up in an office."

"The infamous Orders in Council." Belami nodded. "What's your opinion of them, as a naval man?"

"Orders are orders," the man replied vaguely.

Belami was surprised. Most naval officers would rant against them for an hour. "Did you actually land at America?"

"America? No, I didn't get there."

A few more vague answers were enough to show Belami the man was no officer. He had apparently promoted himself from crewman to captain upon retirement. Belami's next item of interest was the counterfeit coin. When the brandy arrived, he said, "If you're paying with a guinea, I'd like to see it first. I got a counterfeit coin at Dover— indirectly through you, sir. You might have had contact with the infamous Jalbert gang. Do you remember where you got this guinea?" He showed Styger the coin.

"What's that you say?" Styger exclaimed, and looked around in alarm. "A counterfeit coin?" He looked so worried Belami took the notion his money was scarce, and the loss of a guinea a matter of some importance. Belami

9

paid for the brandy himself and said, "Could you describe the man you got this guinea from?"

"Why—I—I really don't recall. How do you know it came from my pocket?"

"You were right in front of me at the desk this morning. Do you recall where you got the coin?"

Styger shook his head. "I was in a game of cards last night with half-a-dozen gentlemen. Tall and short, dark and fair—it might have come from any of them. Why do you ask, sir? Are you a government agent?" He looked askance at Belami's elegant jacket.

"Oh, no, just a concerned citizen."

"Ah. Well, as I rooked you, let me buy the coin back with genuine money."

"I'd prefer to keep it," Belami said, and turned the conversation to other topics.

It wasn't the brandy that did the mischief. Belami rather thought it was the man's pipe tobacco that was turning his stomach queasy. When the ship gave a lurch that sent their drinks sloshing to the table, Belami rose and said, "I'm going to see how my friend's making out. I left him in the cabin nursing a bout of seasickness. Nice talking to you, sir."

"My pleasure. Do you mind if I have a look at your newspaper?" he asked, as Belami left it on the table.

"Help yourself. It's pretty wet from that spilt brandy."

"It'll soon dry," the captain said, and picked it up.

By the time Belami reached his cabin, he scarcely had the strength to open the door. He lay on his bunk, wondering why he had ever left firm land.

On the other side of the ship, the duchess of Charney was asking herself much the same thing as she huddled into the blankets. Deirdre Gower, on the other hand, was as lively as a cricket. It was the first time she had ever left England. Europe spread before her like a fairyland. Paris, Venice, Rome. She'd come home a world-weary sophisticate, dropping phrases in foreign languages. She'd meet princes and potentates—perhaps she'd even have a few affairs.

When she returned to London, dripping with the glamor of foreign travel and wearing risqué gowns, she'd smile condescendingly on Lord Belami and whatever provincial lady he had married. Then he'd be sorry. He'd be trotting at her heels like a pup, and she'd dismiss him carelessly.

"Deirdre, bring the bucket!" the duchess called, interrupting her niece's reverie. And Deirdre brought the bucket.

Chapter Two

The crossing that could take three hours under optimum conditions took eight. The duchess made her influence felt at customs and was rushed through with no problem. She had been thoroughly briefed half a century before and knew the Silver Lion was the best posthouse. It was to this place of faded elegance that she took her niece.

"I'm reduced to a shade after that wretched crossing," she complained. "We shall have a bite to eat and go up to bed."

Deirdre dressed with care for her entrée into cosmopolitan society. A very dashing gown of deep blue silk exposed her arms and shoulders to whistling drafts as the ladies descended to the dining room but created quite a stir amidst the oglers.

"If your vanity has been satisfied by the admiration of this gaping crew, you might put this nice warm shawl on," the duchess suggested, placing a decrepit mauve shawl around her niece's shoulders.

Deirdre kept it in place till the meal was served, knowing that once her aunt was involved in fork work, she'd spare no notice for anything else.

Pronto was detained at customs. "I know I had that curst passport in my pocket," he said a dozen times, but a dozen searches didn't produce it. He finally had to send his valet to open the trunks and root about till it turned up, carefully marking his place in Plutarch's *Lives of the Noble Grecians and Romans*, which he'd been reading all winter.

"I'll carry it for you," Belami said impatiently when they were finally released, and put Pronto's papers with his own.

Night had fallen when they left customs. A damp, cold wind whistled through the streets. "There isn't a carriage to be had," Belami said. "We'll head straight for the Hotel d'Angleterre. It's the best place. We can hire a carriage there for the trip to Paris."

The rooms at the Angleterre were all filled. "We'll have to make do with the Prince of Orange," Belami decided. There, too, they arrived too late. "Damme, it looks as if we must stay at that fleabag, the Silver Lion."

"If we don't find some food soon, my stomach will collapse," Pronto complained. "It's been empty so long it thinks my mouth is sewed shut."

As Pronto spoke only garbled French, it was Belami who went to the desk to arrange accommodations. This left Pronto free to scout out the dining room. The first person he saw was the duchess of Charney, sitting like a ghost at the table. A cold sweat broke out on his forehead and a strange ringing invaded his ears. "By jingo, I'm seeing things. I'm weak with hunger." He rubbed his eyes and looked again. Now he was seeing double visions. Deirdre Gower sat beside her aunt, eating what looked like a very tasty ragout. His mouth watered, but even hunger didn't divert his thoughts. What the devil was Charney doing here? She was supposed to be at Fernvale, sick as a dog. The old liar—it was all a ruse to break off the wedding. His next problem was whether or not to tell Dick.

When they went upstairs to view their rooms, Pronto hung about Belami's door, nibbling his thumb in a way that alerted his friend to trouble. "What's amiss, Pronto?" he asked.

"I was just thinking, Dick, as a hypo what-do-you-call-

13

it question, you know. What would you do if Charney and Deirdre was here?"

Belami's lips clenched and a flash of lightning sparked from his eyes. "I'd leave." Pronto thought of the ragout and the search for another hotel in the miserable wind. "Why do you ask? Are you trying to spoil my appetite?"

"No, no. Nothing of the sort."

Belami frowned and began to dress, wondering if Pronto was ill. As soon as he left Belami, Pronto shot back downstairs like a bullet. He knew he was becoming nearly as clever as Dick, and his next Machiavellian inspiration proved it. He had a "complimentary" bottle of wine sent to Belami's room, and insisted they try it before dinner. When at last they entered the dining room, Pronto flashed a glance at what he mentally called "the scene of the crime" and saw with a rush of relief that the table was vacant.

"By Jove, this is something like." He smiled broadly and strode forward. *"Table pour deux, monsieur."* With a knowing look at his friend he said, "Time to start parlaying the old bongjaw. *Vin et viande*—that's what we want."

The wine, when it arrived, was a remarkably good Beaujolais. It would be a crime to destroy it by unpleasant news, so Pronto put off telling his tale till after dinner. In the comfortable haze of two bottles of wine and a postprandial brandy, the problem eased to insignificance. A clever rascal like himself could keep them apart. "We'll leave early tomorrow," he told Dick. "Lost out on a decent hotel by dragging our feet. We'll check out of here at seven and nip over to the Angleterre for breakfast and hiring the carriage."

"The Tour du Guet should be worth a look while we're here. It's thirteenth century."

"Then it's too old to bother with. Bound to be falling apart. We'll nick straight off to Paris."

"If you like," Belami agreed, but he knew Pronto's

14

tardy habits and didn't expect to see him at seven. They dawdled over coffee and brandy, enjoying the babel of foreign conversation around them and the unusual details of dining in a foreign country. At ten, they had sat long enough and rose to retire.

At the bottom of the stairs, they stood aside to allow three ladies to descend. Belami noticed they were speaking English and said "Good evening," with a smile that explained his forwardness. Fellow countrymen in a strange land automatically formed a freemasonry against the natives.

Smiles were returned as the group passed. The party was composed of two young ladies and one older—mother or chaperone. The older lady was tall, gray-haired, and thin. It was at the daughters that Belami looked more sharply. The younger was blond-haired and blue-eyed, small but buxom with a childishly round face. She shyly averted her eyes as they passed. Belami hadn't much interest in wilting violets. It was at the older, taller one that he continued looking. Her raven hair reminded him of Deirdre. Except for the blue eyes, she bore little resemblance to the other girl. She met his gaze boldly, as an equal. He liked those statuesque ladies with bold eyes. She had a prominent nose, well-shaped, and a firm chin.

He lingered a moment belowstairs, noticing that the chaperone was having difficulty making herself understood by the clerk. He advanced and introduced himself. "I speak French. May I offer to act as your interpreter?" he inquired politely.

"Why, thank you, milord." The chaperone smiled gratefully. "I am trying to inquire for a carriage to Paris for tomorrow."

"It's the Hotel d'Angleterre you must go to. I'll be going there myself tomorrow morning. I'd be very happy to make the arrangements for you, Mrs.—

"Mrs. Sutton, and these are my daughters, Elvira and Lucy," she said, indicating the elder first.

15

"Miss Sutton, delighted," Belami said, with his best bow.

The haughty beauty curtsied stiffly and gave him a scathing glance. This lack of encouragement intrigued Belami. They remained a few minutes talking. Mrs. Sutton announced that she was taking her girls on an educational trip abroad. "My Elvira is artistic," she explained.

Belami used it as an excuse to observe the haughty Elvira. He wasn't imagining the flash of anger in her beautiful blue eyes. They were a deep blue, much prettier than Lucy's. "Then I expect you'll be stopping at Florence," he said.

"We mustn't keep the gentlemen, Mama. Thank you for your assistance, Lord Belami," Miss Sutton said in a firm voice, and taking hold of Lucy's arm, she turned to ascend the stairs.

"Thank you so much," Mrs. Sutton repeated. "I shall be awaiting word here tomorrow morning regarding the carriage."

"Good-looking gels," Pronto remarked a moment later. "But we'll not cozy up to 'em till we're out of Calais."

"Why not?" Belami asked. "I never knew you to spurn a lady's advances, Pronto. Lucy was rolling her eyes at you."

"No, at you. If you'd stopped mooning at the other one long enough, you'd have noticed. No time to be chasing women."

"That's part of the reason we're here, isn't it?"

"No, it's the reason we're going to Paris and Italy. You've got to keep your nose clean in Calais." The poor devil wouldn't get a wink of sleep if he told him about Deirdre before morning. They began climbing the stairs, talking as they went.

"Are you worried that the customs bogeyman will come after you?" Belami joked.

"That's it." Pronto leaped on this excuse. "I didn't like the sharp eyes of him. Could open an oyster with a glance.

16

Regular gimlets. We'll be up and out of here at seven o'clock.''

The walls of the Silver Lion were thick. No more than a murmur penetrated to Deirdre's room as the gentlemen passed, laughing and talking. Something in the tone of the voices, also the firm tread of one, the shuffling gait of the other, reminded her of Dick and Pronto. But then everything reminded her of Dick. He'd never put up at a wretched old place like this. How different this trip would be had she come with him on their honeymoon. She wouldn't be in bed at ten o'clock, listening to her aunt snoring. They'd be out, seeing the city. And afterward, they'd come home together. She wouldn't be lying all alone, with a hot tear trickling down her cheek.

The duchess had left word to be awakened at eight. At eight-thirty she was in the dining room, spooning a very inferior and overpriced gruel into her mouth and discussing how they were to proceed on their journey. "The public diligence is the cheap—quickest way to continue," she outlined. "Only a hundred and eighty-three miles. The guide book says it makes the trip to Paris in fifty-four hours. The time will fly by with so much to see.''

"There will be twenty or thirty other people in the coach, and half of them will be French," Deirdre pointed out. Foreigners, she knew, were anathema to her aunt.

"An excellent opportunity for you to practice the language. That's why I brought you along.''

"A post chaise would only cost two and a half guineas," Deirdre mentioned hopefully.

"Aye, but you have to pay extra to have the heavy luggage sent by stagecoach.''

Deirdre knew a stone was easy squeezing compared to her aunt's purse. The duchess was reputed to be worth a large fortune, but her joy in life was to hold on to it, not squander it on mere necessities. Her bonnet was older than the century, and the sable-lined pelisse could give the bonnet a decade.

17

Deirdre glanced at the tattered copy of the *Liste Générale des Postes de France* and smiled. "Oh, look, Auntie. The public diligence leaves at six in the morning. We'll have to spend another day here—and the rates so high," she added slyly.

The duchess grabbed the book from her hands and examined it with her falcon's gaze. "Nuisance! Why did the clerk not tell us? They're all in it together, fleecing travelers. There's nothing else for it. We must find some English ladies to share a chaise with. Those Suttons we met at dinner last night—they spoke of hiring a post chaise, did they not?"

"Yes," Deirdre said reluctantly. She rather wanted some privacy in which to nurture her wounded heart. On the other hand, company might be the very thing to help her. The older daughter had seemed friendly. The younger though—Lucy—she had been less forthcoming.

When the Sutton party entered the dining room a little later, the duchess lifted her arm and beckoned them to her table. "So comforting to see an English face," she said, beaming. "Pray join us for breakfast, ladies."

"How soon do you plan to proceed to Paris?" the duchess asked Mrs. Sutton, as soon as they had settled in.

"This very day. An English gentleman we met here last night is arranging a post chaise for us this morning."

"I hope he has more luck than we." The duchess sighed forlornly. "I sent a messenger over to the hiring stable, and there wasn't a thing to be had. It looks as though my niece and I must loiter here till something turns up." She shot a sharp glance at Mrs. Sutton as she composed this piece of fiction. She read the considering expression in her companion's eye—the careful weighing up of pros and cons. Commoners were aware of the distinction inherent in noble friends. On the other hand, the carriage would be crowded for a longish trip.

Without a second thought, the duchess consigned her own and Mrs. Sutton's servants to following them in the diligence. "Our last hope of getting out of this wretched place today is joining someone who has had the good fortune to obtain a post chaise. Of course we would have to do without our servants for a few days while they follow behind. I wonder if there is anyone in the hotel willing to go snacks with me."

While Mrs. Sutton looked doubtfully at her daughters, Miss Sutton spoke up. "Mama," she said, "if we leave our servant behind, we could travel with the duchess and Miss Gower."

"Good gracious!" the duchess objected loudly, "I hope you don't think I was hinting! Crowding you good ladies was the last thing in my mind. Of course a poor cadaver like myself wouldn't take up an inch, and Miss Gower is slender as a reed."

"Let us do it, Mama," Miss Sutton encouraged. "The duchess will be company for you, and Lucy and I will have an opportunity to know Miss Gower better."

Before the duchess and Deirdre left the table, the matter was resolved, right down to the details of financing. The duchess was swift to point out that there were only two in her party, whereas the Suttons would occupy three-fifths of the rig. It worked out very neatly: a guinea for her share, a guinea and a half for the Suttons. They rushed upstairs to tend to their packing while the Suttons had a hasty breakfast.

"Truth to tell, I didn't think Mrs. Sutton was the sort to insist on our paying when the sum in question was so small—only a guinea," Charney said to Deirdre. "Incredible how some people squeeze every penny." But on the whole she was pleased with her bargain and Deirdre was not unhappy.

They left Haskins, their female servant, in charge of the trunks and quickly stuffed their essentials into a pair of bandboxes to go on the post chaise. They hastened downstairs to join the Suttons. Within a quarter of an hour, Mrs.

19

Sutton glanced up from her coffee and said, "Ah, there is Lord Belami now, come to tell me about my carriage."

Now why did that cause the duchess to gag and the young lady to turn white as a sheet? The Suttons looked on with the liveliest interest, observing that Lord Belami had turned into a stone statue, staring as though he wished them all at Jericho. No one spared a glance at Pronto Pilgrim, who stood with his eyes bulging and his lips open. Fat was in the fire now.

"Er, Dick," he muttered, "the ladies are waiting. Best buck up and get on with it."

Belami unclenched his fists and willed down the urge to fly at the duchess's scrawny throat. The public nature of the meeting demanded a show of common decency. He strode stiff-legged to Mrs. Sutton and her companions.

"Good morning, ma'am. Ladies," he added, with a very small bob of his head to the others, "I've arranged for your carriage, Mrs. Sutton. You have only to send a note to the Angleterre when you want it."

Mrs. Sutton began introductions. "We've all met," Dick said brusquely.

Deirdre instantly turned to crystal. She daren't look at Dick or she'd betray herself, but a tumult of emotions heaved within her—embarrassment, curiosity, joy, shame, anger, regret. What must he think? He'd think they were following him. She lifted her eyes and smiled uncertainly at her old friend, Pronto. Her eyes, once up from her lap, found courage to turn to Dick. Strange how she could read exactly what was in his mind when he wore that bland mask. He stared with unwonted attention at Mrs. Sutton as he explained the details of the carriage. His voice was unnaturally loud, his speech erratic.

She saw a flicker of his eyes toward her and quickly looked away. Had he looked at her? Her eyes skimmed back, but he was talking to Miss Sutton now.

"I hope you had a good sleep, ladies?"

"Fine, thank you," Miss Sutton answered coolly.

The duchess, never one to minimize a scene, had recovered her wits and pitched herself into the fray with joyful sourness. "So you are taking your trip after all, Belami. We had no notion you planned to abandon your London dissipations. Our news at Fernvale was quite otherwise," she said, with awful emphasis on the "dissipations." "The only reason Miss Gower and myself are here is for my health. My doctor recommended a warm climate for my lungs."

Belami's mobile brow lifted, and he directed a scathing glare at her grace. "I'm under no misapprehension that you put yourself to so much trouble on my account, your grace. Europe is large enough to accommodate us all." His glare flickered left to include Deirdre in this chilly civility. She felt battered to see so much hatred and anger. It was all over then. A lifetime was too short to overcome that much ill will.

"I wish you all a happy trip, ladies," he said, bowed gallantly, and left.

Pronto jiggled uneasily, said "Heh, heh. Nice to see you again, Deirdre," and went darting off after Belami.

"Jackanapes!" the duchess growled in a perfectly audible voice.

"Good gracious! That was mighty uncomfortable!" Miss Sutton exclaimed. "I take it you ladies have had some unhappy doings with Lord Belami."

"My niece gave him his congé last month," the duchess said. Dirty linen was not washed in front of commoners, though a few pieces of it might beguile the long trip to Italy if she felt in the mood.

"He's very handsome!" Lucy said. "Why did you jilt him, Miss Gower?"

"This matter is very upsetting to my niece," the duchess said dampingly.

Lucy could see Miss Gower looked ready to burst into tears. Both Elvira and Lucy developed a strong interest in

Miss Gower and looked forward to hearing her story when privacy could be arranged.

"Now, Mrs. Sutton, shall we send that note off to the hotel and be on our way?" the duchess asked in a rather imperious manner. She called for a waiter, demanded a pen and ink, and wrote the note herself.

As they returned to the hotel for their carriage, Belami was silent as an oyster, which was a vast relief to Pronto. He felt steeped to the gills in complicity, as though he had personally arranged that meeting. After a few blocks, however, he was curious to hear his friend's views and said, "Bit of a shocker, eh? Charney and Deirdre in France."

The very word "Charney" was like a whiplash to Belami. "What news did the old bint hear at Fernvale, I wonder? Who was writing off to her? She hasn't a friend in the world. I'd stake my head she wrote to her relatives asking about me."

"You've hit the hammer on the head there—er, nail. Relatives are always glad to rub salt in the wound—Deirdre's wound, I mean."

"If Deirdre was wearing any wounds, she hid them well."

"She would. You went storming in like Attila the Hun."

"You noticed Charney was quick to let me know their trip has nothing to do with me?"

"It's true. We decided on the spur of the minute. Deirdre ain't chasing you, if that's what you're afraid of." Actually, Pronto feared "afraid" wasn't quite the right word.

"Talk about salt in the wound!" Belami muttered.

"What we've got to do is find out where they're heading, and go off in the other direction," Pronto decided. "Like you said, the continent's big enough for both of us. All of us. If we meet up again, I'll ask Deirdre their destination, and we'll know where not to go."

"I don't intend to change my plans one iota," Belami

22

announced. "Deirdre knows my itinerary. If she doesn't want to see me, she'll know where to stay away from."

Pronto hobbled along, trying to keep pace with Dick's long, angry strides on his own little stumps of legs. "If she stays away from Paris and Venice and Rome and all our itinerary, where the deuce can the poor girl go?"

"She can take a different route—go in a different order. She knows my plans. That's all I have to say."

"She won't have one word to say about anything. Charney rules the roost. She'll tag along wherever she's led."

"She's good at that," Dick growled. "If she were as biddable a wife as she is a niece, she'd be a pattern card for some man."

"That's right," Pronto said. He found it expedient to agree when Dick was in this mood. "Charney says 'Jump,' and Deirdre says 'Which way?' Jumps like a rabbit. No backbone."

Dick clenched his lips more tightly and increased the length of his stride. No backbone, but such a face! He was ambushed by a host of memories. As long as he didn't see Deirdre in the flesh, he could go on being furious with her. One glimpse and he was undone by those stormy, speaking gray eyes that went right through his flesh and touched his heart. Such long lashes, fanning her cheeks. Such sweet lips, quivering in emotion. Her face reminded him of a porcelain statue, a clear, translucent white, tinged with pink on the cheeks.

A muscular spasm moved at the back of his jaw as he firmed his resistance. She knew exactly where he had planned to go—with her. It should be Deirdre beside him now, not that chattering idiot, Pronto. Damme if he didn't feel a tear sting his eyes. He blinked it away and said in a rough voice, "It's colder than Réal's Canadian arctic here. I'll be glad to get to Italy." Of course it was the cold that made his eyes water.

"Cold?" Pronto complained. "The sweat's pouring

23

down my spine. Can't you slow down to a gallop? I'm winded.''

Belami slowed down, but it didn't stop the wind from stinging his eyes. It didn't ease the angry hammering of his heart or dim the image of Deirdre Gower that was burned into his mind.

Chapter Three

Belami's trip to Paris was a virtual dash. His proud "I won't vary my itinerary one iota" was soon revised to "There's no point dawdling in little villages." He stopped at Amiens long enough to peep into the cathedral, but of the ramparts, the wall, and the five gates he had only a glimpse in passing. Pronto didn't even get to see the head of Saint John the Baptist in the church, which he'd been looking forward to with keen interest.

The whole flat plane of northern France passed in a blur. Belami didn't know what route Mrs. Sutton meant to take, but he knew she would stop at Paris. Belami's groom, Pierre Réal, was in alt. Here he was in the home of his fathers, with a better grasp of the language than his master. He was not only permitted but actually urged to set a hot pace. To add to his joy, he was told to keep an eye peeled for Sutton's carriage. He never did see it, but any time twelve miles an hour became too slow for him, he could whip up the team and let on he had.

They arrived at the city gates in the fading light of day, fatigued and bounced to a jelly from their mad dart. Belami directed the carriage to the Hotel d'Orléans in the Faubourg St. Germain. As he signed the register, he quickly ran an eye up the list of patrons. His quarry had not registered, but they would be spending some time in Paris, and the Orléans was a good central base from which to operate.

Belami continued to profess the greatest aversion to Miss Gower's company, but Réal had soon weaseled his way into his master's confidence. "You have the little job for me?" Réal asked archly. "Tomorrow morning you want I take a run around the hotels and see if *la Mégère* has arrived?"

"If they haven't, you might just speak to the clerks and cross their palms with silver. Ask them to notify me here as soon as they check in. It will not be one of the finer hotels," he added, with thorough British understatement.

Réal was a small, swarthy French-Canadian, sharp of eye, sharp of nose and tongue. "*La Mégère*, she don't spend *l'argent* freely." He nodded knowingly. "The shrew" was his endearing sobriquet for the duchess. "*De fait*, she won't put up at an hotel at all, melor'. It will be furnished lodgings and a public dining room for that one. This will be a big job," he pointed out. Though a demon for work—the bigger the job the better—Réal was never one to diminish the importance of his duties.

"Very true. It'll be a small, cheap hostelry, but in a good neighborhood. You might send my valet off to loiter discreetly around Notre Dame and some of the major tourist spots. Have Nick follow them and see where they're putting up."

"It will be done." Réal bowed.

"I wish you wouldn't say that! You make me feel as though you're praying to me."

Réal was desperate when three days passed and still he had failed in his duty. He liked not only to perform to perfection, but to do it with an astonishing speed. After a little cudgeling of his brains, he decided that the reckless haste of their dash to Paris had left *la Mégère* a few days behind. Where she would first be seen was at the entry gate to Paris. The next morning he drove there and spent a tedious day watching carriages arrive.

At four o'clock, his hard little heart nearly burst for joy. From his post behind a tree, he saw the Suttons' carriage bowl up and stop. He recognized *la Mégère*'s raucous voice from ten yards away. When the formalities were through, he followed the coach. For a dreadful moment it seemed it was going to stop at the Hotel d'Orléans. How like fate to steal his glory. His fear ebbed when the carriage continued on past the hotel, around the corner. It pulled up in front of a small hotel called La Licorne, with a gilded unicorn on the hanging sign. His quarry descended and straggled in.

Réal darted back to the Orléans and sought out his master in his room. As Monsieur Pilgrim was not present, he could speak quite frankly, but frankness was not his way. He liked to tease his master before giving glad tidings.

"For three days I have hounded every hotel lobby, every set of furnished rooms in Paris," he began wearily. "I personally go to Notre Dame and all the points of interest on the Ile de la Cité. For the valet—he is a *vaurien*. We do not count on him. *La Mégère*, she was not in Paris."

Belami listened impatiently. "Still no luck, eh? I wonder if they bypassed Paris entirely. I'm convinced if you didn't find her, she ain't here." As he spoke, Belami idly flipped his lucky guinea, which was not proving so effective as a charm.

"I do not say I don't find her," Réal pointed out.

"Where is she?" Belami exclaimed.

"I don't say I do find her too either," he added mischievously. He tapped his temple. "I think—we drive very fast to Paris. *La Mégère*, she don't like the so fast driving."

"That's true."

"Very much true. I drive to the city gate. I see the dusty carriage lumber on the road—all filled with ladies' heads."

"Where are they?" Belami demanded again.

"This five minutes just past, they enter to La Licorne,

a small hotel around the corner from here," he announced, and waited for congratulations.

Belami bounced to his feet and grabbed Réal's shoulders with his two hands. "Réal—you're a pearl beyond price. Choose your own reward."

This was life and breath for Réal. Astonishment, praise, appreciation of his unique perfection. He smiled. "I have no need for *la douceur*," he said modestly, but his hand slid out and palmed the gold coin that was placed in it.

Réal was delighted with himself, but his insatiable craving for praise demanded more. As soon as he left the room, he darted back to La Licorne. A few ingratiating words with the clerk elicited the information that the ladies had taken rooms for a week. He also learned that Miss Sutton had been interested to learn there was a dancing party in the ballroom that same night. The young ladies, the clerk said, had sent gowns down to be pressed.

With a smile as wide as his face, Réal pranced back to Belami's room. His master had been joined by Pilgrim, so that some evasion was necessary. "I thought you might like to know there is to be the small dancing party *ce soir* at La Licorne," he said, but his flashing black eyes said a deal more. "Some English tourists will be attending, I hear."

"Thank you, Réal. Perhaps we'll drop around. What do you say, Pronto?" Belami asked.

"I wouldn't mind hearing some English faces," Pronto agreed. "The people here all sound like fishwives— wretched twangy voices." Réal pokered up, and Pronto rushed on to assuage him. "Not like your nice soft Canadian French."

"My people, they come from Bretagne," Réal said. "The Parisians, they speak very bad French."

"You ought to hear their English," Pronto informed him.

Réal left, and Pronto went to his room to change for dinner. It was a good sign that Dick wanted to meet some girls. Dick was in high spirits all through dinner. He waxed quite eloquent on the advantages of foreign travel. He spoke of staying another week in Paris, then moving on to Italy. "Shall we stop at Torino, Pronto, or skip right along to Milan?"

"Thought we was going to Turin first," Pronto reminded him.

"Torino is Turin—it's the Italian name for it."

"I see it's going to be as bad as France; everybody calling things by the wrong names. I'm all for getting as far south as we can. Paris is colder than London."

"I think you might be right," Belami said. "We'll continue down to Naples." A lady come to ease her lungs would certainly head south.

"But stopping at Venice. I want to see the water roads— the canals. Didn't get to see the head of John the Baptist." An accusing glare accompanied this.

They chatted about their trip till dinner was finished. Pronto leaned back and suggested a glass of brandy to top off, but Dick was strangely eager to get along to the little ball, so they left. When they had entered La Licorne, Pronto looked around in disgust. "What kind of a den is this? You've been led astray, Dick. Let's shab off somewhere else."

"They're beginning a quadrille. If we hurry, we might get partners and have one dance before we leave." Belami hastened his steps toward the doorway, Pronto following reluctantly.

At the Licorne, the duchess had never been in better curl, and it was all due to dear Mrs. Sutton, now called Meggie. The woman was a godsend. She had no more skill for accounting than a sparrow. One had only to remind her there were three in the Sutton party versus two in her own and Meggie would snap up the bill quick as winking. The delightful words, "Let me get this one," came to her lips as readily as a smile.

Meggie also showed a fine discernment in accommodations. She spurned the more expensive spots, but had a genius for discovering cheap places in the right neighborhood. Her hand was as quick to draw forth the necessary pourboires as the duchess's was slow. Nor was this largesse the sum of Meggie's virtues. She was a stern moralist. Her husband having been a clergyman in Cornwall would account for her keeping her gels on a tight rein, though truth to tell they were not at all prone to flirtations. They were good modest girls, even in their dress. No scintillating conversation or high degree of learning was required from such obliging traveling companions as this.

The three young ladies also found much to like in each other. Deirdre favored the elder daughter, Elvira. It was not so much similarity as the attraction of opposites. Elvira was what Belami would call fast. She had a sharp tongue and a knowing eye. Lucy was more demure and somewhat given to sulking. It was Elvira who learned of the assembly that evening. The duchess cast no rub in their way when she learned Meggie was willing to act as chaperone for all the girls.

"Excellent." She nodded. "I shall have an early night. Try not to waken me when you come in, Deirdre." This request was unnecessary. How could you awaken a lady who had dosed herself liberally with laudanum, as the duchess usually did?

At eight-thirty the duchess brought out a marble-covered gothic novel to read while the ladies descended to the small ballroom under the aegis of Mrs. Sutton. The assembly was hardly designed to strike joy into the heart of anyone but a provincial. Deirdre saw at a glance that there wasn't a modish jacket in the room.

The three hedgebirds the master of ceremonies brought forth for introduction were indeed far from handsome, but at least they were English, which was a relief. The three friends all joined the same set and stood waiting for a fourth to complete it. The music began, and still they lacked a fourth. Glancing around the room, they saw a number of young ladies scanning the walls for partners, of which there were none.

"Oh, here are some men just arriving!" Elvira exclaimed. "The master of ceremonies is introducing them—there, the tall one is going to join our set."

Deirdre glanced across the room and saw the unmistakable form of Belami quickly advancing, with a Miss Wiggams on his arm. She froze to the spot and clutched Elvira's fingers. "It's Belami!" she whispered. What was he doing in this out-of-the-way spot? Had he been looking for her? There wasn't a trace of conciliation on his hard face. He didn't look in her direction once, which was pretty good evidence he had seen her.

"We'll all cut him," Elvira said.

"That would be too farouche!" Deirdre replied. Really Elvira sometimes went too far for comfort.

The master of ceremonies made brief introductions; Belami nodded curtly to everyone and from that point on, it seemed as though cutting would not be necessary. His lavish attentions to Miss Wiggams showed he had no interest in reestablishing any rapport with Deirdre. The steps of the quadrille proceeded in nearly total silence, save for the scraping of the fiddles. During *le pantalon* the variations in the dance might be held to account for the lack of talk. Every area performed the steps differently, and attention was necessary to arrive in the right spot at the right moment. By the time the dance had proceeded to *l'été*, however, the strain of silence was beginning to tell.

When Deirdre joined hands briefly with Belami during *la poule*, she met his eyes and said, "Are you just arrived in Paris, Belami?"

"No, we've been here a few days."

"We just got here this afternoon."

"You're wasting no time in finding entertainment, I see."

They parted, and Deirdre considered this exchange. If he had been here for a few days, he might be leaving soon.

31

When they met during *la trenise*, she had her question ready. "Are you staying in Paris long?" she asked, careful to keep any enthusiasm from her voice.

"We're traveling ad lib. Do you remain long?"

"A week, I believe."

"Then on to Italy?" he asked nonchalantly.

"Yes."

They parted. The last chance for conversation was the *finale*, and that would be a regular mêlée of chatter. Deirdre's only consolation was that Dick had asked her destination. Italy, however, was a vast area. She must mention Venice. That was Meg Sutton's destination, and her aunt had taken such a liking to Meg that she planned to hasten along there as well.

She was on tenterhooks till the *finale* arrived. Dick caught her eye and edged closer. "Where do you plan to stop in Italy?" he asked.

A light of gratitude beamed in her eyes and a small smile lifted her lips. "We are going directly to Venice," she said.

"Ah, Venice!"

"Will you be stopping there?"

"Pronto has expressed an interest in falling into the Grand Canal."

Miss Wiggams put her dainty fingers on Belami's arm and he led her back to her chaperone. The other young ladies returned to Mrs. Sutton.

"They have arranged things badly here for the chaperones," the dame complained. "No cards, no introductions. I'm glad I brought my newspaper or I'd be bored to flinders. Well, how was the dance, ladies?"

"Thrilling," Elvira said, fanning herself in obvious boredom. "Lord Belami is here. Perhaps you'd like to retire, Deirdre? I shouldn't mind I promise you."

"Oh, dear!" Mrs. Sutton exclaimed. "Is that who the handsome fellow in your set was? I was wearing my reading spectacles and didn't recognize him. I wonder if we ought not to leave, Deirdre? Your aunt won't want you pestered by him."

Elvira slid a look toward Belami over the top of her fan. "I wonder if he's here on business," she said. "He amuses himself by looking into crimes, the duchess mentioned." The Sutton ladies exchanged a questioning look, but Deirdre missed it. She was peering behind Lucy's head to watch Dick.

"We needn't leave. It's obvious Belami has found himself some entertainment other than pestering me," she snipped.

As Dick had found a flirt, Deirdre soon found herself some entertainment as well, in the form of the second most handsome gentleman in the room, who unfortunately spoke not a word of English. With her school-book French, she indicated a willingness to attempt the next dance with him and went to the floor.

It was from there that she saw Belami and Pronto stroll over to Mrs. Sutton's table and request the young ladies to stand up with them. Belami inquired first for the satisfaction of the carriage he had hired for them, then said, "I have come to claim my reward." He flashed his famous smile at Miss Sutton, who tossed her curls and looked away.

With this lack of enthusiasm, Belami turned his fading smile to the younger chit. "Miss Lucy, may I have the pleasure of the next dance?" he asked.

Lucy, with a pert glance at her sister, accepted with the greatest alacrity. Belami saw the angry surprise on Miss Sutton's handsome face and was set to wondering. Had Deirdre asked the girls to snub him? His heart pumped hard in anger.

Pronto shuffled toward Miss Sutton and mumbled, "Er, care to stand up and jig it with me, Miss Sutton?"

To everyone's surprise, not least Pronto's, the haughty creature accepted. When she rose from her chair, Pronto noticed she was an inch or two taller than himself, but by Jove she was a well-set-up woman.

"Shall we go and join Deirdre?" Pronto suggested.

Elvira took hold of Pronto's elbow with a firm grip, her sister's with another, and said, "Let us form another square. Deirdre most particularly wishes to practice her French." She led them away to the far corner of the room and soon had the set completed.

There were some strange undercurrents here that Pronto couldn't quite fathom. He had figured out by now that Dick knew all along Deirdre was here, of course. Wasn't a complete flat. What he couldn't understand was why Dick didn't just go and ask her to dance. It wasn't as if Charney were here to stick a spoke in his wheel.

But really these were only minor mysteries. What intrigued him more was that Elvira Sutton, a dasher of the first water, was spurning Belami's advances. Of course he knew Dick was only after her to make Deirdre jealous, but she couldn't know that. What absolutely defied explanation was that Elvira seemed very sweet on himself. In the general way, he never cared much for these ladders of girls. Lucy was more in his style, but Lucy was batting her lashes at Belami as hard as she could. Very strange doings all around. It amused him to see Dick trying his charms on Elvira, wondering why he wasn't having any luck.

"Where are you pilgrimaging to, Mr. Pilgrim?" Miss Sutton asked.

"Europe," he said. "How about you, Miss Sutton?"

"The same," she answered, biting back a smile at this odd little man. "Are you and Lord Belami working on a case at the present time? I've heard you two are famous investigators."

Pronto's chest swelled to be harnessed so properly in tandem with Belami in these investigations. "We're taking a holiday from crime. The only crime we've come across is that Dick got hold of a counterfeit coin at Dover. He was within ame's ace of missing the boat, but I got him blasted off.'' Miss Sutton's smile encouraged Pronto to tackle a compliment. ''Seems to me it's a crime for a lady to be so dashed pretty as you, Miss Sutton. Maybe we ought to look into it, what?''

She laughed lightly. ''You are a shocking man! Just what part of me did you plan to look into?''

Pronto blushed and sought a suave extrication. ''I never look a gift horse in the mouth, and that's a fact.''

''Then my teeth are safe,'' Miss Sutton teased. ''But I warn you, sir, my fetlocks, my withers, and especially my flanks are out of bounds.''

''Heh, heh.'' Miss Sutton was a high flyer, and no doubt about it. Pretty warm talk for a maiden! ''Don't worry I'm trying to saddle or bridle you,'' he said. ''Not that I mean to say I wouldn't like to! That is—oh, dash it, Miss Sutton, you know what I mean.''

''Let us abandon this metaphor, Mr. Pilgrim. So you and Lord Belami are in Europe only on pleasure?'' she asked again.

''That's it. Tell me, Miss Sutton, am I wrong, or have you taken Belami in aversion for some reason?''

She gave him a bold smile. ''I never poach, sir. Till we see whether he and Miss Gower are indeed through with each other, I shall keep my distance. Really, Belami is not in my style. Is it all over with those two?''

''The lord only knows. It's been over a dozen times, but he keeps coming back to have his head kicked in again. It wouldn't surprise me if he took it into his noggin to go tagging after her. Er, what is your style, Miss Sutton?''

''I prefer shorter men. Someone I can look in the eye,'' she said boldly as she looked down into his eyes from her clear blue orbs. Pronto was knocked endways by that look.

''Where are you folks heading to?'' he asked.

''Rome,'' Miss Sutton answered firmly.

''Rome, eh? Perhaps we'll meet again there and have another dance. Shall we make a date?''

Elvira gave him a mysterious smile. "Let us leave it in the hands of fate," she said.

By the time the dance was over, Pronto knew his fate was sealed. Wherever Elvira went, he meant to follow. She wasn't the woman he ever thought he'd fall in love with, but there it was. Fate. She was a lively young lady, not one to keep her tongue between her teeth and make a fellow do all the talking. She was a mite taller than him, but she preferred short men. If that wasn't an invitation he was a yahoo.

Both Pronto and Belami returned to Mrs. Sutton's table at the end of the dance. During the intermission, Deirdre's partner took her for a glass of orgeat. Belami sat down and tried to make conversation with the chaperone.

"Is the duchess planning to join the party?" he asked.

"No, she's gone to bed. We must leave soon, too."

Her first speech was music to Dick's ears. It seemed possible he might arrange a private meeting with Deirdre. He ordered a bottle of wine and talked to Mrs. Sutton while Pronto entertained the youngsters.

"I see you've managed to find an English newspaper," he mentioned. "Is there any news from home?"

"This is several days old," she replied. "English papers are at such a premium a gentleman at the hotel offered me his."

Belami glanced at it and noticed a piece had been cut out. When Mrs. Sutton closed the paper, Belami saw a brown stain on the front page. The paper was the *Dover Chronicle*, bearing the date of their departure. "Would you care to have it?" she said.

"I've read that issue, thank you." He frowned at it. "You didn't by any chance get it from a retired sea captain?"

"No—that is, I'm not sure what the man's calling was. I didn't actually know him. Why do you ask?" she said.

"It's a small world. That looks like the paper I gave to a gentleman on the boat. We spilled brandy on it during

36

the crossing. Captain Styger must be putting up here at the Licorne. I may look him up tomorrow.''

He glanced up and saw Elvira staring at him. She looked conscious for a moment, then smiled. She had a charming smile. The wine arrived, and during the intermission some desultory conversation ensued. When the next set began forming, Pronto grabbed Elvira's hand, and Dick went after Deirdre.

She had been keeping a sharp eye on him and hoped for some such move. As he approached, however, her pride demanded a show of pique. She smiled very thinly and said, ''Nice party.''

''Charming,'' he sneered, and lifted her hand from the Frenchman's sleeve to lead her away. She didn't object. In this mood, Dick was capable of any havoc. ''But all good things must come to an end,'' he warned, ''and now it's time for us to talk.''

She leveled a cold stare at him. ''I can't imagine what you and I have to say to each other, Lord Belami. It seems to me we exhausted all our threats and insults some time ago.''

''Speak for yourself. I still have a full budget! Why didn't you tell me you were coming to Europe?''

''Why should I? We're only here for my aunt's health.''

''No doubt your dancing with that French gigolo is an inestimable help to her.''

They reached the far side of the room, and Belami showed her a chair. ''My aunt is getting her sleep. Why should I retire at nine o'clock? I'm not a child.''

Dick saw the chaperone across the room stir restively and decided it was time to abandon his petulant pose. ''Mrs. Sutton plans to leave soon. Deirdre, we have to talk. Meet me down here. The duchess won't hear you go.''

''You can say anything you have to say now,'' she replied. She lifted her gray eyes to his and was set trembling at the look he wore. It was the face of the man she'd fallen in love with. One black brow was arched imperiously over a flashing dark eye, but the gentle smile on his lips told a different story. It spoke of his continuing affection—his love. He seized her hand and squeezed it tightly.

"I can't do what I want to do," he said softly in an intimate voice that sent chills down her spine. He gazed at her lips as he spoke, till she felt them quiver.

"Dick, behave yourself!" she said, blushing.

"Give me half a chance and I shall behave just as you always liked. Come back down and meet me, darling. There's no impropriety in it. Pronto's here as well. We'll just have a dance—that's all."

Deirdre leveled a searching gaze at him. "This is not the way you spoke last month at Fernvale," she reminded him.

"I can't go on being savage with you. It's destroying my sanity. Last month at Fernvale I was a madman. Who wouldn't be, with the wedding put off for the third time? My bovine pride has been coerced by your absence. We broke off the engagement in haste, and I've repented at leisure."

"Also with considerable pleasure, if rumor is to be believed. You were out every night in London."

"Out trying to forget you, most unsuccessfully. You know my erratic temper, Deirdre. My patience was tried beyond endurance, but now that I've had time to think—Oh, damme, here's Miss Sutton, come to claim you."

Miss Sutton was advancing at a swift stride, with a very purposeful glint in her eyes. "Mama thinks we ought to retire now, Deirdre," she said, without even glancing at Belami. That woman's arrogant manner was beginning to bother him unduly.

"Pray tell her we are busy," Belami said curtly.

Miss Sutton looked at him, and he was hard pressed to imagine why she disliked him so intensely. This was no cunning act of dislike to heat up his interest. There was blue fire in her eyes—yet she'd smiled at him a few minutes ago.

"Is that the message you wish me to take to Mama, Deirdre?" she asked.

"No, of course not. I must go, Dick," she apologized.

"You'll do as I asked?" he said. "What we discussed?"

A small smile glowed in her eyes. "Very well." The dimple that occasionally flashed at the corner of her lips peeped out for a brief instant to enchant him. "It was nice meeting you again," she added, to give an air of finality to their parting.

Belami escorted the ladies back to Mrs. Sutton and took a polite leave of them all. He noticed Pronto smirking at Miss Sutton and quizzed him about it when they were alone.

"Tossing your bonnet at the young Amazon, are you?"

"The bonnet's on the other foot. She's a dasher, Dick. Bold as can stare. Very fond of Pronto Pilgrim."

"I admire her taste," Belami said satirically. Elvira's aloofness still bothered him. "What's the secret of your success in that quarter?"

"I'll be dashed if I know. We think it's fate. Do you mind, Dick, when you was telling me about you and Deirdre once before she jilted you—the time you had old Bessler mesmerize Charney, I think it was. You said Deirdre was your other half—that's how it is with me and Elvira. We met and something clicked."

"Your money and her love of same, perhaps?" Belami suggested. "Those ladies are not exactly top of the trees, Pronto. I swear young Lucy dropped a dozen aitches while we were dancing, and was none too steady on her grammar."

"Elvira didn't drop anything but a hint that she liked me pretty well," Pronto said with satisfaction. "I did notice Elvira seems a touch above her little sister. I wonder what accounts for it."

39

"Mrs. Sutton seems genteel enough," Belami said, frowning at this small puzzle. "It's strange to discover that sort of discrepancy within a family."

He idly opened the newspaper as he sat, waiting for Deirdre to return. He looked at the spot where an article had been cut out. Odd how he found himself wondering about that one article more than all the others that were there for him to peruse if he wanted to.

"What are we waiting for?" Pronto asked.

"Deirdre's coming back down," Belami said.

"Eh? Who says so?"

"I say so," Belami told him, and smiled.

"Well, if you ain't a flat, Dick! You're going to let her and Charney kick you around the field again?"

"We're just going to talk, that's all," Dick told him.

"When you two talk, it's either April and May or fighting. Believe I'll just toddle along to our hotel."

"No, stay," Belami urged. "It will look better if she's not alone with me. Don't worry. Nothing will go wrong this time. I've got my lucky guinea," he said, and took it out of his pocket to flip. He glanced at the open paper. "That's what's missing!" he exclaimed.

"It ain't missing. It's right there—in the air. In your hand now," Pronto pointed out.

"No, the article that's been cut out of the paper. It's the one about the counterfeiters, the Jalbert gang." He riffled quickly through the paper to verify it.

"What the devil are you talking about?"

Belami explained about lending the paper to Captain Styger and finding it in Mrs. Sutton's hands. "I wonder why Styger cut it out." Belami frowned.

"Who's to say he did? Maybe Mrs. Sutton cut it out."

"Why would she do that? I wonder—"

"What are you on to?" Pronto asked, with more foreboding than pleasure. He knew that pensive face.

"I'm going to see if Styger's still here, at this hotel."

"Why?"

40

"It's a matter of suspicious coincidences," Belami said.

"That means clues, which means a case," Pronto deduced.

"Styger was at Dover, where the gang eluded the police. He called himself a sea captain, but oddly he didn't know much about the navy. He's the man I got my counterfeit coin from, indirectly, and seemed very upset when I mentioned it. He even offered to buy it back. He asked me if I was a government agent, too. I found that rather odd. And he's been here, in this hotel. It almost seems like fate throwing him in my path. What a crown to our career, Pronto, if we caught an international counterfeiter. I'm going to inquire if Styger's here," Belami decided. "If Deirdre comes, ask her to wait. I shan't be a moment."

He was back soon, still wearing his pensive frown, which Pronto noticed had grown stronger. Certainly looked like the makings of a case. "What's up?" he asked.

"There was never a Captain Styger registered here at all."

Pronto hunched his narrow shoulders. "There goes your clue. Mrs. Sutton must have got the paper from someone else."

"Perhaps, but I have a more interesting explanation. When I described Captain Styger to the clerk, he said there was a man matching my description—an *anglais*, grizzled hair, gruff-voiced, but calling himself Mr. Plunkett. Men don't adopt an alias without a reason. He wasn't registered, but took some meals here the past few days. Enough that they knew his name."

"It's as I said," Pronto explained. "Styger left the newspaper in the hotel—someone picked it up and passed it along to Mrs. Sutton. You're making bricks without straw here, Dick. You don't know the Jalberts ever went abroad at all."

"No one said so, but it makes eminent sense," Belami countered. "Gold is accepted as standard currency abroad.

41

Foreigners would be less familiar with the guinea than Englishmen. A false coin would be easier to peddle in Paris.''

"There's no saying Plunkett is Styger. Plenty of grizzled old *anglais* in Paris. I haven't heard of funny money showing up as far as that goes.''

"Neither have I, but I'll keep an ear out for it. I wonder what's keeping Deirdre?'' Belami looked impatiently toward the door. Charney was asleep, so all Deirdre had to do was wait till the Suttons' door had closed, and she could come down. It shouldn't have taken sixty seconds. But after thirty minutes, he was still waiting.

He had established a foothold, however, and was optimistic that before the week was up, he'd be back in Deirdre's good graces. Ever the optimist, Belami even saw her ensconced in his carriage on the way to Italy. The duchess would sell her soul, if she had a soul, for a free carriage ride.

He and Pronto returned to their hotel. "We'll have a week here before leaving for Venice,'' Belami mentioned.

"Believe I may have changed my mind, Dick. Rome's all the crack. Broken-up rubble of old churches and things. Artistic.''

"If it's Miss Sutton you have in mind,'' Dick said, "their destination is Venice.''

"Ain't. Elvira said Rome, clear as day.''

"Deirdre said Venice. They're all going together.''

"Going to Rome,'' Pronto assured him.

"Then why did Deirdre say Venice?''

Pronto shook his head sadly. "For the same reason she led you down the garden path about coming back down tonight, Dick. To pay you back for everything. The whole lot of 'em are likely chuckling up their sleeves this minute.''

Belami glared. There was just enough plausibility in this explanation to turn him wary. Deirdre had been vexed with his London doings. Was she playing off a stunt on him? It was clear now why Miss Sutton had snubbed him as well. Deirdre had put her up to it to teach him a lesson.

"It's just as well," he said, feigning a show of indifference. "Actually I wouldn't mind having a few days to look into this Jalbert-Styger thing."

"Include me out. I told Elvira I'm on holiday from crime."

"She knew your reputation, did she?" Dick asked. He remembered Elvira's one smile at him—it had occurred when he'd mentioned Styger, and if it was done to distract him, it had succeeded. Now why would she want to distract his attention from Styger?

"No getting away from it. We're famous. But there ain't nothing to look into," Pronto said. "Of course it gives you an excuse to hang around the Licorne. You might spot Deirdre and place yourself in position for another kick."

'Deirdre who?'' was Belami's manner of indicating that the hostilities had been resumed.

Chapter Four

After leaving Belami at the assembly, Deirdre went very quietly into the room she shared with her aunt. Her spirits sank when she saw the light still burning, and the duchess propped up on her pillows reading one of her gothic mysteries. Her scanty knob of gray hair was bound up in a cap, giving her grace more than ever the air of a gargoyle.

"You're back early. You look upset. Did some vile Frenchie get his hands on you?" the duchess demanded eagerly.

"No, Auntie, it was fine," Deirdre said. She conned the possibility of hiding the truth, but knew it was impossible. "Belami was there, which is why we left early," she admitted.

"The scoundrel! I feared he would follow us. I hope you didn't stand up with him?"

"No," Deirdre answered—sticking to the letter, if not the spirit, of truth.

"Good! I should hate to think any kin of mine so soft, after the way he carried on in London since jilting you."

"He didn't jilt me," Deirdre countered. Oh, dear, but he surely would if she didn't return belowstairs tonight.

"He refused to marry you. I call that a jilting. Perhaps nowadays you gels call it true love."

Deirdre had other fish to fry and let this subject die. "I

thought you'd be sleeping by now. Have you not taken your laudanum, Auntie?''

''I got reading Mrs. Radcliffe's *Udolpho* and couldn't put it down. Such a marvelous book! I shan't need a sleeping draught. Just hurry up your undressing and let us get the lamp extinguished.''

Deirdre had no option but to do as she was told. Her aunt should soon be snoring. She'd have to get dressed again later. She didn't think Dick would leave till she arrived.

A sly grin settled on Charney's haggard face. Into the darkness she said, ''I have the strange feeling I shan't sleep much tonight. I want to lie awake and think about business matters. It has just occurred to me I could let Fernvale while we're away. Yes, I have a deal to think about. Good night, Deirdre.''

''Good night, Auntie,'' Deirdre said in a small, sad voice.

The duchess knew. In some magical manner she had figured out that Dick was waiting belowstairs and was doing this to thwart their plans. Deirdre's main goal now was to let him know what had happened.

After an hour's plotting, her eyes closed and soon her slow, even breaths told Charney the girl was asleep. Now the duchess could get down to scheming in earnest. Preventing this particular marriage had become a sort of avocation to the bored old lady. She had no real hatred of Belami, except that he had outwitted her a couple of times in the past.

Still, Deirdre must be rescued from the most handsome, eligible jackanapes in England. Of course, Deirdre would have told him they were remaining in Paris a week. He would not be desperately eager to settle things. The duchess's course then was to leave Paris immediately. By eight-thirty in the morning, they would all be on their way.

The greatest care and some expenditure of money was necessary to execute this scheme. Before going down to breakfast, the duchess called a hotel maid and told her to pack their trunks and the Suttons'. This done, it remained only to convince Meggie that Paris was not worth seeing. She led her victim to a separate small table for breakfast.

"We'll let the gels discuss last night's party in peace," she declared. "They will speak more freely without us, Meggie."

While Elvira and Lucy teased Deirdre about her beau, the duchess brought her persuasions to bear on Mrs. Sutton. She assumed a pitiful countenance and said, "Belami is the most ramshackle rake in Europe. I tell you quite frankly, I don't put an elopement past him. Not that I blame you for landing him down on our heads, though it is a great pity you ever accepted a favor from him in the first place. And to allow your daughters to be familiar with him! He will have an eye for Elvira, certainly. And she a clergyman's daughter! What easy work he would have with her or Lucy."

Meggie showed a very proper concern but was somewhat obstinate on leaving Paris immediately. "We could remove to another hotel," she suggested.

"That wouldn't stop Belami for two minutes. It is the very sort of prank to interest him. No, we must leave France."

At the end of breakfast, Mrs. Sutton was still showing a remarkable stubbornness, but to soothe her friend she reached for the bill. "It's my turn, I believe," she said, and handed the waiter a gold coin.

The waiter looked at it suspiciously. "It's English money—a gold sovereign," Mrs. Sutton explained. "They've been accepting them in payment here at the hotel."

"Stupid Frenchies," the duchess said. "It is *argent anglais*, my good lad. Now be off with you."

The waiter left, but the duchess was not willing to let him off with the rudeness of speaking French. She collared the one servant in the establishment who spoke English and gave him a piece of her mind.

"A thousand apologies, your grace," he said with pleasing humility. "There have been some reports of counterfeit coins from England circulating in Paris. Yours was not a counterfeit. It was a perfectly good sovereign. I regret the inconvenience."

"A demmed impertinence, I call it," the duchess said. Her wrath was as much for Meggie as the waiter.

"Do you really feel Deirdre is in danger?" Meggie asked.

"She is in peril for her life. But of course you want to see that rubbishing old heap, Notre Dame. Who can blame you?"

Mrs. Sutton looked abashed at this plain speaking. "You make me ashamed for myself, your grace. We shall leave at once. I'll tell the girls."

A sly smile alit on Charney's face. "Don't tell them," she said. "Let us surprise them, Meggie. I don't want to give Deirdre an opportunity to write to Belami. She is not a totally unwilling victim, I fear."

They left, and within fifteen minutes the hapless young ladies were being herded into the post chaise. Only Deirdre expressed any surprise or dismay to see the luggage on top.

"What's going on?" she asked.

"We are leaving Paris," the duchess announced, with a triumphant grimace. "Come along, Deirdre. You don't want the Frenchies to mistake you for a fish with your mouth gaping open. Hop in."

Elvira put her hand on Deirdre's elbow and whispered in her ear, "I left Belami a note at the desk. He'll follow you."

Deirdre gave no verbal reply, but smiled gratefully at her friend. Without further ado, she clambered into the carriage, where many secret smiles were exchanged, causing her grace any amount of worry. But she was in good

47

humor. The war was never quite over with Belami. She had won a battle at least.

At his hotel, Belami had decided that as he'd made the first gesture, the next must come from Deirdre. If it had not been a stunt but only some interfering by Charney, Deirdre would write to him. It couldn't be impossible for her to send off a note. She wasn't kept bound and gagged in her room after all.

Pronto was not such an eager sightseer that he objected to spending a morning at the hotel with his boots on the fender of a cozy fire, with a pitcher of Irish coffee beside him.

"What we'll do is run along to Notre Dame this afternoon," he suggested to Dick. "Bound to be the first place the ladies go. And if they ain't there, you can put Réal on their scent."

"I've seen Notre Dame. I'm going to spend some time at the Louvre."

"The picture place?" Pronto asked suspiciously. "I'll give that a pass. Can see all the pictures of popes and saints I want to in England. We don't want to miss the place where they used the guillotine. Didn't get to see John the Baptist's head. Don't want to miss out on the guillotine as well."

"That'd be la Place de la Concorde, on the Right Bank."

"Not much chance of a head lying around, I daresay."

Both gentlemen kept a close eye on the desk, hoping to be paged for a message, but by noon none had come, and they went out to lunch. Belami went to the Louvre as he'd planned. Sure that Pronto would bring him home a note, Belami was already formulating plans to detach Deirdre from her chaperone that evening or, in the worst case, add the duchess to the party.

He returned to the hotel at five, his feet tired from walking and his mind whirling with images from the Louvre. Pronto wasn't back yet, so Belami picked up a newspaper, ordered a bottle of wine, and went to his room. He riffled desultorily through the pages, glancing at the political news. On page three, the words *fausse monnaie anglaise* seemed to jump out at him. Counterfeit English money! He read on eagerly. Three shops in the Montmartre district had received false coin, in each case a guinea. There were no other reported cases of counterfeit coins in Paris, but merchants were warned to be on the lookout.

A tingling on his neck alerted him that a case was beckoning. The Jalbert gang in Paris? He thought of the newspaper seen last night—but the Licorne was nowhere near Montmartre. Three coins—perhaps a victim like himself who picked the counterfeits up at Dover? If the whole gang was involved in it, there should be more than three guineas around. He took his own counterfeit out and fingered it.

A swell of impatience surged up in Belami. He should have done some investigating before he left England. How many men were in the Jalbert gang, for instance? Were they young, old, any physical characteristics that would easily distinguish them? Was one of them a grizzle-haired man with a ruddy complexion, posing as a sea captain? But really he needed his time free to rewin Deirdre. This was not the moment to intrude into a case uninvited.

As he flung the paper aside and poured a glass of wine, he heard Pronto's telltale scratching at the door. *"Entrez,"* he hollered.

Pronto poked his head in and asked, "Are you alone?"

"Of course I am. What happened to you? Did you fall off the steeple at Notre Dame?"

Pronto's face was smeared with grime, and as his corpulent frame came into the room, his whole toilette was seen to be similarly soiled. An unpleasant aroma accompanied him.

"Heh, heh. No, I didn't go to Notre Dame after all."

"You didn't go to Notre Dame! But I counted on you, Pronto. You were supposed to meet Deir—the ladies."

"Dick, you won't believe it," Pronto said, mincing forward and picking up the bottle of wine to wet his whistle.

"Did you see them? Where? What did she say?"

"I didn't see them," Pronto said, batting the question aside. "I went to that Concorde place—nothing worth looking at. Guillotine's gone; they've cleaned up all the gore. I met this fellow there with a boat, Dick. You'll never guess what."

"You fell into the Seine!"

"Devil a bit of it. I fell into the sewer. This fellow, Henri—he took me on a boat ride through the sewers. There was never anything like it. The whole city's built on a honeycomb of sewers. And that ain't the best of it! There's millions of dead bodies down there. The place is built up with masonry roofs and galleries and I don't know what all. They've taken the bones from cemeteries and made patterns with them along the sides of the galleries. I tried to pry a couple loose, but they're stuck in there like a nut in its shell."

"Good lord." Belami laughed. "You come to Paris, the most highly cultured city in Europe, and spend your day riding around sewers!"

"We don't have 'em in England. Broaden ourselves, you said. See things we don't have at home. By Jupiter, there ain't anything like this in the whole world."

"You'll love Rome. So you didn't see the ladies then?"

"They wasn't there. The duchess would love it though."

"Yes," Belami agreed, and glanced at his watch. Five-thirty, and still no word from Deirdre. It was beginning to look very much as though she had made a cake of him. A jolt of anger stabbed him. "Well, Pronto, what shall we do this evening? I wonder if there are any good wakes we could take you to. It'll be hard to top the catacombs."

"Deirdre didn't send you a note?"

"I haven't heard from her," he answered offhandedly. "What do you say we go to the opera tonight? If you start soaking now you might be clean in time."

50

"Charney won't spring for tickets to the opera."

"I'm not going to see Charney. Madame duChêne is singing this evening. I'm a great admirer of hers."

"Opera singing, eh?" Pronto asked. "Believe I'll pass. I'll drop around at the Licorne and see what Elvira has in mind. Let you know what Deirdre's up to," he added.

"All right," Belami answered, well pleased with the plan.

He knew by the glazed eye of his friend that Pronto was woolgathering. He thought it was the incomparable Elvira that caused that moonstruck look, till Pronto spoke to disillusion him. "Millions of dead bodies, all done up in herringbone and x's and parallel lines. It'd be a shame for you to come all the way to Paris and not see the sewers. But be careful of the rats. Place is swarming with 'em. Shifty-eyed rascals. Reminded me of Charney."

The gentlemen went their separate ways. Madame duChêne proved to be rather more buxom and more piercing of voice than Belami liked. He left at the first intermission and went back to his hotel. Pronto was there, pacing the lobby. He ran forward. "Disaster, Dick!" he exclaimed. "They've gone. Elvira, Deirdre, Charney—the lot of them. They sneaked out at the crack of dawn this morning. Left no forwarding address, no notes for us, nothing."

Belami was stunned. "But they just got here! They've only changed hotels."

"Leave the Licorne when Charney had found just what she wanted? There's nothing cheaper in the decent part of town. No, she only left that dump to go to Italy—or back to England."

"You're sure there was no note left for me?"

"I asked—three times. The clerk was beginning to think I was up to something. There was only one message left all morning, and it was for a Mr. Plunkett. They've shabbed off, Dick. I didn't think Elvira would serve me such a turn."

"Plunkett?" Belami asked. A quick frown pleated his brow. "Plunkett might be an alias for Captain Styger."

"If it is, there ain't much news for him. I read the note. The clerk let me have a peek at it for a half crown. It said 'Change of plans. Leaving immediately. Claude.' I thought for a minute it was from Elvira, till I saw the signature. Her name ain't Claude. Mine ain't Plunkett, so there you are."

"So Plunkett was planning to meet someone at the Licorne. I wonder if he's staying at Montmartre."

"Don't see that it matters to us."

Pronto listened with very little interest to Belami's suspicions regarding Styger-Plunkett. "All based on a bit of spilt brandy. Pretty slim stuff."

"Agreed, but I shall have Réal go to the Licorne and see if the note's been picked up, and, if possible, discover who wrote it. It's obviously someone staying at the Licorne."

Pronto shook his head. "Someone who *was* staying at the Licorne. 'Change of plans. Leaving immediately.' Claude left the note early this morning. He's your man. No mystery there."

"His last name's a mystery."

"I'll leave it to you, my friend. I'm more interested in finding Elvira. I'll stick around a day till Réal finds out where they went. If they've left Paris, I'm off to Rome."

"Venice," Belami countered.

"Italy."

Réal was sent for and came to meet his master in the lobby. "You require the carriage?" he asked in a thin voice. He had met a very charming French seamstress and was on his way to pick her up.

"No, Réal, but I'd like you to run around to the Licorne and make a few inquiries for me." Belami outlined his questions.

"*Sacrebleu!*" Réal scowled, but duty had its way. "I go at once, melord."

He scampered around the corner and made the inquiries. Belami was still in the lobby when he returned. "The maid who packs the trunks, she hears talking of Venice, not another hotel in Paris. The note for Monsieur Plunkett, it is picked up by a red-faced man tonight. There was no Claude staying at the hotel. No gentleman of the initial C, first name or last."

"The clerk didn't get a look at Claude?"

"He don't see who leaves the note," Réal said curtly.

Belami recognized by the symptoms that Réal had a tryst and said, "Thanks, Réal. You're free to join your lady now. I hope I haven't interfered too much with your plans."

"Lady?" Réal asked, eyes wide in contradiction.

"Female—the redhead you were talking to at the Louvre this afternoon. *Très jolie*. Enjoy yourself—use the carriage if you want to impress her."

"I have no plans for the evening, me," Réal insisted. "*Mais si* you are positive you are finished with duties, I drive over and see Notre Dame by moonlight," he said piously. "*Ma mère* in Canada will have a letter full of these descriptions."

"Good lord, do you have a mother? Run along then. The redhead will love Notre Dame by moonlight. *Bon soir.*"

Réal was gone in a flash. Belami went at a slower pace to his room. Paris, city of romance. Réal had found a woman. Pronto was in love. And here was he, jilted, abandoned. He might as well have spent the day in the sewers with Pronto for all the enjoyment he'd had. If Réal were correct—and Réal was always correct—the party had gone on to Venice. At least Deirdre had told him the truth. Why had Elvira told Pronto Rome was their destination? Trying to get rid of him, no doubt.

He thought of the Jalbert gang, of the various groups who had checked out of the Licorne this morning, and found he had indeed built bricks without straw. It was perfectly normal that a few of the Jalbert coins had turned up in Paris. Most English came to Paris via Dover. The three coins at Montmartre were mere accidents. If Styger had been in on it, there would have been some of the counterfeit money at the Licorne, and none was reported. Why waste time when every day was taking Deirdre farther from him?

He stretched out on his bed with his eyes closed, picturing himself and Deirdre floating down the canal in a gondola. Yes, they'd set out for Venice tomorrow.

Chapter Five

Deirdre found Venice as beautiful as Dick had told her it would be. What charmed her more than the rest—more than the canals and the islands joined by bridges, more than the beautiful old buildings and the gondolas—was its greenery after the sere fields of northern France and the snow of Switzerland. When they got into the gondola at Mestre for the last short lap of their journey, a sense of peace entered her heart. The gentle swaying of the boat after the jostling of the carriage, the fresh breeze from the water, and the spiring cypress trees all conspired to enchant her. Then they passed a small island and before her lay a fairyland of azure water on which gondolas moved effortlessly, like water beetles on a pond. From the sea soared the towers and domes of Venice, gold-plated by the lowering sun.

Even the duchess, who had come with the intention of being disappointed, admitted it was "a pleasant change." The hotel chosen was the Léon Bianco, on the banks of the Grand Canal. It too was a pleasant change, being less decrepit than other hostelries patronized. It was late by the time they were settled in and had ordered dinner. Deirdre was too realistic to expect any evening activity other than reading her guidebook while the duchess slept.

When her eyes became tired, she closed the book and went to the window, high above the Grand Canal, to gaze down on the evening activities of Venice. Gondolas glided like humpbacked whales over the black water. When she opened her window, she could hear the haunting echo of Italian melodies gently wafting on the air. There would be lovers in those romantic boats, going to rendezvous. Would she ever be joining them?

It was beginning to look very much as though she would not. Dick should have overtaken them before now. Tomorrow her aunt meant to register with the British consul, Mr. Richard Hoppner. They would learn then whether Lord Belami had already arrived, and if so, where he was staying. If this failed, she had one more clue to follow. On their honeymoon, they were to have stayed with the Conte and Contessa Ginnasi. The conte, a friend of the late Lord Belami, had made the offer through Dick's mother. Their palazzo was on the Grand Canal—one of those old gray stone buildings she was looking at now, with water lapping around its mossy foundations. And if Dick wasn't with them, she would have to assume he hadn't followed her after all.

Why would he not? Elvira had left him a note explaining their hasty departure. He would understand why she couldn't return belowstairs at the Licorne. Of course he'd come. Out in the black velvet shadows beyond the window a doleful bell chimed. Deirdre closed the window, lest the noise disturb her aunt's sleep.

The next morning there was too much novelty in the scenery to be actually depressed, even when Mr. Hoppner had no word on Lord Belami. There was the fascination of going everywhere by boat, sailing under the omnipresent arched bridges, and of looking at the foreigners, always with an eye alert for Dick. The Suttons had decided against going to the British consul with the duchess. Mrs. Sutton said, very properly in the duchess's opinion, that those formalities were only for the nobility. She and the girls would go shopping. They were famous shoppers. In every new town, they had to con the shops.

When Deirdre and her aunt returned to the hotel, Mrs. Sutton was glowing with pleasure. "You must let me take you to the Merceria this afternoon, your grace. The Pantheon Bazaar in London is nothing to it, I promise you. It's the shopping district here, just under that clock tower in Saint Mark's Square. Such bargains in silks and cottons! And gloves—the finest kid, going for an old song."

"I've put my finger through my evening gloves," the duchess admitted. Both finger and thumb had been peeking out for a whole season, till the leather was worn away with trying to patch it. "Deirdre would like some new ribbons, I daresay. Yes, we'll go with you," the duchess allowed graciously.

Over lunch, Mrs. Sutton seemed excited. "I'm afraid you'll think I'm extravagant." She blushed. "A beautiful pearl in a jewelry shop window caught my attention. It's a teardrop pearl, very unusual, and very large. About the size of an acorn—a little smaller in width. I mean to buy it for Elvira's twenty-first birthday. I promised her something special, but the occasion passed and so I owe her a treat."

"What are they asking for it?" the duchess demanded.

"A thousand pounds," Mrs. Sutton said.

The duchess choked on her coffee and turned quite livid. "Are you insane?" she demanded. "What on earth would someone like you want with such a thing? A clergyman's widow, spending a fortune on jewelry."

Mrs. Sutton was accustomed to these slurs on her social standing. "My uncle from India left me a considerable sum of money," she said.

"Hmph." So that explained how the silly woman could afford to jaunt all over Europe in a private post chaise. Odd she hadn't mentioned it before now. "You ought to put it in consuls or real estate," the duchess advised.

"I've already done that. Uncle McMaster left me a veritable fortune."

No further objections came to mind, so the duchess decided she'd go along and have a look at this pearl as big as an acorn. If it were a real bargain, she'd buy it herself.

In the gondola, Deirdre scanned the waters for a sight of Dick. "Still looking for him?" Elvira asked.

"Yes. I wonder if he got the note in Paris?"

"I told the desk clerk twice that if Lord Belami didn't pick it up, he should send it on to the Hotel d'Orléans. He'll come," Elvira said, and patted her arm.

Lucy, as usual, was in the sulks. Deirdre thought her sister's getting such a valuable jewel might account for it this time and decided to drop her a hint. "Will Lucy be getting a present, too?" she asked in a low voice.

"Yes, when she's twenty-one."

"She's a little put out. As your mama has plenty of money, would it not be thoughtful to buy some trinket for Lucy, too?"

"Indeed it would! You have the heart of an angel to think of it." Elvira smiled.

"What are you two whispering about?" Lucy demanded.

"Goose!" Elvira chided. "Why must you always think we're talking about you? I swear the child's as jealous as though I were her beau."

But Deirdre could understand the younger girl's feelings. Since she and the duchess had joined up with the Suttons, Elvira had developed a close friendship with herself. Elvira occasionally suggested they "sneak off" on Lucy. They had long discussions on men and love and marriage—discussions that Elvira felt were a trifle warm for her little sister.

"I heard Deirdre say 'Lucy,' " Lucy announced.

"If you must know then," Elvira told her, "we were discussing a present for you. I mean to ask Mama to buy you a pearl, too. Now are you satisfied? You've spoiled my surprise."

"Oh, Elvira!" Lucy exclaimed, and threw her arms

58

around her sister. "Do you really mean it? Am I to get a teardrop pearl, too?" Her blue eyes sparkled with joy.

"I doubt they'll have two. Your mama said it was quite unusual," Deirdre pointed out. Lucy's smile faded.

"No, I insist Lucy have one just like mine. If they don't have two, I shan't take it," Elvira said firmly.

They disembarked at Saint Mark's Square, and Mrs. Sutton hastened them all along to the Merceria, with hardly a glance at the magnificent architecture all around. Cathedrals and towers soared into the blue sky above, and in the square, pigeons strutted about as though it belonged solely to them.

"There is the shop, Casa Cerboni," Mrs. Sutton said, pointing to a small storefront. "It's right in the window."

They all hurried forward to admire the piece. Deirdre stared at the most beautiful pearl she had ever seen. It was as Mrs. Sutton had described it, an inch long, about half an inch at the widest part. The pearl had a rosy glow against its black velvet setting. The top of the teardrop was encased in a gold cap, with a hook attached for hanging on a chain.

"It's beautiful!" she gasped. It struck her at once how well the piece would suit statuesque Elvira and how gaudy it would look on little Lucy.

They went inside, where the jeweler recognized the Suttons from their morning call. Signor Cerboni did a brisk business with tourists and spoke English fairly fluently. He got the pearl from the window and set it on the counter. It was the duchess's bony fingers that reached out to take it up.

"This is mighty handsome," she declared, and stuck the pearl between her teeth to test its authenticity. It grated as a pearl should, but one compliment was more than she had meant to utter. "Very smooth on the teeth," she said doubtfully.

"There is no doubt of its authenticity," Signor Cerboni declared. "I got it directly from the Rusconi estate. The pearl's history is well known. It was given to Lucrezia Borgia by her bridegroom, who bought it from her father, the pope, in 1493. It is a great bargain, ladies. The only reason it is going at such a price is that pearls are not in the highest fashion in Italy.''

The duchess pried at the setting. "Odd they would set such a valuable pearl in tin," she said.

"It is eighteen-carat gold, signora!" the jeweler exclaimed. These English eccentrics!

"You may call me Duchessa."

Signor Cerboni looked at her tattered gloves on the counter and smiled blandly.

"It's a pretty enough trinket, for five hundred pounds." The duchess shrugged.

"The price is one thousand," Mrs. Sutton reminded her.

"Surely you jest! A thousand pounds for this spurious thing, mounted in tin. You must be mad, Meggie."

"The price is not open to bargaining," the jeweler said, and snatched the pearl from the duchess, before she got it pried loose from its moorings entirely.

"I'll take it," Mrs. Sutton said. "Could you deliver it to the Léon Bianco for me? I don't like to carry a thousand pounds in the streets. You will accept English gold coins, I presume?"

"But certainly, signora. I shall have it delivered tomorrow morning, if that suits you?"

Deirdre nudged Elvira's elbow. "Lucy's present," she whispered, and Elvira spoke to her mother.

The duchess stepped back and spoke to Deirdre in accents of disgust. "I could have got a couple of hundred pounds knocked off the price if Mrs. Sutton had her wits about her. These new nabobs spoil shopping for the rest of us."

At the end of this speech, the door opened and a very elegant lady entered the shop. Deirdre had never seen anyone so lovely in her life. The woman looked like a Dresden doll, small in stature but perfect in every proportion. Beneath her fashionable bonnet, a wave of jet black hair sat on a high forehead. Her skin was pale and translucent, every feature finely drawn. The eyes in particular were magnificent. Great, dark eyes, wide-set, fringed with long lashes.

Signor Cerboni looked up and exclaimed, "Ah, Contessa!" There was some rapid Italian conversation in which Deirdre understood only the word *"diamante."* The contessa had a lovely musical voice, soft as a dove's.

Charney saw no reason why a duchess should wait on the pleasure of a mere countess and elbowed the lady aside. "You have the address, sir? Léon Bianco, on the Grand Canal."

The beautiful contessa turned and smiled at her grace. "Then we are neighbors!" she exclaimed in a prettily accented voice, and offered a small hand gloved in blue kid to match her gown. "I live just across the canal."

"You speak English!" her grace said, allowing a small smile to reveal her yellowing teeth. "The Duchess of Charney, and this is my niece, Miss Gower. These are the Suttons," she added, with a nod to the rest of the party.

It seemed impossible the contessa's eyes could grow any larger, but they widened in astonishment. "It is impossible!" she exclaimed delightedly. "Not Deirdre Gower and her aunt! But I have been hearing about you ladies for two days now!"

"I daresay word of our coming has preceded us," the duchess allowed. She was finding the contessa a respectable person, possibly one who threw lavish dinner parties and balls. "I don't believe I caught the name—"

"Forgive me! Surprise has robbed me of my manners. I am Contessa Ginnasi."

Deirdre stared in dismay. This couldn't possibly be the wife of the late Lord Belami's friend. Contessa Ginnasi should be a lady in her sixties. She had a dreadful premonition where the contessa had heard of them. Dick!

61

And he was staying with this sinfully beautiful lady. A young, beautiful lady, married to some old relic. She knew now where Dick was, and why he hadn't bothered trying to find her.

"So nice to meet you, Contessa," Deirdre said, with a cool jerk of a curtsy. "We really ought to be going now, Auntie."

The contessa placed her hand on the duchess's sleeve, a thing not normally tolerated, but permitted on this occasion. "Do wait, just a moment. I have such a surprise for you!" she smiled, revealing teeth like a set of matched pearls.

"We can allow you a moment," the duchess decided, while she scurried around in her mind for what the surprise could be. "I say, are you some relation to old Conte Ginnasi, who was politicking in England eons ago? Don't tell me he's still alive! Is he coming to meet you?"

"My dear Guy seldom goes out," the contessa said.

"You are the conte's daughter-in-law, are you?" the duchess asked, trying to figure out a reasonable relationship.

"Ah, no, I am Guy's wife. We married five years ago when the old contessa passed away." The contessa flashed a glance to the door. Her face lit up like the sun. "Here we are! Not the conte, you see, but the baron!" With a dramatic gesture of her arm, she welcomed Belami into the shop.

Any hope or doubt that Dick had planned this meeting vanished when Deirdre looked at his shocked face. He looked as guilty as a poacher caught with his bag jiggling. His eyes darted first to Deirdre, then to the contessa, to the duchess. He wished the floor could open up and swallow him.

"*Mio* Belami," the contessa said, and went forward to take his hand. "See who I have found for you!"

"Good day, Lord Belami," Deirdre said, and turned

purposefully to her aunt. She fully expected to see Charney on her high horse, but it was no such a thing.

That sly old dame was ransacking her mind to figure out what was afoot here. Ginnasi—of course, that was where Dick had planned to batten himself and Deirdre in Venice! Obviously he was staying at the Palazzo Ginnasi—free. These palazzi were enormous buildings. Two more guests, herself and Deirdre, would never be noticed. The Suttons were well enough for traveling companions, but it was time to dispense with them. That Belami was obviously the contessa's lover was no impediment. It would open up Deirdre's eyes once and for all to what kind of a rake he was.

"Nice to see you again, Belami," the duchess said, and offered her hand.

Dick reached out and shook it as one in a trance. What was going on here? No abuse? No insults? No stalking out of the shop? "Sorry I missed you in Paris, your grace," he said.

"We didn't stay a minute. So chilly—we much prefer Italy. One does get tired of the racket of hotels though."

"Have you been here long?" Dick asked, darting a quick glance to Deirdre.

As half a day seemed rather short to have tired of their hotel the duchess said, "We have been on the road forever. Hotels are all alike. Where are you putting up, Belami?"

"The contessa was kind enough to offer me rack and manger," Dick said. He was beginning to understand his function now. He was to ease the skint's path into Carlotta's home.

Deirdre stiffened like a frozen reed at this news. "Let us go now, Auntie," she said.

"We must get together soon," the duchess said to Contessa Ginnasi. "Do come to our hotel for dinner. I should so like to see the dear conte again. Ah, but he doesn't go out, you said."

63

"You must come to us," the contessa answered. "Come tonight!"

Deirdre felt such a rage she could no longer stand still. She strode toward the door and met Pronto Pilgrim coming in.

Pronto looked from Deirdre to the rest of the group. "Oh, oh! Fat's in the fire now," he muttered into his collar.

"Mr. Pilgrim," Deirdre said stiffly.

"G'day, Deirdre. No point cutting up stiff at me. I ain't the one arranged this business. See you've met Carlotta. Quite the dasher, ain't she?"

"Is that her name?"

"Must be. It's what everybody calls her. How's Charney taking to Dick's following you here?"

"Following me?" she asked with an angry glare. "I'm not the one brought him here. It's that—Carlotta."

"No such thing," Pronto said, but just as the conversation was beginning to get interesting, he spotted Elvira and drifted off on wings of love.

"Miss Sutton," he said, and bowed most ungracefully. "Here I am, at your service, ma'am. Like you said—fate."

Elvira smiled condescendingly. "Mr. Pilgrim, isn't it?"

"Of course it's me!" he answered. Pretty cool, and him scrambling over mountains to meet her. But he noticed she was smiling and his heart softened. "You're bamming me, you sly rascal. When can I call on you, Miss Sutton?"

"You should really say good day to Mama and my sister first," she pointed out, and led him forward. They showed him Elvira's pearl. "I want Lucy to have one just like mine."

"That's sweet of you," Pronto said, much impressed at her kindness. "Didn't realize your mama was a nabob."

"She isn't," Elvira teased. "Her uncle was a nabob and left her his fortune when he died."

Pronto frowned. He already knew winning Elvira would be difficult. If she was an heiress into the bargain, it'd be

64

impossible. What he had to do was snap her up fast, before she went home where all the fortune hunters would be hounding her. As he looked at her tall, beautiful body, her full breasts, and noble face, he knew she was worth every effort.

"Sorry to hear it," he said.

"He died a year ago. We're not in mourning."

"Didn't mean that. Hope you don't take the notion I'm after your money. I cared for you before you told me."

Elvira's throaty laugh echoed in his ear. "You are too ridiculous, Mr. Pilgrim. I never for one moment thought of you as a fortune hunter. Why you strike me as a gentleman who doesn't have to worry about money."

"Matter of fact, I do own an abbey," he remembered, and looked hopefully for approval. It certainly looked like approval, or interest at least, shining in Elvira's eyes.

"There you are then." Elvira smiled. "You own an abbey; I own the pearl. And the rest of the world may whistle for envy."

"So when may I call on you?" he asked.

"Why don't you come around to the Léon Bianco later?"

"I'll be there," he promised. Inching his way behind Mrs. Sutton for privacy, he lifted Elvira's hand and kissed her fingers. A fine, sturdy paw the girl had. Nearly as big as his own, only long and artistic, whereas his was short and pudgy.

There were sounds of leave-taking across the shop. Pronto went reluctantly forward, feeling he ought to greet Charney. *"Bonjouro,"* he said, and made a leg.

"Mr. Pilgrim. Still tagging along with Belami, eh? How are you liking Europe?"

"They've got dandy sewers in Paris," he told her. He was right—her eyes were exactly like the sewer rats'.

The duchess suspected this was a joke. She never connived at jokes and ignored it. She gathered up the Suttons and left.

"The contessa has invited Deirdre and myself to dinner this evening," she announced. "We shall be seeing a good deal of the contessa and her set. As you mentioned this morning, you will find your own friends. I fear these upstart Italian nobles take themselves very seriously. I hinted that you and the girls might accept an invitation as well, but the contessa didn't take me up on it."

"We certainly don't expect to glide into society on your coattails, Duchess," Mrs. Sutton said, as friendly as ever. Really, the woman was better than a gift.

They went on to a few other shops, but for Deirdre the day was destroyed. She had found Dick at last, only to find him involved with a woman so beautiful there was no hope of winning him back. He had been stiff and unfriendly and, worst of all, he looked palpably guilty. She dreaded the ordeal of dinner at the Palazzo Ginnasi worse than a trip to the tooth-drawer. And like a bad tooth, the pain refused to go away.

Chapter Six

While Deirdre fretted and got dressed in her best blue gown that showed off her shoulders, the duchess was chirping merrily. With careful flattery and encouragement, the contessa would be made to see the benefit of harboring an English duchess under her roof for an indefinite period. Connections would be made that greatly reduced the cost of further travel: carriages provided free, noble doors opened to her in Naples and Rome. She dashed a note off to Fernvale, urging her bailiff to find an occupant for the estate on a six-month lease, renewable. This done, she turned to her niece.

"Bring along a shawl, Deirdre. It will be chilly in the gondola, and drafty as bedemmed at the palazzo."

Deirdre picked up her silver-spangled shawl that wouldn't keep off the breath from a gnat, but it looked good. The Ginnasi gondola was waiting for them at the landing. In the starry dusk of twilight, they were whisked across the Grand Canal to the left bank and a little north to the palazzo, nestled in beside the Accademia. The Palazzo Ginnasi was a fairly ugly old stone building of great antiquity. Moss climbed a few feet up its walls. The duchess took one look and was struck with the notion that she would pay not to stay there, and that was saying a good deal. Her joints would seize up entirely in those moist drafts.

But when the footman led her up the walk from the landing to an entrance on the north side, she observed that the breezes, while damp, were really not at all chilly. Once in the palazzo, she discovered a delightful surprise—fireplaces, which had been absent in Italian hotels. The heat from them mingling with the moisture created a balminess similar to a conservatory, an atmosphere in which not only plants but also octogenarians might thrive.

The contessa awaited them in her saloon, a chamber of faded grandeur in which the duchess felt very much at home amongst the other antiquities. There were threadbare Oriental carpets, draperies sagging with age and dilapidation, ornate gilt-trimmed sofas covered in shredding satin—all of it topped by a fine chandelier with its lights turned as low as seeing would permit.

But it was the hostess that was of more interest to Deirdre, and her youthful eyes could see well enough that the contessa was as beautiful as she remembered. This evening she wore a dramatic black gown that revealed a pair of alabaster shoulders and hinted at other attractions as well.

"Duchess, Miss Gower, so kind of you to come," the contessa said, striding forward to shake hands. "My husband will be here in a moment. Belami has gone to fetch him."

The ladies made polite greetings and were shown to one of the sagging sofas. Within a minute, Belami appeared at the door pushing a hooded bath chair. In it sat the conte, a shriveled little gentleman of some seventy-odd years, wearing a deep blue velvet jacket of ancient cut. At his throat a fall of white lace gleamed.

He greeted them in a quavering voice. *"Ah, Duchessa! Lei è molto gentile—"*

"Inglese, caro," the contessa reminded him.

Even while he welcomed the duchess, his black eyes turned to ogle Deirdre. *"Che bella!"*

"Mind your manners, Guy," his wife scolded, and

nodded for Belami to push him up to the fireplace. The duchess hastened to occupy the chair closest to him and Deirdre stood, struck dumb that the beautiful young contessa should have shackled herself to this wreck of humanity. The conte was obviously a skirt chaser, but why on earth had Carlotta married him?

Deirdre became aware that both the contessa and Belami were staring at her, both in much the same way. They looked curious, alert, expectant, and it made her very nervous.

"What a charming palazzo, Contessa," she said.

"*Grazie*. May I offer you a drink, or would you rather have Belami show you the gardens while it's still daylight?" Before Deirdre could answer, the contessa continued. "Do show Miss Gower the garden, Belami, and I'll tend to Guy. He'll become snappish if I don't get him his posset."

"Deirdre?" Belami offered his arm, and in some confusion Deirdre accepted it and was led out the door.

"You are looking very beautiful this evening, Deirdre," he said as they went along to the door.

"Thank you," she said stiffly. "The contessa is lovely."

"She's a diamond of the first water," he replied unwisely.

"It's odd that she should have married such an old man."

They had reached the door. Belami opened it wide and smiled at her, one of his peculiarly intimate smiles that always disarmed her. She felt as if she were the only woman in the world when Dick looked at her like that. She felt suffocated, and always fell speechless.

"Therein lies a tale," he said, and led her outdoors.

The place was less a garden than a tangle of weeds from which an occasional flower peeped out. At the four corners of the plot, classical statues reared up on pedestals,

69

staring disdainfully at the mess below. The vestige of a curved path led into the small jungle. "Is it safe to take you down the garden path?" Belami asked, glancing at her skirts. Their eyes met briefly. "An ill-chosen phrase." He smiled.

"I've survived your garden paths till now," she answered tartly, and followed as Dick pushed aside the weeds and bushes.

When they were in the center, he stopped and turned to face her. The smile was transformed to a severe, questioning face. "Why did you do it?" he demanded.

"It was my aunt's idea to come!"

"I mean why did you bolt on me in Paris? I waited for ages that night—and then to learn you had left without even sending me a message."

"But I did leave you a note!"

"The hell you did!" he exclaimed angrily.

"Dick, I did! At least Elvira did," she added, and explained the nature of their departure.

"There was no note," he said simply.

"It must have gone astray. Elvira doesn't speak French—perhaps the clerk misunderstood."

Dick frowned uncertainly. "It was only your telling me you were coming to Venice that kept me from hating you," he said. "If you hadn't come here, I don't know what I would have done. Elvira told Pronto your destination was Rome."

"But it was Elvira who insisted on coming to Venice."

"There's something strange about that woman," Belami said.

Deirdre tossed her shoulders. "You're just annoyed that she doesn't care for you. The contessa is not so immune to your charms, I think?"

"Carlotta's a man-izer. It stands to reason, being married to old Guy."

"Why did she marry him?"

"It's called making a good match. Guy's a conte, he

owns this heap," he said, looking around the derelict garden and to the house beyond. "Carlotta was an actress, and his mistress. When the old contessa died, they made it legal. Guy won't last long, and once he's gone, the contessa will be in a position to make a really stunning match."

"Did she tell you all that?" Deirdre asked.

"The best stories are contained between the lines."

"That's true," Deirdre replied enigmatically, and looked away to where the sun was setting in an amethyst sky streaked with amber. Between the lines of Dick's story, she read that he was carrying on with the man-izing contessa.

Belami gazed at her profile, her pale face limned against the dark foliage, and felt a wrenching inside. He reached out and turned her to face him. His hands remained on her arms as he gazed at her, and when he spoke, his voice was husky. "Don't even think it," he said softly. "You know you're the only woman I ever loved, Deirdre."

He pulled her into his arms and lowered his lips to hers. It seemed an omen of good luck that in this country where songbirds were rare, a nightingale chose that moment to utter its plaintive warble. He crushed her against his chest and the kiss deepened. Deirdre raised her arms to his neck and clung as though her life depended on it. This wasn't the time to be difficult, when she hoped to lure him away from the palazzo.

After a lengthy embrace, she pulled away and looked shyly at him. "If you know what I'm thinking, Dick—"

"I do, but the contessa is just a friend. The Ginnasis are in desperate financial trouble. I'm staying here as a paying guest. There's nothing between Carlotta and me. Don't ask me to leave. The contessa is helping me."

"You're not on a case," she objected.

"I am, rather. I've been haphazardly following an English counterfeiter—Jalbert's the name. I got one of his false coins at Dover. A couple turned up in Paris, and as

I made the journey here, I came across a few more people who'd been duped. It's difficult for me in a foreign country, but Carlotta has connections. One of the coins turned up at Mestre. It's obvious the Jalbert gang were on their way to Venice. Carlotta knows bankers and merchants and some of the other sorts as well.''

Deirdre frowned, not understanding. ''People from the demimonde,'' he said bluntly. ''She's acquainted with criminals from before her marriage—someone like that would be the first to know if a new colleague is in town, and where to find him.''

''Why do you have to be the one to catch the gang?''

''I have an inkling what one of them looks like,'' he said, and told her about Captain Styger. ''Counterfeiters prey on the innocent. The man's English. If it isn't for an Englishman to catch him, who should do it? Besides,'' he added more realistically, ''it'll be great fun.''

But it wouldn't be much fun for her to know Dick was off on an investigation with the beautiful Carlotta. She pouted attractively. ''You can help me, too,'' he added. ''You'll be in all the shops. Keep an eye open at the hotel as well. Perhaps Jalbert will turn up there.''

Before there was time for more persuasions on either side, a servant came and called them to dinner. The dining room was better lit than the saloon, and in better repair. An impressive array of fine china and silver gleamed on the white linen cloth. The conte had his bath chair wheeled up to the table. Seating arrangements were bound to be irregular with three ladies and only two gentlemen. They were further thrown out of kilter when Carlotta sat beside her husband to feed him. She cut up his food as though he were a baby and fed him, beguiling him with baby talk all the while. In spite of this trying job, she also managed to entertain her guests.

The duchess in particular pelted the hostess with questions. ''How many rooms do you have here, Contessa?'' she asked.

"Forty or fifty. You must see the Tintoretto organ shutters in the music room. They are one of our show pieces. Dear Tintoretto—Michelangelo's drawing and Titian's colors was his motto. Unfortunately the colors have faded till they more closely resemble a London fog."

"I mean how many bedchambers," her grace persisted.

"Twenty-five, more or less," the contessa said vaguely.

"Such a shame, all that space going to waste. At Fernvale, I keep the place full of company."

Dick's lips moved unsteadily as he smiled across the table at Deirdre. He well remembered the company of bats and mice, and beetles, during his brief visit.

"I hope you and the dear conte will feel quite free to put up with me if you ever come to England," the duchess said grandly. It seemed safe enough. The conte was scarcely able to get down to his own saloon. The contessa smiled, but she didn't make any offer.

Undeterred, the duchess forged on to clarify her meaning. "Such a pleasure to be in a home, after weeks of hotels. You are fortunate to have such good friends in Italy, Belami."

"I am very much aware of it," Belami said.

The contessa was mashing milk and butter into the conte's vegetables and ignored these broad hints. "Here you go, my little Guy," she said merrily, and lifted the fork.

The duchess noticed a smear of green on the conte's lace fichu. Lord, what an infliction the man was. She very firmly lifted her own forkful of meat and chewed it up on the few remaining steady teeth in her head. Perhaps the conte might be more amenable to her hints.

She bared her teeth in a smile and said, "How very much at home you make me feel, Conte. I was used to feeding my husband just as your dear lady is doing. How I miss feeding him, and wheeling his chair about the garden on fine days, reading to him by the fireside when the weather was inclement. You must let me come one day and take over your chores, Contessa.''

The contessa lifted her head. Aha! She'd hit the magic chord here. The minx hated every moment of her loving act. ''That is kind of you,'' Carlotta said. After dinner she requested Belami's help in getting the conte back to the saloon.

She pushed the bath chair aside and whispered, ''Do you want me to invite them here?''

''I have nothing against it,'' Dick said.

''She won't expect to pay, but I must say I would appreciate some help with Guy.''

''She won't lift a finger once she's here.''

''To hell with her then.''

Dick frowned. Charney would be in a rare pelter if she were crossed. On the other hand, free board would put her in alt—and Deirdre would be here. ''I'll pay,'' he said. The contessa gave him an encouraging smile.

She held the door, Dick shoved the bath chair through it, and the contessa went to sit beside the duchess. ''I have just had a marvelous idea,'' she said, smiling. ''Don't refuse me. You and Miss Gower must stay here with us. We'd adore to have you.''

''Eh?'' the conte demanded, and was completely ignored.

As the gondolier rowed the guests home afterward, the duchess was in high glee. She forgot temporarily that Belami, who came with them, was a villain. ''A charming couple,'' she told him. ''Deirdre will do well to involve herself with the contessa's set. And mind you don't be exposing your chest like that trollop,'' she added aside to her niece.

In the darkness, Dick took Deirdre's fingers and squeezed them. ''I'll bring the Ginnasis' boat for you tomorrow morning, your grace. What hour will be convenient?''

Breakfast was obviously too early to go, but lunch could be had free of cost. "Say, eleven," the duchess decided.

Belami accompanied them from the landing to their hotel and left them at the bottom of the stairs. The duchess was so happy that she allowed Deirdre to remain behind a moment.

"How did you arrange it?" Deirdre asked. "Are you paying for us, Dick?"

"It was Charney's offer to help with the chore of husband-sitting that turned the trick. I hope this convinces you there's nothing between Carlotta and me."

Deirdre smiled mischievously. The world was suddenly bright again. "If there is, I'll soon discover it," she warned, and scampered upstairs.

Pronto was sitting in the lobby and called when Belami passed. "Figured you'd bring the ladies home," he said. "I'll grab a ride back to the palazzo with you. I'll be leaving it *demanini*, Dick. I'm moving here, to the Léon Bianco."

Belami could usually figure out Pronto's few insertions of foreign speech. They were some strange admixture of French and Italian. "Why?" Dick asked.

Pronto rubbed a hand over his luxuriant brown curls and sighed. "Elvira. Bit of a nuisance having to leap into a leaky boat every time I want to see my *amoro*. Rates here ain't any steeper than Carlotta's. I'm taking Elvira to see the Doge's Palace *demanini*. By the by, she was wondering if you'd come in the morning and take a look at that pearl her mama's buying."

"I'll be here to pick up the ladies," Belami said. "They're removing to the palazzo. I'd be happy to have a look at the pearl, but why do they want me to see it?"

"The duchess gave Mrs. Sutton the notion the pearl was a fake. Told her she couldn't do better than to have my old *compagno* take a look at it."

"Cerboni wouldn't sell a fake. He's a reputable jeweler, but I'd like to see the piece. Well, shall we go?"

They returned to the gondola. As the oars splashed through the water, Pronto leaned back and gazed up at the stars. "Just like a dream," he said softly.

"It's beautiful here," Belami agreed.

"I didn't mean this old creaking boat. I meant Elvira. She's mad for me, Dick. Said she'd missed me."

Belami frowned into the darkness. "I'd be wary of strange ladies if I were you."

"No reason to be jealous. You've got your Deirdre— and Carlotta. That minx is hot for you. I saw her cornering you in the hallway this morning—the old conte was peeking around the lid of his basket, too. You'd best be careful."

"Carlotta was only asking my opinion of her bonnet."

"Why'd she have you by both hands then?"

"She's affectionate," Dick said, but he was a little worried that her affection would get out of hand.

"She was affectionate to me, too. Came to my bedroom when I was undressing. Told me I have nice hands," he said.

"You're becoming quite the accomplished flirt, but I still say be wary of Elvira. She told Deirdre she'd left me a note in Paris. As you very well know, there was no note. She told you they were going to Rome."

"Explained that," Pronto said. "Thought I was just a trifler. Didn't want to get her heart broken, so she told me that bammer. Very sensitive," Pronto added gently.

"What did you two do this evening?"

"It was the four of us. The mama and Lucy tagged along. Took the *signoras* out for dinner and a walk around a couple of *piazzas*. We're going to paint some bridges one of these days. Some old gaffer tried to strike up an acquaintance with Mrs. Sutton. An Englishman, he was."

"This seems to be a city of romance."

"He didn't get much romance I can tell you. She made short shrift of him. I had the notion he followed us from the *restauranto*. Knew it was the same fellow by the pipe he smoked. One of those big ones, you know, with the white lining."

Belami jerked to attention. "A meerschaum pipe?" he asked.

"Eh?"

"What did he look like?"

"I told you—big one, white lining."

"The man, Pronto."

"Oh, the man. Gray hair, high color. A bluff old gent."

"By God, it was Styger."

"Didn't give his name."

"It's the man who had a counterfeit coin on the boat. I think he's one of the Jalbert gang! Now what could he want with Mrs. Sutton?"

"Trying to make a date with her, I daresay. Heard us talking English at the restaurant. Lonesome, very likely."

Belami rubbed his hand over his chin. "She had his newspaper at the hotel in Paris. We're coming across some mighty strange coincidences here, my friend."

"Coincidences—that's another word for clue," Pronto said accusingly. "If you're suggesting the Suttons have anything to do with the Jalberts, you're off the mark. They're rich as Croesus. Had an old nabob uncle stuck his fork in the wall last year and left them a fortune. Why, ain't Mrs. Sutton buying a great big pearl for Elvira tomorrow, and paying cash?"

"Cash! Counterfeit guineas if I know anything," Belami exclaimed. "They'll buy the pearl and disappear."

"Now see here, Dick, I've gone along with you on many a case, but when you try to involve Elvira's mother, you go too far. I won't have you bouncing her gold on the counter and weighing it—dashed insult."

"I shall be exceedingly discreet," Belami promised, but he was quivering with excitement.

Pronto was in such a foul mood when they reached the palazzo that he said *"aurivderci"* very coolly, then went to his room and locked the door, in case Carlotta came to

77

admire his hands. Belami locked his door, too. As he lay in bed reviewing the doings of this strange day, he wondered why the Suttons had especially invited him to be present during the purchase of the pearl. There wasn't a chance in a thousand Pronto hadn't told them his suspicions of the counterfeiters. They had discussed it a good deal during their trip.

Was Mrs. Sutton, that woman who looked like the incarnation of a clergyman's wife, connected with the Jalbert gang? It seemed incredible. Lucy, too, was a very ordinary sort of girl. But Elvira . . . There was a cat of a different stripe! And after all her evasionary tactics, she *invited* him to oversee the purchase of the pearl.

She didn't match the rest of that ordinary family. She was better spoken, more sure of herself, more intelligent. He had suspected before that she had been reared separately from Lucy. Perhaps reared in some circumstance that brought her in touch with the Jalberts? Could it be Elvira the man with the pipe was trying to speak to, not Mrs. Sutton?

As Belami lay in bed thinking, he could see no way to learn the truth but to tackle Elvira himself. He must do it discreetly. Compliments would help—perhaps a mild flirtation. She really was a very handsome woman; making up to her wouldn't appear unusual. It was well Deirdre was removing from the hotel—though whether moving her into Carlotta's orbit was a good idea, he had grave doubts.

Chapter Seven

Deirdre and the duchess had a farewell breakfast with the Suttons the next morning. At eleven Belami and Pronto came, the latter with his luggage to check into the hotel. When Signor Cerboni arrived, the group went to a private parlor to view the pearl. Belami took it and the jeweler's loupe to the window to examine it in daylight. He saw at a glance that the pearl was genuine and the setting, too, had the rough appearance of fifteenth-century work.

He remembered his plan to befriend Elvira, and was pleased when she joined him. "Mr. Pilgrim tells me you are an expert, Lord Belami," she said. The teasing look in her eyes did not denote agreement with this notion. Quite the contrary.

"You strike me as a young lady who knows her own mind," he answered with a flirtatious smile. "I never was an oyster and claim no intimacy with pearls, but this certainly looks genuine to me."

"I thought so, too," she said, and reached for the pearl. Their hands brushed. Elvira, who hadn't a clumsy bone in her body, lost her grip on the pearl. Belami, quick as a cat, reached out and grabbed it before it fell. Their eyes met and held. Some spark of emotion flared between them. Elvira took the pearl and turned away.

Belami put his hand on her wrist to stop her. "Pronto

has been singing your praises to me, Miss Sutton," he said.

She lifted her eyes and directed a challenging look at him. "You would know better than I to what extent Mr. Pilgrim's opinion might be relied on."

"I prefer to judge for myself. I judge you to be a young lady of the world." He said no more but allowed his eyes to admire her a moment before wandering to Lucy and Mrs. Sutton. "Rather more so than your sister," he added thoughtfully.

"I have had more advantages than Lucy."

"You, I think, have had the advantage of a larger society than . . . ?"

"We're from Cornwall. I was sent to a seminary in Bath to be educated. Lucy was a frail child and remained at home."

Was it possible the haughty Elvira was uncomfortable in a mild flirtation? She certainly seemed ill at ease. "That would account for it." Belami nodded.

"And now perhaps you would be kind enough to return my hand," she said, looking boldly at him with a smile in her eyes. "Miss Gower will think her kindness toward me ill-paid. She might mistake this interlude for a flirtation."

"I'm sure we both agree she would be quite mistaken," Belami said, but ambiguously. His tone hinted at romance. And Elvira was interested. He could see it in her eyes. Interested and—what? Guilty, no doubt, because of Deirdre. He accompanied her to the table, where they sat side by side.

Deirdre was not such a demon of jealousy that she resented their brief absence. Belami indicated his satisfaction to Cerboni, and they both looked expectantly to Mrs. Sutton for the money. She set on the table a black leather box and unlocked it to reveal one thousand English guineas twinkling in the light from the window. They certainly looked genuine to Belami, but then so did the

80

counterfeit coin in his pocket. He reached for it and discovered to his dismay that it was missing. He had changed jackets before leaving the palazzo and most particularly put the coin there to check against Mrs. Sutton's money. His pockets were deep enough—it seemed unlikely it had fallen out. His eyes slid to Elvira, who had turned aside to speak to her sister.

It struck him that this morning was the first occasion Elvira had ever voluntarily said a word to him. Had she taken the coin from his pocket while they spoke? Was that why she "dropped" the pearl, and why she had looked self-conscious? He adopted his drawling voice that told both Deirdre and Pronto he was in a pelter and said, "We have agreed the pearl is genuine. Shall we now put the money to the test?"

Elvira's head turned slowly. If ever contempt glowed in a woman's eyes, it glowed in Elvira Sutton's now. Signor Cerboni looked quite alarmed. "What do you mean?" he demanded.

"Have you not heard, signore?" Belami drawled. "England is overrun with counterfeit gold coins—guineas, exactly like this," he said, and lifted one from the leather box. He bounced it on the table. It appeared to him that it rang true. The weight also seemed right, though without his own counterfeit for a comparison, he couldn't be positive. That's why Elvira had stolen it!

Again Belami glanced at Elvira, who smiled triumphantly at him. "Are you satisfied, milord?" she asked.

"Not yet," Belami countered, and tested another from the bottom of the box. It also rang true.

"Would your lordship like to test the money with acid? You'll find no copper present, I assure you," Elvira said.

"I wouldn't expect to find anything but gold till I got inside the coin," Belami replied. He turned aside to Cerboni. "The counterfeits have an iron slug inside. If you're in any doubt, you might cut one of these apart. Gold cuts easily."

Cerboni was sufficiently alarmed that he wished to make this experiment on the spot. "The kitchen here at the hotel should be able to provide some tools," Belami informed him.

They went off together and were back in a few moments with a mutilated guinea, solid gold to the core.

"Are we all satisfied?" Elvira asked. "Quite sure you wouldn't like to have it assayed, Lord Belami? A pity we can't take it to the Fraternity of Goldsmiths."

Belami glared and took another coin from the box. "I assure you it would pass the Trial of the Pyx," Elvira said. He knew from the weight it was genuine, and he knew from Elvira's angry face that she regretted her last revealing speech.

It would be difficult to say who was more angry with Belami. The duchess deeply resented the delay in getting to the palazzo, Deirdre was angry that her friends had been insulted, and Pronto was in the boughs. Belami felt like a fool, but strangely the Suttons were unfazed. Elvira, with her taunting smile, looked like the cat who has just swallowed the cream.

The purchase was completed, but there was still one more item of business. "Mama, you are forgetting Lucy's pearl," Elvira reminded Mrs. Sutton.

"It slipped my mind with the scare Lord Belami put into us," the mother said. "We want to buy another pearl exactly like this for my other daughter, signore," she explained.

"It will be very difficult to find another like it," Cerboni said. "These teardrop pearls are rare. I have a very nice pearl necklace that would suit the young lady," he added.

"We realize Lucrezia Borgia did not possess two identical necklaces, signore. Just find us the pearl, and we shall have it mounted," Elvira said.

"I don't have anything remotely resembling this piece,"

82

Cerboni insisted. "I have not seen such a thing in Venice."

"Then might I suggest you try outside of Venice?" Elvira said patiently, as though to a child. "Surely in Rome or one of the large centers you could find something. We would be willing to pay handsomely for it," she added enticingly.

A greedy smile lifted Cerboni's lips. "I shall return to my shop and begin investigations this very morning, signorina."

The jeweler soon left, and it was time for the others to depart for the palazzo. There was a moist leave-taking amongst the young ladies, who promised to meet again soon.

"I'll see you later, Pronto," Belami said. "What are you doing today?"

"Elvira's going to paint the Rialto. A picture of it, I mean, not the bridge itself. I'll bear her company."

"Keep in touch. You know where to find me."

Deirdre found Dick quiet as they proceeded along the Grand Canal to the Ginnasis' place. The duchess, however, wasn't about to let him off so easily.

"You must have felt a flaming jackass, Belami, trying to pull off one of your stunts and coming a cropper," she said merrily. "You've met your match in young Elvira Sutton."

"She knows her business," he agreed.

"Aye, she is quite an expert, speaking of assays and Fraternity of Goldsmiths and I don't know what all, like a professional gentleman."

"And the Trial of the Pyx," he mused. "Your average young lady don't carry that bit of esoterica in her head, even if she's attended a good seminary in Bath."

"Bath? They are from Cornwall," the duchess told him.

"Elvira was educated in a seminary at Bath, unlike Lucy."

83

"It's odd Meggie never mentioned it. Did she tell you that, Deirdre?"

"No," Deirdre said, frowning, "though I suspected some such thing. She is better educated than Lucy."

"And better educated than her mama," the duchess added. "That goosecap had no notion that the Italian language was based on Latin. I mentioned to her that I would feel quite at home, having a sound education in Latin. 'What good will that do, your grace?' she asked me. 'They speak Italian in Venice.' I noticed young Elvira smiling behind her fist."

Belami listened quietly, interested to see these chinks appearing in the Suttons' background. He kept thinking of that missing counterfeit coin from his pocket. Pronto would have told Elvira that he always carried it as a good-luck omen. Had she stolen it while they talked by the window? He'd looked in the gondola, and would look again in his bedroom, but he was quite sure he wouldn't find it. Yet there was no reason for her to take it—the Suttons' coins were legitimate, so any comparison would have been harmless. Why had Elvira wanted him to be there at all? Was it to authenticate not the pearl, but the coins? Was that it?

While the duchess and Deirdre were being installed in their rooms, Belami called for Réal.

"I have a job for you," he said.

"This is most excellent news." Réal smiled. "It is very *ennuyante* in this watery place."

"You don't care for the Grand Canal?" Belami asked.

"Pshh! You call this creek a grand canal? In Canada, there we have *real* waters. The Saint Laurent, wide as an ocean, and the mighty lakes. The job, melord?" he asked eagerly.

"Go to the Léon Bianco and keep an eye on the Suttons," he said. "I'm particularly interested to see if any of the party speak to a certain gentleman," he added, and

84

described Captain Styger. "If Styger shows up, follow him."

"You wish I enter also into the ladies' chamber for the searching?" Réal suggested.

"An excellent notion, but don't get caught."

Réal looked at him as though he were an idiot. "I don't get caught, me. What I am looking for? Which clues?"

"Letters, money—a large quantity of gold coins in particular or anything that suggests counterfeiting. Also names or addresses. Whatever strikes you as out of place in a ladies' chamber. Take as long as you require. I shan't need your coaching services on these wet Venetian roads."

Réal left and Belami went in search of Deirdre. She was busy settling into her new home till lunch time, when the whole party met at the table. The duchess intended to fulfill her bargain for the remainder of that first day and offered to sit with the conte in the afternoon. Carlotta graciously accepted and looked at Belami, who was careful not to meet her gaze.

"That leaves us free to explore Venice, Deirdre," he said.

Carlotta snapped an angry glance at him but said nothing. Her amorous interests were by no means limited to Englishmen. She had a young Italian nobleman, Marchese Laderchi, in her eye as well, as a potential replacement for her aging conte.

Belami and Deirdre explored the shady streets and shops of Venice, ending up, not quite by chance, at the Rialto. Belami realized Elvira wouldn't actually be on the bridge when her aim was to paint it. He knew when he saw one stationary gondola jiggling nervously that it was his friend, and had his gondolier pull alongside.

"Will you sit still, Pronto!" were the first words heard from the boat, uttered in a vexed tone by Miss Sutton.

"Elvira!" Deirdre waved. "We're just going to one of the cafés for wine. Will you and Pronto join us?"

"I'm dry as a desert," Pronto mumbled.

They pulled in at the nearest landing. Before going to the café, Deirdre wanted to see Elvira's picture. "This is beautiful! Look," she said, and handed Dick the small canvas.

He viewed a superior painting of the humpbacked bridge, lined with small shops. Considering that it had been done in an unsteady gondola, and with Pronto there to help, it was extraordinarily well executed, in the style of Canaletto.

"You're a talented lady," he said to Elvira.

"Why, thank you, milord. Would you care to test and see that the pigments are still wet? We wouldn't want you to think I was trying to pass off a Canaletto as my own effort. Till the paint has dried a few months, it shall remain a Sutton." A bold smile gleamed from her blue eyes.

Belami felt no attraction to her, though she was very pretty and very much in his style. "I have a good eye, Miss Sutton. I can see a bridge by daylight."

"And quote Mr. Shakespeare very appropriately, too, sir."

"A pity the picture isn't smaller, and I could steal it from you—slip it into my pocket," he joked.

Elvira's lips quivered in amusement. "What *can* you mean, milord? Come, let us go for that wine. Pronto, carry this," she said, handing him the painting. "And get my paint box, will you? There's a good fellow." The box was open, with wet pigments out loose. Pronto frowned at it in confusion.

"Why don't you just leave all that in the gondola?" Deirdre suggested. She was unhappy to see Elvira behaving with so little consideration of Pronto.

Pronto tenderly returned the canvas to the boat and took Elvira's arm to follow the others to the café.

"What are your mother and sister doing this afternoon?" Deirdre asked Elvira.

"Shopping and looking at churches, in that order, I fear. Tomorrow we must go to see the churches, Pronto. Shall we go together?'' she asked, smiling brightly at Belami and Deirdre.

"Be happy to take you, my dear," Pronto said. He pulled his head back, which in no way limited the range of his voice, and added, "Don't encourage 'em. We'll want to be alone."

Once they were installed at the café, Belami said, "It's rather chilly here. I'll get your shawl from the gondola, Deirdre."

"I'm fine, Dick."

"I don't want you to take a chill," he insisted, and hastened back to the gondola. He was happy to see the gondoliers had left to take some refreshment. Belami climbed into Pronto's boat and looked around for clues. The only items Elvira had left behind were her painting and paint box. The latter was a large wooden affair, difficult to search as it was smeared with wet pigments. He carefully lifted out the top rack and looked beneath. In the jumble of tubes and brushes he saw some white powder. By tilting the box he shook enough of it to one end that he could take a sample, which he wrapped in his handkerchief.

Then he hastily got Deirdre's shawl from his own boat and went back to the café. It was obvious that Pronto wished privacy for his courting. As Belami had the same desire, he and Deirdre soon left.

"It's so odd to see Pronto in love," Deirdre said. "He was carrying on nonsensically while you were gone, Dick. Holding her hand beneath the table and gazing at her as though she were a goddess. I shouldn't be surprised if he made her an offer."

"She'll never have him."

"Probably not," Deirdre agreed. "On the other hand, Pronto is a little higher socially than the Suttons. That might be an incentive. I don't like the way she treats him—almost like her servant."

Belami and Deirdre enjoyed a leisurely row along some

of the smaller canals, while he tried to repair the ill feelings that had grown up between them.

"If you hadn't broken our engagement, we'd be in Venice together now," he reminded her.

"We are in Venice together. And I didn't break the engagement. You did. I wanted to get married."

"You wanted to honeymoon at Fernvale, with your aunt sitting on our tail."

"I didn't want to," she explained earnestly. "I just couldn't leave Auntie when she was ill. She really was sick, Dick. She very nearly died."

Dick put his arm around her. "She's better now. We could get married in Venice. Let's do it, Deirdre," he urged.

The sun slanted down on them as they drifted along the water. It was quiet in this small branch off the Grand Canal. "I'll need time to prepare her," Deirdre said.

"Don't take too much time, or she'll find some other reason to turn me off. I'll go to Hoppner and see to the formalities of an Italian wedding. I'd like us to have our honeymoon here, as we planned."

"Yes, that would be—" Belami's lips silenced her as he drew her into his arms for a quick, stolen kiss.

The afternoon was drawing to a close, and it was time to turn the gondola toward the palazzo. Belami went to his room and drew out his handkerchief containing the white powder from Elvira's paint box. He tasted it—not flour or starch or any food stuff. It was coarser, not as white as starch or as silky to the touch. It tasted like gypsum. Plaster of paris? Perhaps Elvira did a bit of sculpting as well as painting.

He poured water on the powder. It quickly absorbed the water and swelled in volume. Within a few minutes, it began to harden. It was plaster of paris then. It could be perfectly innocent—or it could be that Elvira was more closely connected with the counterfeiting than he had supposed. The counterfeit coins were so good that he was sure they'd been made in a mold from real coins. The first step would be to take plaster imprints. . . .

Elvira had given him a very knowing smile when he made that ambiguous joke about stealing her painting and putting it in his pocket. She knew exactly what he was referring to, and the knowledge amused her. He paced the room, wishing Réal would come back.

It was much later that evening when Réal returned. Dinner was over, and a long evening in the saloon with the Ginnasis and their guests had followed. Carlotta had spoken of having a masquerade ball to honor her English friends. Belami fully expected this cost would be laid in his dish, but Deirdre had been excited at the idea. He liked masquerade parties himself.

It was after eleven when Réal came tapping at his door and stepped in. Réal wasn't swaggering, which was a hint of failure. "There is nothing amiss with the Sutton ladies," Réal told him. "No large quantity of coins, no letters, no names or addresses. No things of any interest to us. Me, I find it strange there is nothing at all."

"People only bring the essentials along when they travel," Belami said doubtfully.

"Only one small thing is all I find," Réal said.

Belami looked up eagerly, hoping Réal had been teasing him. "Well, what was it?"

"A razor, all new and sharp, by the water pitcher."

Belami blinked. "A man's razor?"

"The ladies, they don't use the razors, *non*?"

"They don't—usually, though I have a few aunts who have been known to shave their upper lips and chins as they advance into middle age. Mrs. Sutton isn't particularly hirsute, however. I wish I could ask Deirdre if Mrs. Sutton ever used it. There was nothing else indicating a man's visit? No boots, no neckcloths—no pipe?" he asked hopefully.

Réal shook his head. "Just the razor."

"I'm going to tap on Deirdre's door and see if she's still

up and about. Thanks, Réal. The lookout is still on. Night is the likeliest time for a clandestine visit. Send Nick during the day, and you take the night shift.''

Réal nodded and left. It grieved him that he had brought home such a paltry clue. He would exceed his orders in eagerness if not in finding clues. He went back to the Léon Bianco and took up a position that gave him a view of the door.

Belami tapped on Deirdre's door. She was in her dressing gown and couldn't ask him in.

"You'll think I'm unhinged," he said, "but would you happen to know if Mrs. Sutton had any reason to use a man's razor?''

"She uses it all the time," Deirdre told him. "She uses Elvira's razor for a fruit knife. Elvira keeps one in her paint box, you know. She uses it to sharpen quills and cut pieces of canvas—all sorts of things. It came in handy when we were traveling. I've used it myself to peel an orange. Why are you asking?''

"Merely curious," he said evasively. The razor wasn't in Elvira's paint box—it was by the water pitcher.

"Has this something to do with the Jalberts?''

"With Elvira. She's involved with them. It was just a hunch—till she stole my counterfeit guinea this morning.''

"Dick, she didn't!''

"It's missing. I've looked high and low for it." He went over his other suspicions in some detail. "You didn't see anything of my suspicious sea captain on the trip?'' he asked.

"Not a glimpse. They all behaved in a perfectly normal way.''

"I'm keeping an open mind, and an open eye. I'd best let you get to bed now. You look very fetching in that dressing gown," he added, touching a wisp of lace at her collar.

His fingers moved to her throat, caressing it. Belami peered up and down the darkened hallway, and when he saw the coast was clear, he drew her into his arms. He was about to kiss her when he heard some sound from the next door—the duchess's room. Without waiting to hear her abuse, he hastened along the hall to his room.

Belami made a mental list of his various clues. More than ever he regretted that he knew so little about the Jalbert gang. He had no idea how many people were involved, where they were from, or what they looked liked. He'd ask Hoppner if he knew anything tomorrow when he went to inquire about the wedding.

The interval till he and Deirdre could get married would be busily filled with catching the Jalberts . . . and of course trimming the duchess back into line . . . and making sure Pronto didn't propose to Elvira . . . and evading Carlotta . . . and courting Deirdre. On this happy thought, he extinguished the lamp and went to bed.

Chapter Eight

When the duchess heard Belami's errand the next morning was an innocent trip to see the British consul, she had no objection to Deirdre's accompanying him. Upon learning that the duchess already had Hoppner's acquaintance, Belami made his inquiries regarding a wedding in Italy on behalf of a "friend."

"Would it be difficult for two English people to marry in Venice?" Belami asked.

"I would advise them to avoid the technicalities and find an English minister to tie the knot. I could recommend one, if that would be of any assistance to your friend."

Deirdre and Belami exchanged a relieved smile that didn't fool Mr. Hoppner for a minute. Then Belami asked the consul if he had any news on the Jalbert gang.

"Is that why you're here?" Hoppner asked. "I wondered when I heard you were in the city."

"My visit isn't official," Belami said.

Hoppner gave a wise wink. "Mum's the word, but if I can be of any help, don't hesitate to call. You might find these interesting," he said, and handed him a few newspapers.

They parted on the best of terms. Belami and Deirdre strolled to a café to peruse the papers. As she sipped her coffee, Deirdre looked more at her partner than the papers. She loved Belami in any of his guises, but this was her favorite. His dark eyes flashed with intelligence and an eagerness to get solving the case. She was eager, too. Helping Dick added zest to her humdrum life.

"You're famous, Dick," she said proudly. "Imagine, Mr. Hoppner way over here in Venice knows your reputation. Did the government send you?"

"No, but if I'd had my wits about me I'd have approached them and got my trip gratis. Here it is," he exclaimed, and read the headline. " 'Jalbert Gang Elude Capture at Dover.' "

He scanned the article and described the gang to Deirdre. "Two men, Alfred Jalbert and son Claude. Both married. It doesn't say whether the spouses were at Dover, but they aren't at their home in London. The counterfeiting equipment was there, but they got away with the molds and could set up shop elsewhere. Alfred sounds remarkably like my Captain Styger—it even mentions the pipe. Claude's described as slight of frame, fair-complexioned, handsome. Did you see anyone like that during your trip?"

"No. If they've joined up since leaving England, what you're looking for is an older couple and a young couple," Deirdre said.

"Yes, *if* they've joined up. Any reports I've had of Jalbert dropping bad coin along the trip describe him as traveling alone. Listen to this, Deirdre," he added, and read another item. "As well as false coin, the Jalberts have also been active in selling forged paintings. An alleged Carpaccio they sold to a woman in London has been proven to be forged."

She knew by his excitement that he considered this a clue. "You're thinking of Elvira's painting," she said, "but she can't be one of them."

"She could be Claude's wife," Dick suggested, and looked for her reaction.

"Then why would she be traveling with the Suttons?"

"The gang has broken up for the trip. They're less likely

to be captured if they travel with innocent tourists. I suspect the Suttons had planned this trip before the Jalbert gang was captured and Claude induced the Suttons to come along so he could be near his wife."

"How could she have even met Claude when she was in the seminary and he was in London?"

"Getting counterfeit money into circulation is the hardest part of the operation. When the fakes are spotted in one county, they must move on to another one. I daresay the Jalberts have been all over England, leaving their steel guineas behind them. Elvira could have met Claude in Bath or Cornwall. I wish we were back in England where I could check on some of these suppositions. Elvira's in this up to her *beaux yeux* and laughing at me from the side of her mouth."

"The Suttons are rich. Mrs. Sutton paid a thousand guineas in cash for the pearl."

"The Suttons aren't the Jalberts," Dick countered. "Their having money wouldn't do the Jalberts any good unless it was in Elvira's hands. Quite possibly Mrs. Sutton doesn't even know about the marriage."

"I'm sure she doesn't. They would have made some slip during all the time we were with them. They seem like such ordinary people."

"I wouldn't call Elvira ordinary. She may have run away and married Claude, and her mama brought her here to get away from him. I don't know the details, but I know that woman is up to something."

"Just because she doesn't like you." Deirdre shrugged.

"The feeling is entirely mutual. She didn't leave me that note in Paris. But Claude *did* leave a note telling someone that they were all leaving earlier than planned. The way I see it, Claude paid a running visit to Elvira that morning, and she told him about the early departure. The Licorne was their meeting place. Styger-Jalbert kept in touch with them there, and very likely with Claude, too.

I didn't think to ask if Styger ate alone. Whose idea was it to go to the Licorne?"

"It was Elvira's," Deirdre admitted. "It was Elvira who particularly wanted to come to Venice, too. She chose the Léon Bianco. She had a friend who recommended the two hotels."

"A husband is more like it. The great attraction in Venice was that the Jalberts are here. Who is this friend?"

"It's a girl she knew from Bath. Her name is Jane something—she's in Italy. It could be the friend who's married to Claude."

"Is she in Venice?"

"She's somewhere nearby."

Dick considered it a moment and shook his head. "No, it don't fadge. If Claude's in Venice and married to Elvira's friend, Elvira wouldn't have to be acting as go-between. He could see Jane himself. It's Elvira he's married to. That would account for all her odd behavior."

"Oh, dear!" Deirdre exclaimed, and set her coffee cup down with a thump. "Pronto!" she said, with a wild eye at Belami. "He's in love with a married woman."

"Good lord! He's courting her to the top of his bent. You may be sure there's a jealous husband out there, keeping an eye on him. I'd best warn him."

"Oh, my, yes," she agreed. They gathered up their papers and dashed off to the gondola to go to the hotel. They found Pronto taking a leisurely breakfast alone in the dining room.

"*Bonjouro*, Deirdre, Dick. Care for a *caffé*? They make a decent breakfast here, if you can stomach bread and fruit. Stay away from the meat," he added behind his hand.

"We haven't come for breakfast," Belami told him.

Pronto narrowed his eyes and said, "I knew it. You've been deducing again. What have you found now?"

"It's about Elvira, Pronto," Deirdre said gently. In his

95

concern, Belami began to empty his budget much less gently.

Pronto bridled like an angry horse. "Now see here, you're way out of line, traducing an innocent girl. I won't hear a word against her. Whatever you've got to say, bear in mind you're saying it about the woman I love."

"Don't be a sapskull," Dick said. "She's making a May game of you. We have reason to believe she's already married."

"What reason?"

Belami explained his reasoning in some detail. Pronto's face went from anger to incredulity to contempt. "And I thought you was a clever man. This is a bag of moonshine. All your clues are based on this old piece of newspaper from England saying that Claude Jalbert's married. It don't say he's married to my Elvira. You'd best come up with some new coincidences, for it don't wash that Elvira's married to a counterfeiter just because she made a fool of you. That's what burr you've got under your saddle."

Belami took a deep breath and tried again. "She is. I feel it in my bones," he insisted. "She stole that guinea from my pocket. She lied to Deirdre about leaving me a note. She led the ladies to the Licorne where Alfred Jalbert picked up notes. She was in Saint Mark's Square the other night when Jalbert was there. And how do you account for her knowing so much about counterfeiting—the Trial of the Pyx? How did she know that? And," he added importantly, "she had plaster of paris in her paint box. Does she use that in her work?"

"How should I know? We have better things to talk about than plaster of paris!"

"She doesn't do sculpture, only painting," Deirdre said.

"Well, it's used for making molds in counterfeiting," Belami said.

Pronto just shook his head. "You've made a fool of yourself once already, Dick. That business of bouncing Mrs. Sutton's money around the table yesterday—don't mean to rub it in your nose, but you looked nohow. Don't do it again. Your rubbishing clues are all circumstantial. You lost your coin yesterday. Don't blame Elvira because you're clumsy. She *did* leave you the note in Paris. Those demmed Frenchies misplaced it. You know about the trials and pixies and all that—I don't see us calling you Mr. Jalbert. Your nose is out of joint because she likes me better than you, and that's the top and bottom of it.''

"Perhaps she finds you easier to fool," Belami said.

"Maybe you're wrong, Dick," Deirdre said. "Elvira wouldn't lead Pronto on if she didn't care for him—if she were already married, I mean.''

"Would she not? She knows I'm after the Jalbert gang. Their little business is no longer viable. When Claude's clamped into irons, she'll some other protector.''

"You *do* admit I'm number two with her, then, do you? Big of you.'' Pronto scowled.

"No, *bigamy*," Belami joked. "A lady's only allowed one husband at a time.''

"Where is Elvira, Pronto?" Deirdre asked. "I'll run up and say hello to her while you and Belami talk.''

"She's gone.''

Dick and Deirdre exchanged a wild stare. "Where? When?" Dick asked.

"She's gone to visit a friend. Left this morning.''

"Was it Jane, her friend from England?" Deirdre asked.

"That's it. Miss Blackwell. It's some place that starts with a *v*. Just between Verona and Vicenza. Or was it outside Valdagno? Something like that. Italy has too many *v*'s to suit me. The place is full of them. It's via this and via that, Venice and Vesuvius. *Veni, vidi, vici.*" His voice petered out.

"Why?" Dick asked.

"Demmed if I know," Pronto replied, shaking his head. "Do you remember in the old schoolbooks, they was always sticking in a *v* instead of *u*, making it impossible to read?''

"Why did Elvira go away?" Deirdre asked, as Dick seemed in some danger of exploding.

"Visting her friend," Pronto said. "Already told you."

"When will she be back?" Deirdre asked.

"Two or three days."

"When did she leave?" Belami said.

"This morning, around eight-thirty. I walked her down to the landing and saw her into the gondola. They only have the one servant, and she didn't want to leave her mama short handed. Watched her start out for Mestre. That's where you've got to go first to get out of this place," he explained.

"You sent her off alone in a gondola?" Belami frowned.

"Dash it, I hadn't had a bite of breakfast. I offered to go with her. Elvira insisted I go in and have my breakfast. But I didn't. I hobbled back up to bed instead."

"I expect Claude was missing her," Belami said archly. "A man likes to have his wife with him in romantic Italy." His glance turned to Deirdre, where it softened.

"He will if I have anything to say about it," Pronto said. "I mean to pop the question when she gets back."

A sense of urgency was added to Belami's worry. He remembered his spies, and hoped Réal might have more detailed information as to who had met Elvira at Mestre. He and Deirdre left a very disgruntled Pronto behind, muttering into his cup.

"What do you make of this?" Deirdre asked.

"She's gone off to meet Claude and report that I'm making waves here in Venice. If they planned to dump their guineas here, they'll have to change their plans."

"I wonder if she intends to come back at all. It would almost be best if she didn't."

"Possibly she was just waiting to collect that jewelry from her mother and take it to her husband to finance their journey elsewhere," Belami suggested.

They went directly to the Palazzo Ginnasi, where Réal was pacing the dock, waiting for them.

"Réal, any news from the Léon Bianco?" Belami asked. "Did you happen to see Miss Sutton leave this morning?"

"But yes, I see everythings," Réal said comprehensively. "She goes in the boat to Mestre, where she hires a carriage."

"Hires?" Belami asked. "You're sure it wasn't there waiting for her?"

"She hired a carriage, with very bad horses, like all the horses in Italy."

"Where did she go from there?" Belami asked eagerly. He felt the blood pulsing in his veins, pacing his heart faster.

"She went west, to some place starting with a *v*," Réal said, and looked fearfully for his master's approval.

"You mean you let her get away!" Belami gasped.

"You said. 'If Styger shows up, follow him.' Styger, he don't show up. I come back to the hotel. Nick—he was late," Réal said, hoping to dissipate the blame. "H'as usual."

Belami grimaced. "I wish you'd stayed with her. She could have led us to the gang. I wager she's meeting Claude."

Réal was racked with grief. For five minutes he had stood, trying to determine which course he should take at Mestre. What victory he could have brought home, if only he'd followed Miss Sutton. Regret turned to anger and he lashed out. "If some peoples would say what they mean, it will be making my job much easier. Follow Styger, you said."

"You're right," Belami said placatingly. "The trouble is, I need a dozen men, not just you and Nick. Did anything of interest happen last night at the hotel? Any callers?" he asked hopefully.

"No callers. Miss Lucy and the mother went out—to visit churches. I hear talkings of Saint Mark's."

"Hmm—I wonder who they met there. You didn't—"

"I stayed watching the hotel, like I am told to do,"

Réal answered grimly. More coals of shame were heaped on his head that he hadn't read his master's mind from afar. He left very soon, his body so suffocated with remorse and regrets that there was only one way to subdue it. He must hire a boat immediately and return to Mestre, to see what he could learn of the travels of Miss Sutton.

It was late in the evening when Réal returned. He didn't know whether he had real news or whether he would add to his shame by the unlikely tale to be told. He found Belami with all the others in a small saloon sorting through costumes from the contessa's attic for the masquerade ball. Réal stood, willing Belami to look at the doorway. Such was the intensity of his wish that Belami turned at once and discovered his groom.

Belami hastened to the door and asked, "Why aren't you at the hotel?"

"I am just going. Before I leave, I have other newses for you. I went to Mestre this afternoon," he said.

Belami was hard pressed to imagine why Réal was shifting uneasily on his feet. He feared some ill news was about to be revealed. "Well, what is it?"

"The hired carriage of Miss Sutton, it goes to Mira, a short distance from Mestre. There it goes to a small inn. Miss Sutton hires a room."

"That's odd. Did she meet the Blackwells?"

"She meets no one," Réal said.

"Is she still there?"

"No, she disappeared. She locks herself into the room carrying one small case from the carriage. The maids, they think she is sleeping. Many hours later they are worrying, and knock. There is no answer. They open the door with the key—Miss Sutton, she is gone. Her case is gone. No one is going to visit her all day, and Miss Sutton isn't leaving her room also. She disappeared," he said, and stifled the urge to cross himself, for obviously the forces of Satan were at work here.

Réal stood trembling with anxiety to see the effect of

his news. A rush of glory entered his breast when Belami clipped him on the arm and said, "Good work, Réal!"

But Réal was never one to take undue credit. "Possibly I am misunderstanding the servants," he admitted. "I do not speak the Italian very good, though I know the paternoster and Ave Maria by heart."

"Hmm, that's a distinct possibility. I have the deuce of a time understanding the language myself. What's the name of the inn at Mira and where is it, exactly?"

He got the name and the directions. Réal went to the hotel and Belami returned to the saloon to tell Deirdre what he had heard.

"We must go to Mira at once," she said. "I'll sneak out tonight. You can question the servants at the inn."

"I read and write Italian better than I speak it. The idioms confuse me." He glanced toward Carlotta and knew she would be a better interpreter.

Before Deirdre could change his mind, the duchess joined them. "This robe will do for you, Deirdre," she said, and handed her niece a heavy brocade gown. The sleeves were long and full, stitched with gold threads. Slashes in the material revealed white cambric inserts below. It was more interesting than beautiful, but the greater deterrent was that the stiff old material looked extremely uncomfortable.

"I rather like this one," Deirdre said, showing a simple sheperdess's gown of blue mulled muslin. The sleeves and skirt were full, the top featuring a blue velvet weskit that laced up the front. A wide-brimmed leghorn bonnet went with it.

"I have always wondered at that taste for the common in you," Charney said, and cast a darkening eye at Belami.

Dick set the straw bonnet on Deirdre's head and smiled. "Perfect! I wish I were a sheep."

The duchess thought a wolf was more like it, but she said no more. Actually Charney was in high spirits. The palazzo was very much to her liking. What fun to wheel the conte, ten years younger than herself and in so much worse shape, around the house. She delighted in pointing out to him features that his dim eyes missed. Hands fallen off statues, spots on the carpet, dirty windows. And when she tired, there was always a fine fire raging in the grate, with a bottle of wine left permanently at the ready. Lavish compliments on this inferior brew had informed her that it came from the conte's own vineyards. She meant to see a large quantity of it sent to England before she left. The long days left her plenty of time to tease the conte about his wife's never being home.

"You might give these a try," Charney suggested to Belami. She handed him a short velvet jacket and a pair of long silk hose. A grotesque feathered hat completed the ensemble.

"I think not. I'm wearing a domino," he replied firmly. "I'll ask Carlotta if she has any."

It made a good excuse to speak to the contessa without arousing suspicions. "I have a favor to ask of you," he said when he was alone with her. "Can I meet you later tonight, after the others retire?"

Carlotta slanted a long look at him from below her lashes. "I was beginning to think you'd never ask," she purred. "Your room or mine?"

"I want you to go to Mira with me," he said. A nervous glance toward Deirdre and the duchess accompanied his answer.

"Perhaps that would be best. The duchessa is a regular Argus. Shall we say, around midnight?"

"As soon as the others retire."

She tapped him playfully with her fan and glided over to push her spouse out the door, into the hands of his valet.

It was ten-thirty. Carlotta yawned extravagantly. "I'm for bed. Duchessa, would you care to have anything sent to your room? Some cold meat—wine?"

"I am feeling a little peckish," the duchess admitted. "Bring that gown upstairs, Deirdre, and we'll see if Haskins can do anything with it. It smells of camphor. It must be laundered at least."

Deirdre looked a question at Belami. "Good evening, ladies. I'll see you tomorrow," he said, and bowed.

He remained below with Carlotta. The duchess had observed signs of the growing friendship between her niece and her rakish ex-fiancé and was determined to quash it.

"They will want to be alone," Charney said. "It would be gauche of us to be forever hanging around. You know Belami must be carrying on with some woman. Better the contessa than you, my dear. That one can handle him if I know anything. Shocking the way she bear-leads the dear conte."

"He's not carrying on with her," Deirdre said.

But as she peeped over the bannister, she saw very clearly that Carlotta was carrying on with Dick, and he wasn't fighting her off as he should. He allowed the hussy to put her arm through his and carry him off like a trophy to the saloon, where they would be alone. The tinkle of Carlotta's silvery laughter hung on the air. Carlotta had a very suggestive laugh.

Chapter Nine

Belami explained to Carlotta why he wanted to take her to an inn at Mira in secret at night, but her sultry glances said as plain as day that she thought it was a mere excuse.

"Such elaborate explanations are not necessary, *caro mio*. I will be happy to interpret anything you like. I am a very experienced—interpreter." She smiled.

"Perhaps it would be better if I took one of your footmen. I don't want to put you to so much trouble. I just thought the innkeeper would be more helpful to a contessa."

"He will," she assured him. "Shall we go? We must be back by breakfast. The conte doesn't trouble me in my bedroom, but he does expect to see me at the table."

"We'll be back long before morning," he said earnestly.

The contessa smiled her Gioconda smile. "We'll see."

In the gondola, Carlotta rested her head on Belami's chest and captured his hands in both of hers. It was the least mischievous thing her busy fingers could be doing, so he didn't object. "What a moon!" Carlotta sighed, turning her face, pale in the moonlight, up to gaze at Belami. She had a lovely face, shaped like a heart, with those great soft eyes glittering. "Venetian nights were made for love," she crooned.

Belami desperately searched his mind for something to

distract her. "I have read there are over a hundred islands altogether in Venice," he said, and felt like a fool.

"I've made love on ninety-nine of them."

Belami laughed nervously. "And about four hundred bridges, I think."

"I haven't made love on many bridges," she said. "Except the Rialto, where there are all the shops. I've never made love at Mira before," she added, and began stroking her white fingers up his arm. "My favorite place for making love is in a gondola. Feel the gentle swaying of the water, *mio* Belami." Her hands strayed to his chest, where they soon sought out the buttons of his jacket.

"Quite a stiff breeze," Dick said, and did up his buttons as quickly as she unfastened them. "Now behave yourself, Carlotta," he scolded when her fingers out ran his.

"You know how you can make me do anything you want, *carissimo*," she said in a husky voice, and put her arms around his neck. "Just by doing—this." She pulled his head down and kissed him, very long and hard, till his lips were stinging.

It was a long trip up the S-curve of the Grand Canal, around the island and to the canal of Mestre. Belami's ingenuity was stretched to the limit. He sang, he quoted everything he could lay his tongue to, he kissed Carlotta and thought of Deirdre. She had been suspicious at his remaining downstairs with Carlotta, and a suspicious Deirdre wasn't likely to stay in her bed once Charney was asleep. She'd be up prowling by now. At least she couldn't very well follow him. The Ginnasis only had one gondola.

They went to Taverna Vecchia, a modest whitewashed inn standing in a small yard. "Tell them we want the room at the far end of the hall, the right side of the staircase," Belami instructed.

The contessa relayed this information to the innkeeper, then turned to Belami. "It's taken. I told him the one next to it would do."

"No, no! It must be that room. Tell him I'll pay the client's bill if he'll change to the next room."

"Darling, they'll think we're mad!" Carlotta laughed.

"Just give him the message."

Carlotta gave the message, and the innkeeper with a shake of his head went upstairs. He soon returned and led the new arrivals to the required chamber, muttering something unintelligible to himself. Belami caught the word *"imbecilles inglese"* and smiled sheepishly. When they were installed and the innkeeper had left, Belami took the lamp and began searching the room.

"What are you looking for, *carissimo*? It's right here," Carlotta said, pointing to the bed. She had thrown off her wrap and was beginning to remove her dress.

"We're looking for any sign that Elvira Sutton was here." He opened the clothespress, and drawers of the dresser, looked under the bed. "There's nothing." He pulled the bell cord and the innkeeper returned.

"Ask him about Elvira's visit—if this is the right room, how long she stayed, and whether she met anyone. See if the name Blackwell rings a bell."

Carlotta talked for about five minutes, asking questions and frowning. Then she dismissed the man. "She came to this room, locked herself in, and wasn't seen again. No one named Blackwell was here at all," she said.

Belami went to the open door and looked up and down the hall. "There's no fire door upstairs. If she didn't go out through the lobby, she had to climb out that window."

He opened the window and looked down. "She'd have broken her neck if she jumped."

Carlotta joined him at the window, her arm carelessly around his waist. "Unless there was someone there to catch her," she said.

"That must be it. Claude was there waiting for her. But why did she bother stopping here?"

"Perhaps Claude knows the purpose of a bed," the contessa said. Her voice was becoming just a trifle thin.

"Elvira came alone—she could hardly wait at the docks. This must have been where she waited for him," Belami thought out loud.

"Now are we finished with business?" As Carlotta spoke, Belami felt her body rubbing seductively against his. Her gown was open to the waist, revealing sights that took his mind from business.

"Yes, we might as well go."

"The room is paid for. Two rooms—it seems a waste."

Dick cupped her upturned face in his hands. "You're a beautiful woman, Carlotta. If I weren't engaged—"

"She'll never know!"

"Yes, she will. She has a sixth sense where I and other women are concerned. And really I don't feel at all like—"

Carlotta lifted his hand and kissed his fingers. "I can take care of that," she tempted.

"I know it very well. That's why we're leaving." He buttoned up her dress.

It was a vast relief that Carlotta sulked all the way home. She sat with her eyes closed, pretending to be asleep, but Belami could feel the resentment emanating from her stiff body. Once he was assured she didn't mean to continue seducing him, his mind was free to think of other matters.

Elvira had gone to a great deal of trouble just for a few days with Claude. Was there more than love involved? Was it some arrangement being made to unload the false money? Was she ever coming back? That was the important question. If she didn't, he'd lost the trail of the Jalberts entirely. There was no point wasting Réal at the Léon Bianco. He'd send him to Mestre tomorrow—and if Elvira showed up with Claude, Réal would follow him and learn where the Jalbert gang were staying. One of Carlotta's footmen would come in handy as interpreter.

When they landed at the palazzo, Carlotta wrapped her cape around her and strode angrily into the house without a word. Belami followed, trying to soften her up to beg the loan of a footman.

107

"Carlotta," he said softly, and put his hand on her elbow. "I'm sorry. You've been a perfect angel, and I've been a fool. I thought you understood about my engagement."

"You don't have an engagement. You have a mousy provincial who doesn't think enough of you to marry you. The duchessa has no intention of allowing this match. If you ever hope to marry that chit, you'll have to carry her off by main force—to some inn, where you will paralyze her with boredom while you look in closets and under beds. I had heard the *inglese* were cold, but not that they were frozen. *Buona notte, signore.*"

"Things are different in England," he said simply.

Carlotta looked at him with rising interest. Belami was much more conciliating than he'd been earlier. "You are not in England now. When in Rome—and when in Venice also—"

"I'm just a tourist."

"Then you must enjoy the sights while you are here." She looked an invitation from her sultry eyes. "One of the more interesting sights will be on display in my chamber, in about five minutes."

"But—"

"I'll be expecting you," Carlotta said, and fled upstairs to prepare for her visitor.

For the contessa, love was a battle; sex her weapon. Men had all the advantages of superior physical strength, wealth, and education, but God in his wisdom had hobbled them with one fatal weakness—lust. Belami would come, and before he left the room, he would have promised to redeem her diamonds from the pawn shop. Guy was becoming tiresome about the Ginnasi diamonds. His latest request sounded very much like an order. "You will wear the diamonds at my masquerade ball," he had said. "The duchessa would like to see them." Diamonds could not be at the jeweler's forever, having a clasp fixed.

Carlotta called her woman and made a grand toilette.

108

She knew virginal white was not her color. For gentlemen, she was the fantasy temptress. She wore assorted wisps of black lace that allowed tantalizing glimpses of white velvet skin to show beneath. Her black hair was carefully tousled to add a note of abandon. Perfume scented the air, and in far corners of her elaborate chamber, dim lamps burned. When all was ready, she dismissed her servant and arranged herself on the counterpane. Then she waited. And waited. And waited.

While she waited, Belami went to his room and undressed. It was demmed uncomfortable, having to offend your hostess. An offended Carlotta might make any amount of mischief. For openers, she'd be rude as only a clever street urchin could be to the duchess and Deirdre. He wouldn't bother asking Carlotta for the loan of the footman. He really should go to her and explain though. Money was the best explanation. He opened his metal box and picked up a handful of gold coins. With them in the pocket of his dressing gown, he went softly to her room and tapped at the door.

Carlotta called "Come in," and he slowly opened the door. His heart sank to see her elaborate preparations. She patted the counterpane beside her and said in a pouting way, "It took you long enough, caro."

When Deirdre went upstairs with her aunt, she had no intention of remaining there, but getting away was extremely difficult. The duchess had a sharp nose for trouble, and knew by Deirdre's restless roaming around the chamber that she was planning some foolishness.

"Come and sit with me while I eat this snack," the duchess ordered. She cast a greedy eye over the plate. The ham was tasty but very thinly sliced. The bread, however, was excellent. So light and fluffy she could eat twice the amount on the plate. Green grapes and cheese completed the repast. With a glass of Ginnasi's red wine, it made a fitting dessert.

"Would you like me to get you your sleeping powder now?" Deirdre asked, when the plate was empty.

The duchess shot a gimlet glance at her. "Not tonight, dear. The wine will work as well. It works a little slower, of course." The duchess had another glass. With her stomach full, she became expansive. "You may leave now, Deirdre," she decided. Then on an afterthought she added, "I'll look in to say good night after I've read a few chapters of *Udolpho*." She had no intention of doing it, but the threat would keep Deirdre in her room. Deirdre left, and the duchess drew a luxurious sigh, called Haskins to prepare her for bed, took her glass of laudanum, and was soon snoring.

Deirdre paced her room, waiting for the visit. She spent half the time at the door, listening for sounds of Dick and Carlotta coming upstairs. After three-quarters of an hour they had still not come. She tiptoed down the hall to her aunt's room, quietly opened the door, and saw exactly what she expected to see. The room was dark, and in the gloom the stertorous sounds of the sleeping duchess rent the air. Within minutes, Deirdre was downstairs, prowling the saloons. All the lights had been extinguished and the servants had retired. An eerie, pale moon washed the rooms in silvery light. They had gone out together. She knew it as surely as she knew what they were doing. The only question was where. She went out the palazzo door, down to the landing. The gondola was gone.

Her heart was as heavy as her steps when she went back inside. She remembered Carlotta's white fingers clutching Belami's sleeve, that silvery tinkle of laughter as she carried him off. With a weary sigh, she went into the dark saloon and sat on the sofa. She dreaded the morning, and the next morning, and the masquerade ball. She was sorry she'd come to Venice. She'd try to encourage the duchess to continue on to Rome. Her own reason for coming on this trip had been to forget Dick. Well, she'd forget him. She curled up on the sofa and began her forgetting by a

110

long remembering of their rocky past, which was littered with a dozen Carlottas.

After a while, her eyelids became heavy and she fell into a doze. She was roused some hours later by a sound, but when she sat up and listened, she heard nothing. There was no clock in the room, but her mental clock told her she had been asleep for some time. She peeped out the window and saw the gondolier just coming up from the landing. Her instinct was to dart up to Dick's room and demand an explanation. Of course he'd have some story ready for her. No, she wouldn't lower herself to ask. She'd just wait a moment till everyone had settled down, then she'd go to her room. And tomorrow she'd be as cold as an iceberg when Dick came smiling around.

She listened at the bottom of the stairs. There wasn't a sound. She crept up to her room and quietly went in. After undressing, she lay in the darkness, staring at an invisible ceiling. Strange there were no tears. Her tears had all been shed. She felt only a searing hot anger. Sleep wouldn't come again that night. She was wide awake when she heard the floorboards creak outside her room.

Deirdre didn't really think it was Dick. He'd had his bout of lechery for the night, but curiosity impelled her to go to the door and peek out. In the pitch-black hall, she couldn't distinguish the figure. Not till the contessa's door was opened and a wan beam of light fell on Dick's head and shoulders did she recognize him. When the contessa's door closed, she went silently into the hall, drawn to the door like a moth to light. She heard Carlotta's soft and sultry laugh, heard the telltale clink of coins falling on the counterpane, and felt ill. She would not stand at the keyhole like a kitchen maid. She returned to her room and lit both lamps to read the guidebooks and maps. Tomorrow she must convince her aunt to leave Venice.

At breakfast, the contessa was full of smiles, and Dick looked as tired and troubled as Job.

"I hope you slept well, Duchessa?" Carlotta asked. The

contessa occupied her customary place at the table, spooning gruel into her husband.

"Extremely well." Charney grinned. "It is that excellent Ginnasi wine that accounts for it. It is better than a sleeping draught. You must allow me to buy a few hogsheads to take home with me, Conte."

"It doesn't travel well," Carlotta warned. She was familiar by now with the duchess's meaning of the word "buy."

"No matter," Charney said merrily. "Even if it goes a little off, it will be better than French wines. I insist you allow me to take some home and puff it off to my friends. You will have every ounce of it sold next year if I know anything."

Carlotta turned her smile to Deirdre. "Did you sleep well, Miss Gower? You look a little peaked this morning."

"I slept fine, thank you. The traffic in the hall hardly bothered me at all. I hope you weren't ill, Contessa?"

The contessa looked slowly from Miss Gower to Belami. "I never had such a good night before," she said enigmatically.

"I certainly slept like a top," Belami said, with that heartiness that heralded a lie. "It's the refreshing Venetian air that accounts for it." A second thought cautioned him that this lie might prove troublesome. "I took the liberty of going for a cruise down the canal with your gondolier before retiring, Contessa. I hope you don't mind."

"You must make yourself quite at home, Belami," she replied. "We begrudge our guests nothing, do we, Guy?" she asked, remembering her spouse.

"Too cold," the conte said. This apparently referred to his gruel as Carlotta beckoned for a servant to remove it.

After a short breakfast, Deirdre left the table with her aunt and tried her luck at getting away from the palazzo.

"Leave today?" Charney asked, bewildered. "You forget the masquerade ball being thrown in our honor. It would be a slap in the face to leave before it takes place.''

''Could we not return to the Léon Bianco then?'' Deirdre asked. ''It would be livelier than here.''

''I don't know what you are about, my dear. Palazzo Ginnasi not lively? Why, the conte has a wonderful library.''

''But it's not in English.''

''We didn't undertake the expense of coming to Italy to read books in English. There is more to this fit of sulks than a dislike of Italian books,'' the duchess said, and examined her niece from narrowed eyes. ''Belami has shown his true colors, eh? I knew all along he was carrying on with that trollop the conte made the error of marrying. Better you should see what Belami is now than after you're shackled to him. That alone makes the trip worthwhile. If you are unhappy with Belami, however, there is no need to see much of him. Don't be rude, for the contessa likes him tremendously, but on the other hand, you need not go out with him. You can take my manner toward him as your guide.''

Deirdre could think of nothing more likely to terminate Dick's interest in her. She would do it, providing he bothered to seek her out at all.

Chapter Ten

When Belami came looking for Deirdre later that morning, he was met with two frosty stares. "I'm taking the gondola to Mestre this morning, Deirdre, and thought you might like to come with me. There are horses for hire there. Some exercise would do us both good."

"I plan to visit Lucy today," Deirdre replied, without even looking at him. "A walk around Venice will be enough exercise. Will you come with me, Auntie?" she asked.

"No, my dear. Take Haskins. I have promised the conte to read to him today. He likes to keep his English brushed up. Perhaps your contessa will go to Mestre with you," the duchess suggested to Belami.

Belami heard that "*your* contessa" and knew why he was being given such a chilly reception. "The contessa is making calls this morning," he said.

Deirdre stared coolly at him. "I am flattered that you should make me your second choice, Belami, but my plans are made. As the hotel is closer than Mestre, perhaps you would be good enough to allow me first turn at the gondola?"

On this curt speech, she rose and strode from the room. When he heard her coming down the stairs later, he darted to the dock and was there when she arrived.

Deirdre took one look and stopped before she reached

the landing. "If you are in that great a hurry to reach Mestre, I shall wait till the boat returns," she said.

"I want to see Pronto. I'll go with you, and go on from there," Belami replied indifferently. "There's no need for you to come, Haskins." The servant nodded and left.

"Very well." Deirdre stepped into the boat and turned her head adamantly away to stare across the water, oblivious to all the charm of ancient domes and sun-dappled water. She didn't look when she felt Belami sit beside her, but she took the precaution of removing her nearer hand. The gondolier cast off and the boat began plying toward the right bank.

Belami decided to behave as though he had nothing to hide. "I went to Mira last night," he said. "I spoke to the innkeeper. What Réal told me appears to be true."

Deirdre continued gazing silently across the water, and he plowed on. "The real reason I'm returning to Mestre is to watch out for Elvira's return. I don't have to go. Réal will be there, if there's anything you'd like to do today."

"I don't require your company for anything I wish to do," Deirdre said, speaking into the wind.

He refused to take offense. "Carlotta said she'd be happy to have the Suttons at her masquerade, if you like."

"I'll mention it to them."

He sat silent a moment, then spoke. "Why are you acting like this?"

"Because I'm a lady," was her stiff reply. "Ladies don't make scenes or use foul language. You may count yourself fortunate that I have some self-control."

"I think your self-control slipped a little last night! You've been spying on me again, Deirdre. What did you see?"

"That it should be necessary for you to ask that question gives a good indication of your character. I saw enough to know that I want nothing more to do with you."

"That's going to be difficult when we're staying under the same roof."

"Not for long if I have anything to say about it!"

"Whatever you saw," he said comprehensively, "it's not what you think."

"Of course not," she said with heavy sarcasm. "The laws of nature are suspended where you're concerned. Your creeping into her room in the middle of the night and giving her money had nothing to do with your being at Mira with her earlier."

"I didn't want to get Charney turned against me. That's the only reason I didn't want to take you."

"Why did you take her?"

"Because she speaks the language. The innkeeper would go out of his way to answer a contessa's questions, whereas if I took a servant, he might not have given us the time of day."

"Or night!" she shot back.

"Nothing happened at Mira!"

"You must be slipping! I made sure your performance in her boudoir was an encore, not the main performance."

"There was no encore, and no performance."

"Then why did you give her money? I heard it rattle on the bed."

He leaped on it like a tiger. "You *were* spying!"

"I was not spying! I heard such a racket in the hall I just peeped out to see if someone was ill."

"Stockinged feet don't make much racket."

"Gentlemen who are sneaking into a lady's bedroom in their stockinged feet and dressing gown in the middle of the night must be a little careful, I daresay." And he still hadn't explained why he was giving Carlotta money.

"I was just talking to her."

"No, you were just paying her, Belami, and we both know why. I don't want to hear any more of your excuses. I don't want to see any more of you than is absolutely necessary. I don't want to be engaged to a man I can't trust around the corner. I want you to leave me alone. Just

116

leave me alone. Don't say one more word or I'll push you into the canal."

"Fine!" Belami clapped his hands together and exercised great self-control to keep from shaking her. "You're quite right that we wouldn't suit. I couldn't be married to a woman who doesn't trust me."

"I suggest you find yourself a congenital idiot, preferably one who is deaf and blind."

Deirdre snapped open her umbrella and used it as a shield for the remainder of the trip. When the gondola docked, they got out and walked in silence to the Léon Bianco. The first thing they saw was Pronto. Latched on to his arm was Elvira Sutton, and a very comical couple they were, Pronto hopping along to keep pace with her longer strides. When he spotted them, Pronto came forward, smiling from ear to ear.

"She's back," he announced, rather unnecessarily.

"Elvira!" Deirdre exclaimed, and rushed to greet her.

Elvira blushingly held out her left hand, on which Pronto's signet ring decorated the third finger. "Congratulate me!" She smiled. "We're engaged." Her deep blue eyes flashed a triumph beam at Belami.

He was sent reeling but soon recovered speech. "It is unlike you to utter a solecism, Miss Sutton. You must know it's the gentleman who is congratulated on his victory. To you we offer our best wishes. You returned earlier than expected, did you not?"

She smiled at Pronto. "Shall we tell them?" she asked.

"It's all right with me," Pronto said proudly.

"I cut my visit short," Elvira explained. "The truth is, I had an understanding with my friend's brother. My friend Jane Blackwell, from Bath. When I told him I had fallen in love with another, I was uncomfortable with them, so I left immediately and was home last night. Jane is angry with me, I fear."

"You never said Jane had a brother!" Deirdre exclaimed.

"I felt so horrid, hiding it." Elvira blushed. "But he had to be the first to know of my change of heart. Till I had told Mr. Blackmore, I couldn't accept Pronto's offer."

"Just where exactly do the Blackmores stay—or is it Black*well*?" Belami asked. His brow rose in interest at this slip, the first Elvira had made thus far.

"Blackwell," Pronto told him. Elvira nodded.

"They were staying with friends outside of Vicenza," Elvira answered with a clear, untroubled gaze. "I never did get to the house. I told them as soon as Robert and Jane met me at Mestre. We went for a drive in his carriage, had lunch at an inn—I'm sorry, Lord Belami, I can't give me the name of the inn," she added mischievously.

"Perhaps you could give me the name of the friends the Blackwells were visiting?" he asked.

"What do you want to know that for?" Pronto demanded.

"I don't, really," Dick said. Why waste time following this cold trail? Elvira hadn't met the Blackwells at Mestre. There were no Blackwells. She'd met Claude at Mira, and whatever she was up to, she'd gotten clean away with it. Why hadn't his spies seen her come back? "What time did you return, Miss Sutton?"

"Shortly after dinner. It was just coming on dark. I sent a note off to Pronto at once. He spent the evening with us and asked Mama for my hand."

"She said yes." Pronto smiled.

What had Nick said last night? The hotel was quiet. Only three arrivals—a French couple and a few English gentlemen, none of them asking for the Suttons.

"Where are you off to now?" Deirdre asked.

"We're going to Cerboni's to buy Elvira a wedding ring," Pronto said. "You folks care to tag along?"

"Do come, Lord Belami," Elvira urged, with still that laughing light in her eyes. "We have every confidence in your ability. You will know if Cerboni is trying to palm

118

us off with a counterfeit diamond. You come, too, Deirdre. We'll all go.''

She took Deirdre's hand as the ladies walked separately a few feet in front of the gentlemen. ''This engagement is very sudden,'' Deirdre said.

''It has been brewing ever since Paris. I like Pronto amazingly. Don't you like him, Deirdre?''

''Very much. Much better than his friend.''

Elvira peered at her companion and swallowed a satisfied smile. ''I agree with you there, but I shall soon have Pronto under cat's paw and detach him from that fellow.'' This speech had the effect of causing Deirdre's shoulders to stiffen. It was one thing for her to denigrate Belami; for Miss Sutton to do it was another matter. She disliked the speech about managing Pronto, too.

When they reached Cerboni's shop, Pronto and Elvira demanded to see the diamond rings. ''Something larger than that, if you please,'' Elvira said, pouting, when the man showed them a tray of modest rings. ''You insult my fiancé to suggest he thinks no more of me than that. We want four or five carats, don't you think, Pronto?'' she asked, batting her eyelashes at her fiancé.

Pronto smiled fatuously. ''No, by Jove. Nine or ten.''

Elvira proved a knowledgeable fiancée. She took her time over the selection, always seeking Belami's advice. ''This one is so flawed even I can see the crack with the naked eye,'' she complained of one. And later, ''You don't think this one gaudy?'' she asked, when she had made a tentative choice of a ten-carat, emerald-cut diamond.

''Very impressive,'' Dick said stiffly.

''My hand is large; I can wear it,'' Elvira decided. ''This is the one, Pronto.''

As Pronto scribbled out a check, Elvira continued speaking to Cerboni. ''Have you had any success in finding a teardrop pearl for my sister yet, sir?''

''It's very difficult, but I have sent out inquiries.''

"We have brought a deal of business your way," Elvira said. "The least you can do is find us a matching pearl."

"If anyone has such a thing, he is not eager to sell it. And if a jeweler approaches to buy it unsolicited—well, it would raise up the price, Miss Sutton. You might have to pay twice as much."

Elvira listened, her intelligent eyes betraying that she understood his reasoning. "Never mind. We'll pay whatever is asked. My sister has got her heart set on having the mate to my pearl. You just find it, and let us worry about paying. There will be other jewelry purchases to be made soon as well, my good man. We don't dally when we want something, so you'd best get busy. My mama plans to give me a set of diamonds for my wedding present. I am going to look in the other shops now."

"Diamonds! Why, I have the best selection in Venice," Cerboni exclaimed, and began showing Elvira diamond necklaces.

"This one is pretty," she said, holding an elaborate matched set against her throat. "How much is it?"

"Roughly ten thousand in British currency," Cerboni told her. His eyes shone with greedy interest.

"Cheap at half the price," Elvira said, and placed it back on the counter.

They all left the shop. Belami wanted to get his friend alone for a good Bear Garden jaw, but Elvira had taken control of him. "Pronto is taking us to the Lido this afternoon," she said when Belami tried to arrange a meeting. There was no invitation for Belami to join them. That evening, Pronto was taking the Suttons to a concert.

"I hope Pronto will also take you to Contessa Ginnasi's masquerade party," Belami said. "I'd like to see him once more before he's married. Your family is invited to the party."

"What fun!" Elvira clapped her hands. The large diamond flashed in the sunlight. "I shall go as the Queen of Sheba, and you must be my Nubian slave, Pronto."

"Eh?" Pronto looked aghast till Elvira squeezed his fingers and smiled.

It saddened Belami to see his old colleague caught in parson's mousetrap with such a shrew, but he felt powerless to prevent it. Pronto was a very willing victim—and Elvira was demmed attractive.

"Now we must go home and show Mama my ring," Elvira decided. She took Pronto by the elbow and carried him off.

Belami cast a glance, half-sad, half-angry, at Deirdre. "I may say good-bye to that good friend," he said.

"At least we know now that Elvira's not married to Claude. But we can't let him marry her, Belami!"

Belami felt a sting to hear himself demoted from "Dick." "I thought you liked Elvira."

"I did—before. She behaves differently now. She's too greedy and too managing."

"Too managing, and too mysterious by half. How the deuce did she get back into the hotel without my spies seeing her? I for one don't believe she went to meet these Blackwells. She must have been wearing a disguise when she returned. Why would she do that if she isn't up to something havey-cavey?"

"It was disgusting the way she conned Pronto into buying her that huge diamond," Deirdre said.

"I don't begrudge a bride her ring, but I do resent that she won't let him off the leash for a moment."

They walked back to the gondola, their anger with each other not forgotten, but temporarily submerged in worry for their old friend.

"We should look on the bright side," Deirdre said. "At least Elvira is well to grass. And their money was genuine."

"So it was—Elvira was at some pains to see that I was aware of the fact. I wonder . . ."

"What?"

"I wonder how the Suttons plan to pay for the rest of

121

the jewelry and whether I'll be invited to attend that session as well. That first purchase may have been made to establish their bona fides. Cerboni now feels they are well-to-do tourists. Pronto's purchase reinforces the idea. Cerboni won't look too closely at the color of their gold next time around.''

"Elvira didn't say how her mama would pay. Probably by check. I shouldn't think they'd carry thousands of pounds in gold around with them.'' ·

"No more should I, not if it's genuine money. Of course a big purchase paid for in cash would be a clever way to unload the counterfeit coins and have something they could sell in return for *real* money. Réal didn't find any such cache when he searched their rooms." Dick stopped walking and frowned.

"What's the matter?" Deirdre asked.

He looked at her, one brow riding at a quizzical angle. "What's wrong is that we've just enlarged our circle of suspects. We, at least I, thought only Elvira was involved with the Jalberts, through Claude. Now it seems she's not married to Claude. What we've been saying suggests that the whole family is involved."

"Oh, dear. That can't be true. Elvira manages her mama as easily as she manages Pronto. She's pulling the wool over their eyes—using some stunt to get hold of her mama's inheritance."

"That inheritance is beginning to smell as fishy as everything else about Miss Sutton. Did she ever give a name for this nabob uncle?"

"It was Mrs. Sutton's uncle, her father's brother. What was her maiden name? It sounded Irish—Mc something. McMaster, I think. Yes, that was it."

Belami increased the pace and soon handed Deirdre into the gondola. "Aren't you coming back with me?" she asked.

Belami cast a surprised look at her. "This is a good

sign. You weren't at all eager for my company when we left this morning.''

Deirdre remembered why she was angry and sniffed. "I am not eager for your company. I only thought we might think of some way to save poor Pronto. He's my friend, too.''

"That's exactly what I plan to do. Rescue Pronto. Maybe I'll even find a way to rescue Belami while I'm about it. He's not the rake you imagine, you know.''

Deirdre tossed her head angrily, but she was not so immune to his pleadings as she pretended. Something in her wanted to believe him. "How do you plan to rescue Pronto?'' she asked.

"Very carefully. I can't let him know what inquiries I'm instituting about his ladylove or he'd marry her to spite me—and after all we've been through together, too.'' His accusing eye spoke more of herself than of Pronto. "Why is it I attract such hardhearted friends, do you suppose?''

Deirdre gave him a withering stare. "Any friend of yours needs a hard heart. You give it such a battering.''

"That's what I get for trying to be a Good Samaritan. It's well that virtue is its own reward. There don't seem to be much else in it for the virtuous.''

He shoved the gondola adrift with his boot and stood looking till it was underway. Deirdre wasn't facing him, but she turned around just once and looked back. She looked—doubtful. And ravishing, as she always did, never more so than when he wasn't allowed to touch her. What had made him fall in love with Deirdre Gower? She was pretty, but not an incomparable. A provincial little prude was what she was, and it seemed hard that he, who counted himself up to all the rigs, should be ridden over roughshod by her.

Then she turned away, and his thoughts drifted to Pronto. Hoppner was his best hope. He'd have to cast some official block in the way of that marriage. Papers would have to be found to be irregular. Belami's heart thudded angrily. Why was he so furious with Elvira? He usually felt some troublesome attraction to his female quarry. Carlotta, for instance, was rather sweet in that raffish way of the demimonde, but for Elvira Sutton he felt nothing but anger and a determination to unmask her and save Pronto.

Chapter Eleven

Belami turned his steps toward the British consul's office and was shown into Mr. Richard Hoppner's office.

"Good morning, sir. I'm back on behalf of that friend of mine who is interested in getting married in Venice," he began.

"Is it time to offer my congratulations, Lord Belami?" Hoppner asked roguishly.

"To the bridegroom, you mean?" Belami replied, feigning dullness. "I fear not. The fact is, I have come to believe the match is a poor one and want some new information. What can be done to delay a marriage of foreigners here in Venice?"

"Providing they plan to use an English cleric, as I suggested, nothing can be done," Hoppner told him.

"If their papers weren't in order—" Belami suggested. He remembered Pronto's passport, still in his own care.

"A couple of witnesses to identify them is all that's required really. If youngsters are determined to marry, they will find a way."

"That's true." Belami nodded and went on to his next question. "Do you happen to know of any British tourists in Venice with some connections in India? I'm trying to learn something about a nabob named McMaster."

"Old Brian McMaster?" Hoppner asked. "The Irishman who was British resident for one of the nawabs at Jaipur?''

"That's probably him.''

"We have a fairly large contingent of nabobs here,'' Hoppner told him. "They can afford to travel, and like our warm climate. McMaster never did come to Italy himself, but his friends often speak of him. A colorful gentleman, to judge by their stories. He was already in failing health when he returned to England. He stayed at Tunbridge Wells trying to recuperate there, but he didn't last long. What is it you want to know about him?''

"He's dead now, I take it?''

"Oh, yes, some five years ago.''

Belami's eyes lit up. The Sutton inheritance was supposed to be only a year old. "Any notion who his heirs were?''

"There's no question there. He left his entire fortune to the East India Company School at Haileybury, where young lads are trained up for the EIC. Being an orphan, he considered John Company his nearest relative.''

"An orphan, you say?'' Belami asked. A peculiar smile played over his lips.

"That's right, an orphan and a bachelor. He left the bulk of his estate to the school to set up a library. Was there any particular reason . . .''

"Not really. I heard someone mention McMaster the other day—their name was also McMaster.'' Belami figured he knew where the Suttons had hit on the name McMaster. Watering spots like Tunbridge Wells were a haunt for disreputables hoping to con some money out of the nabobs.

"A coincidence,'' Hoppner said.

Belami was in a fever to get on with his case and made an excuse to leave very soon. He was desperate to see Pronto alone. He hoped to at least put a doubt in his head about his fiancée. His hopes for success weren't high, but he left a note for Pronto at the hotel asking him to come to the palazzo that afternoon.

To his considerable astonishment, Pronto came. He arrived around three. Luncheon had been a particularly gruesome meal. Carlotta was out with friends, leaving Belami and the conte alone with the duchess and Deirdre. Such conversation as had occurred was mainly the duchess telling the conte to eat his lunch "like a good boy," and Deirdre refusing all her suitor's overtures with a cool "I shall be busy today, Belami."

Pronto bounded out of a hired gondola, very nearly upsetting it, and went in search of Belami. "Well, I'm here. What is it you want?" he asked.

"Need you ask?" Belami said, putting his arm around Pronto's shoulder. "We are best friends, Pronto. I've missed you. Let's have a glass of wine and talk."

"I'll have the *vino*, but if you're planning to bend my ear about Elvira, don't. Fact is, I just came to pick up my passport. Don't fear I'll lose it, for Elvira's going to keep it for me."

Belami didn't want to start the visit on a bad foot and sent off for the passport. He also requested that Miss Gower be informed of Mr. Pilgrim's presence, hoping that would nudge her out of her sulks. It was a good enough excuse for her to do what she'd been wanting to do all afternoon—join Belami.

After a few glasses of wine to get Pronto back in humor, Belami began raising some more important matters than mere chitchat. "It's like old times, we three friends together again," he said leadingly. "I'll certainly miss you when you're married, Pronto."

Deirdre felt a stab of regret. She'd been missing Pronto, too. He was her semiofficial mender of fences when she and Dick were at odds, as they so often were.

"You ain't losing a son, Dick, you're gaining a daughter. It'll be the four of us together, solving cases. Elvira's

127

sharp as a needle. Be no end of help to us. We'd like you and Deirdre to be our witnesses when we get married.''

"When will the wedding take place?" Deirdre asked.

"Day after tomorrow—on Saturday.''

"That soon!" Deirdre exclaimed, and shot a wild glance to Belami. "But that's the day of the contessa's masquerade party. You won't be here for it," she said.

"Of course we will. We're getting married in the morning and going to the masquerade party at night. That'll leave the afternoon free for—for getting ready. Heh, heh. Got it all worked out. I found a preacher from Bath who'll do it up brown for two guineas. We're getting married at the hotel.''

"Surely not at an hotel," Deirdre objected. "It seems so tawdry—that is, so unromantic.''

"As to romance, a hotel is as good a place as any for that. *Molto bieno*," Pronto said. A lecherous little smile flitted across his face at remembered indiscretions. "An excellent place for romance ac-tually. You don't say that anymore, Deirdre. You remember how you used to quiz her about it, Dick?" Pronto was becoming maudlin from the wine. He smiled fatuously at his companions. "Shall we drink a bumper to marriage? Why don't we make it a double wedding?''

Deirdre stared coolly at Belami. "Finding someone to marry you shouldn't take more than two days," she said blandly.

Pronto lowered his brows. "He's already found you. Are you cutting up your larks again, Deirdre?''

"I? Your memory is faulty, Pronto. It was always Belami who behaved badly.''

"That's true. And if it wasn't Dick chasing the light skirts, it was the duchess misunderstanding everything. Pity I can't be here to keep you two apart—er—together. You should take a leaf from Elvira's books, Deirdre. She never cuts up stiff.''

"She seems a trifle managing to me," Deirdre ventured.

"That's true, but then I need a manager. Elvira's managing everything. The honeymoon, our finances—even our costumes for the masquerade party."

"Your finances?" Dick asked sharply. "Just what does that mean? I hope you haven't given her your money?"

"No, she'll manage it after we're married is all I mean. About this slave thing—ain't what you think," he muttered. "I was a bit worried myself when she talked about nude slaves. Told her point-blank I wouldn't go to a party naked. It's Nubian slave."

"She'll have you painted black?" Deirdre asked.

"Only my face and hands. Cut quite a dash. That way, Elvira'll be able to recognize me if we get separated. The Italian fellows are bound to be all over her. She'll easily spot a black face, and can come running to her *esposo*—me."

"Elvira strikes me as a lady who can handle herself," Belami said. "She organized this trip her family is taking, I believe? Deirdre mentioned Elvira was the one who chose hotels and the route, and so on."

"A regular sergeant major." Pronto smiled and poured himself another glass of wine.

"Why is it she chooses such modest hotels when the family has inherited money from McMaster?" Belami asked.

"Bit of a nip cheese if you want the truth, Dick. Like old Charney. We'll never outrun the grocer with Elvira handling our blunt."

"Old Brian McMaster was it, the nabob uncle?"

"That's the fellow."

"I heard somewhere that McMaster was an orphan," Dick said, and looked to Pronto for his reaction.

"Can't be, he was Mrs. Sutton's uncle."

"I also heard he left his money to set up a library at the East India Company School," Dick continued.

129

"Might have bought them a few books. A regular nabob."

"You have only Elvira's word for all this," Dick suggested.

Pronto set his glass down, lowered his brow, and glared. "Are you starting on Elvira again? I warned you, Dick."

It was time for the gloves to come off. "Pronto, you don't know a damned thing about the woman. What's the rush to get married? Wait till you get back to England and we can find out something about her."

"I know all I have to know. She loves me, and I love her. I don't care if she ain't an heiress. I've thought of that, for there's no saying her mama will give her anything but the diamonds. I ain't marrying Elvira for her money."

"I'm not talking about money," Belami said. "You don't know *anything* about her at all. All we know about any of the Suttons is that they're three women traveling together, calling themselves rich, but traveling like paupers, with only one female servant. That's not the way rich people travel."

"The way Charney travels," Pronto replied sagely.

"She's different. We know who and what she is," Dick replied discreetly. "The Suttons don't behave like nouveau riche people."

"Told you, she's a nip cheese. As to having the money, why look at all the jewelry they've bought. What reason do you have to mistrust Elvira?" he demanded hotly. "A rubbishing piece cut out of a paper, and the guinea you lost."

"There's more than that," Dick said. "There's this mysterious trip to visit the Blackwells, for instance."

"Nothing mysterious about it. Elvira went to break it off with Robert Blackwell."

"She didn't go to see the Blackwells. She went to an inn at Mira and disappeared," Dick said, and went on to explain his findings. "And furthermore, why didn't my man see her when she returned to her hotel?"

"Because he was either drunk or chasing after some serving wench."

"But what if you're wrong?" Dick asked. "What if Elvira is who and what I think she is?"

"If she was married to Claude Jalbert, she couldn't very well marry me, could she? And she is marrying me, Dick. That's what's sticking in your craw. You've been trying to get Deirdre to have you for a dog's age, and I can get my girl to the altar as quick as blinking. It's either sour grapes or dog in a manger—either way, it ain't very flattering, my friend. You'd do better to try to nab Deirdre than scotch my match. Maybe it's my fault," Pronto said, becoming sentimental to consider his friend's ill fortune, while he himself was so blessed.

"You need me here to oil the wheels and turn the duchess up sweet. I've let you down, Dick. Always suspected you couldn't get along without me. I'll give you a hand any way I can, but you've got to stop picking on my Elvira."

Dick caught Deirdre's eye and indicated that he'd like to be alone with Pronto. She left and Dick drew his chair closer to his friend. If he couldn't detach Pronto from Elvira, he certainly didn't plan to let her have sole access to him. "Truer words were never spoken," he said with a sad, conning smile. "I do need you to help me with Deirdre. Things are going badly for me. Deirdre has taken the notion I'm carrying on with Carlotta."

"Keep your bedroom door locked. That's what I did."

"I shall, but meanwhile how can I win Deirdre back? She hardly speaks to me. I need your help badly, my friend."

"Thought as much. Sorry I abandoned you, Dick, but you see my position. A man just engaged, the wedding looming up on me. Dozens of things me and Elvira have to do. I can't just skip off and leave her to order the dinner and pay the parson and all that."

"Surely you can spare me an occasional hour."

Pronto reached up and patted Dick's shoulder. "Any time. I didn't like to admit it, but Deirdre's got a point. Elvira's a beautiful girl and I love her, but it's time I let her know who's the man. Take this Nubian slave thing, Dick. Can't say I relish getting myself covered in boot polish on my wedding night. It's a bit more than the face and hands. It's the arms and legs, too. And the chest and back. Everything but—but the rest of me. About this Queen of Sheba, I was wondering if I couldn't be the King of Sheba."

Eager to abet any revolt, Belami took up this topic. "Nothing is mentioned of the king. The queen's important lover is King Solomon—according to legend, he fathered King David on her. You might go as Solomon, covered in grandeur. Solomon was famous for his wealth as well as his wisdom."

"It'd be a demmed sight better than boot blacking. That's it. I'll go as Solomon. Have to powder my hair, won't mind that. Any news on how I should behave?"

"You could look up the queen's visit to Solomon—it's in Kings in the Bible. In the Koran, there's a peculiar allusion. It seems Solomon heard the queen had hairy legs and feet. To get a look at them, he led her over a glass floor which she mistook for water. She lifted her skirts— the legs were as reported, I believe."

Pronto was much struck with this tale. "Solomon didn't seem to mind, eh? Mean to say—David."

"Her other charms appear to have overcome any little excess of hair." Belami smiled. "Hardly a nice trick to play on a lady."

"I wonder Sheba didn't slip on that glass and break her neck. Or the floor. Funny thing to be in the Bible."

"The Koran, actually. Yes, it's an unexpected thing to find in such a serious book."

"I didn't mean that. The funny thing is, Elvira's legs *are* a trifle hairy. A trim ankle, but pretty hairy withal.

Anyhow, I mean to go to the party as King Solomon. How about you?''

''With a great lack of imagination, I shall wear a domino over my evening clothes.''

''To hell with King Solomon. Sorry about that—didn't mean to blaspheme. To hell with the Nubian slave is what I really meant. But, Dick, if you should happen to see Elvira before the ball, don't mention it. She's got her heart set on me being her slave.''

Belami encouraged this rebellion. ''Put your foot down early. It's the only way to maintain ascendancy over the ladies.''

''I'll say I didn't have any boot blacking. And I'll not let her bring her mama and Lucy on our honeymoon either. I'll hire them a guide is what I'll do. An English *guido*— they'll feel quite comfortable. Met an Oxford scholar t'other day at the Lido. Out of blunt. Mentioned he had to cut his trip short. He'll be delighted to continue it without expense.''

''I drew the line at sharing my honeymoon with Charney.''

''You ended up with no honeymoon at all. I shan't go that far. If she insists on having the ladies along, I'll let her. We'll have separate carriages though, and I won't wear boot blacking on my wedding night. *Mille grazios* for your help, my friend.''

''*Prego*. What's Elvira doing this afternoon?''

''Seeing the modiste. Getting a dress sewn up. Later we're seeing the hotel manager about the wedding breakfast. I'll tackle her about the honeymoon now. When will I see you again, Dick?''

''I'll drop around the hotel tomorrow about ten.''

''*Domani* it is. If I ain't up, just pound the door hard.''

Belami accompanied Pronto down to the landing. ''How'd Carlotta go visiting when their boat's still here?'' he asked.

"Her hostess must have sent a gondola for her. Deirdre and I were using this one."

"What the Venetians need is some water horses."

Belami's lips quivered. "I really do miss you, Pronto."

"Me, too," Pronto said, and clamped his arm. *"Aurevoirderci."*

Pronto left, and Belami stayed outside, enjoying the unusual view. As he gazed across the water, he saw a boat making great speed toward him. He recognized the wiry body of Réal poling a small, light craft forward.

Soon Réal hopped onto the landing. He took Belami's elbow and turned him aside to foil any invisible eavesdroppers. "News of the most serious," he said importantly.

"Did you find out where Miss Sutton went?"

"Of this lady I hear nothing, but I find the house of the soi-disant Captain Styger."

"By God, I knew it! Where is it? Is Styger there?"

"It is nearby Mira, a mile from town. The house is emptied. The Styger is gone away for two days. I had the great fortune to meet with a girl who speaks French and Italian—a seamstress—very pretty, with black hair. She was at the Taverna Vecchia, but lives neighboring at Styger's house."

"Did Styger have any callers?"

"But yes, this is what I have to tell you," Réal said. "He has a call from a very beautiful lady with jet black hairs, only he is not at home."

"Elvira!" Belami smiled.

"But no. The caller came today. It was—" He stopped for dramatic effect. "Milady Ginnasi. A small lady, dressed all in black, the neighbors said, and I saw with my own eyes the contessa in a carriage at the dock later on."

"Carlotta?" Belami exclaimed. "Good God, is that where she's been all day? And she missed Styger then?"

"She do, but she had her gondolier climb in at the window and went inside her own self by the door."

Belami's head was reeling. This new element needed some serious thinking, but meanwhile he hadn't learned what he'd sent Réal to find out. "Was Elvira there yesterday?"

"No ladies were there yesterday. Only one gentleman—young, handsome, according to Marie."

"Does a young gentleman—Claude—live with Styger?"

"He is living alone, even without servants. Nobody is calling till yesterday, when a young gentleman calls. Marie saw him by a window—with no good details of his looks, except young, slender, which she decides is handsome. Then today, the Contessa Ginnasi calls. This is very strange, *non*?"

"This is completely baffling," Belami admitted. "The caller must have been Claude, but where is Claude staying? How do you know Styger's gone for a couple of days?"

"I find out from Marie where he is buying milk and butter and eggs. He asks for none to be delivered till two days."

"What time did Claude call yesterday?"

"Around noon-hour time."

"Elvira would have had time to visit Claude . . . and whatever her errand was, it had to be related to Styger—who then went on a short journey. What could it be?"

"This cannot be learned," Réal said simply. "What can be done is for you to talk to the contessa. Sweet talking," he added, lest his mentor not catch his meaning.

"I doubt if she knows any more than I do. I tipped her the clue the counterfeiters were at Mira—she only went to see if she could gain anything from them. Blackmail, more or less, but I'll speak to her—sweetly."

"I followed her gondola. It is went to the Saint Mark Square landing. I do not follow, as I want to report at once to you this important findings." Réal peered from the corner of his eye to see that this won approval.

The master nodded, then narrowed his eyes and deduced. Carlotta had no luck finding the Jalberts at Mira, but he'd told her Elvira was involved. Damme, she'd gone to the hotel. She'd spoil the whole thing! He hopped into the gondola and handed Réal the pole. "Get to Saint Mark's landing, as fast as you can."

The boat Réal had hired was light. He put his wiry strength into the oars and skimmed across the surface like a butterfly. When they were halfway there, they spotted Carlotta returning and Réal turned the boat around.

"I go back quickly so the contessa doesn't see us," he said. With a superhuman effort, he got the gondola landed a few minutes before the contessa arrived.

Carlotta wore a suspiciously smug smile. "Good afternoon." She smiled at Dick. "I'm back from my visit. Did you miss me?" They began walking toward the palazzo.

"More to the point, did your luncheon partner not miss you?" Belami asked, and took her arm.

She laughed merrily and moved her reticule to her other hand. "You've found me out. Well, I confess. I had a tryst with my marchese. Guy hasn't been asking questions?"

"No, Carlotta, it is I who have some questions to ask. About your trip to Mira," he said, and opened the door.

Her flashing black eyes met his. "How did you know?"

"I'll ask the questions. What were you doing at Mira?"

"It's where I rendezvous with my marchese," she teased.

"Your memory is faulty. You told me you had never made love at Mira. You didn't choose Captain Styger's house for your initiation, I think."

She shrugged her shoulders and pouted. "I didn't discover anything. The place was empty—a total mess. The man doesn't even have a servant."

"Why did you go?"

"Why, to help you, *caro*."

"Try again," he suggested.

"Don't be an ass, Dick. If there are counterfeiters hiding nearby, it stands to reason they don't want anyone to know. Why, I shouldn't be surprised if they'd pay for it to be kept secret."

"That's what I thought. Did you speak to Elvira when you went to the Saint Mark's landing?" Her frank answer didn't surprise him, but he felt a little uneasy. The lovely contessa wore an air of excitement—of smugness—as though she were getting away with something. Her hands betrayed nervousness as they clutched at her black kid reticule. Rather a large reticule, and bulging with something.

"I merely delivered invitations to my masquerade party. That should be quite a party," she added, with a pensive look.

Carlotta noticed that Belami's eyes were trained on her reticule. He saw a square protrusion showing through the soft leather. Her fingers closed over the telling bump. Just as he reached for it, a servant came into the hall. "I must go and relieve the duchessa," she said. "Where's your lady today?"

"I've no idea."

"Such a lukewarm lover," she chided, and swept away, her hips swinging insouciantly as she went toward the staircase.

Deirdre was indeed getting short shrift in the midst of the confusion. He'd enlist her help in discovering what Carlotta was hiding. What could it be? Stolen counterfeit coins wouldn't make a square bulge—but the dies for making them would. Had the vixen waltzed off with Styger's counterfeit dies? It should indeed be a lively party if that was the case.

Could this be turned to his advantage? The Jalberts would want those dies back. And he wanted Pronto back. It would leave him with the jobs of getting the dies from Carlotta, then recovering them again after he'd bought

Pronto's freedom by giving them to Elvira, but at least he'd have Elvira right under his nose. He waited till Carlotta had disappeared, then went prowling the rooms in search of Deirdre.

Chapter Twelve

Deirdre, curious to hear what Dick had said to Pronto, went to the saloon in search of him. "Did you manage to talk some sense into him after I left?" she asked.

"When love comes in at the window, sense goes out the door. But then we know that, you and I," he added, with an intimate smile.

"I never blamed your lack of sense on love, Belami."

He saw he was still in her black books and shifted his mind to business. "Our only hope is to unmask Elvira before the wedding. Will you help me?"

"What can I do?"

"It involves Carlotta," he said, and told her what he'd learned from Réal. "She took her reticule to her room. She will have hidden the dies by now, but I hoped you might slip in and have a look around. The dies would be bas-relief imprints of the coin—you'd recognize them. A separate die for the front and back."

"Very well," Deirdre replied, but far from appreciating Belami's forbearance for staying out of the woman's room, she wore a face of accusation. "That will leave you free to amuse the contessa while I perform the search," she said tartly.

Belami counted to ten and answered fairly civilly, "We can reverse roles, if you prefer. My fear was that Carlotta would come in and find me in her room."

"I'm sure that possibility filled you with dread."

As they were talking, the contessa pushed her conte's bath chair into the saloon. The duchess was with them. "We have had a charming afternoon," the duchess declared. Her eye darted to the fireplace to see that the wine was present and the fire glowing invitingly. "I took the conte to the library and had him show me some of his tomes. An excellent collection. A pity it ain't in English." She turned to her niece and continued, "Deirdre, would you mind slipping up to my room and bringing down my reticule? I want to show the conte my new patent pen. They don't have them in Venice yet."

Belami directed a meaningful look at Deirdre. When he moved to Carlotta's side and engaged her interest, she knew her search wouldn't be interrupted. She tapped at Carlotta's door before entering, to ensure no servants were present. There was no answer so she went quietly in and stared at the lavish bedchamber. The walls were frescoed with nymphs and cavaliers, cavorting amidst a water garden. Dull gilt trim embellished the painted furnishings. The bed in particular caught her attention. It wore a pink satin counterpane and canopy. Laying in readiness for the contessa was a dashing black lace nightgown and peignoir. Deirdre lifted the gown and fingered it, noticing it was transparent. Was this what Carlotta wore when Dick went to visit her?

She shook away the troublesome thought and went to the dresser to wrench open a few drawers. A welter of gloves and handkerchiefs, ribbons and stockings, all liberally sprinkled with powder from the silver powder pot on the dresser, greeted her eyes. How could such a well-polished product as Carlotta issue from this awful mess? She turned from the dresser back to the room. Now where would she hide her reticule in this chamber? Her eyes were drawn back to the bed. At the head of it were half-a-dozen lace-edged pillows. Deirdre slipped her hand under them and felt the soft kid reticule. She pulled it out, noticing that it bulged with something. Something hard and square and rather heavy.

Her heart beat faster as she unfastened the clasp and pulled out a morocco-bound copy of a book. It was small, about twice the size of a chapbook, but still large enough to fill a lady's reticule. It contained excerpts of Boccaccio's tales from *The Decameron*, all in Italian. With a tsk of annoyance, Deirdre returned the book to its bag, the bag under the pillow, and went to get her aunt's reticule. Dick didn't look at her for a moment after her return to the saloon. Carlotta, however, was wearing that smug look Dick had mentioned.

"Here's your reticule, Auntie," Deirdre said.

The duchess drew out a cheap patent pen and handed it with great ceremony to the conte. "For you." She beamed. "You will have the jump on your friends, Guy. These are all the crack in London, I promise you."

The conte accepted the token with sufficient grace to satisfy the donor.

It was some minutes before Belami casually worked his way to Deirdre's side. "No luck," she said in a low tone.

"Couldn't find the reticule, or was it empty?"

"It was full—of a book. Square, lumpy just as you said, but no dies."

Belami glanced around the room, his gaze settling last on Carlotta, who lifted a well-arched brow and smiled. That knowing smile told him all he needed to know. She knew he'd be searching her room and had replaced the dies with the book to tease him.

Carlotta was expansive over dinner. She flirted outrageously with her tired old conte, who smiled his gratitude at her attentions. "I want to have a party, Guy," Carlotta said.

"You're having a masquerade party, my pet," he reminded her. With a little waggle of his head he added, "What, are you becoming forgetful? That's my job."

"You're not forgetful," Carlotta said, and pulled his

141

chin playfully. "I meant another party. We've been so dull all winter, Guy. Let us entertain the duchessa's friends. The Suttons—is that the name, Duchessa?"

The duchess had no objection to any entertainment thrown in her honor, so long as it came without expense. "If you think it worth your while, go right ahead," she said grandly. "They are not the sort of people I should bother to entertain, but they're well enough in a foreign country. At least they are English," she added, with no intention of giving offense.

Carlotta's black eyes snapped and she answered testily, "I shall invite them anyway. You will enjoy to see your friends, Miss Gower."

"That would be lovely," Deirdre replied. She knew Dick wanted to keep in touch with Pronto, and this seemed a way to do it. "You knew Miss Sutton is engaged?" she asked.

"But of course! I must invite that funny Pilgrim, too."

"I'll be happy to deliver the invitation," Dick offered.

"Excellent. Let us make it for tomorrow evening," Carlotta said. "Ask them to come in the afternoon. I'll show them around the palazzo. The frescoes are considered worth the trip. Don't you agree, Miss Gower?" she asked, and slanted a smile at Deirdre. "Especially those in my bedchamber."

"I haven't seen those," Deirdre answered coolly. "I particularly admire the ones in the library, however. Miss Sutton is artistic; she will like to see them."

"What is Miss Sutton painting in Venice?" Carlotta asked.

"She did the Rialto, but I don't believe she's done any painting since then. She is just newly engaged, you know."

Carlotta cast a bright smile, first at Deirdre, then at Belami. "I know, but as she's English, I didn't think romance would feature prominently in the engagement."

Belami stared in fascination. Now the cat was beginning to show her claws. Carlotta must be very sure of herself.

Till now, she'd been more amiable. He was under no mis-apprehension as to her reason. She was sunk in debt and hoped to rescue herself through him, but this was no way to set about it. She had found another source of money then—the dies. She was inviting the Suttons here to make some mutually satisfactory arrangement for their return. They were worth nothing to her—she wouldn't know how to use them, but the Jalberts could put them to use again later, when the storm died down. The conversation contin-ued in this baiting way till dinner was over. After dinner, Carlotta entertained them with some music. When the conte began snoring in his bath chair, the contessa's duties were over. She wheeled him into the hall and called for his valet.

"I'm ready for bed myself," the duchess announced. "Your music was a lovely soporific, Contessa. It has set me to nodding. You youngsters will excuse me? Don't lin-ger too long, Deirdre. Belami and the contessa will have things to talk about." She foresaw no danger to Deirdre's virtue when a very pretty harlot sat ready to entertain the rake, Belami.

"So happy you enjoyed my musical sleeping draught, your grace," Carlotta said. When the duchess had hobbled from the room, Carlotta turned a laughing eye to Belami. "Do we have things to talk about, Belami?" she asked. "Or are you too lulled to sleep?"

"The Italian *conversazione*s are famous, Contessa. You set the subject—Deirdre and I will be happy to oblige you."

"The Italian *conversazione*s are a dead bore. Nothing but idle gossip and bad wine. If you will excuse me, I shall retire before I wake up." Stifling a yawn, she turned away

Dick rose and bowed her from the room. At the door-way she turned around for one last taunt. "It won't be necessary for you to have my room watched. I shan't be leaving it tonight. *Buona notte.*"

"I wish I knew what that woman is up to," Deirdre scolded. "She knew perfectly well I was in her room. That jibe about the frescoes!"

"Of course she knew. She hid the plates and put that book in her reticule to taunt me. God knows where the dies are in a palazzo this size."

"Do you think she's inviting the Suttons here to try to sell the dies back to them?"

"I don't see why else she's doing it. She must be in a hurry if she can't wait till the masquerade party."

"I couldn't believe at first that Elvira was mixed up in this business, but since she conned Pronto into this hasty wedding, I know she is." Deirdre sighed.

"Of course she is," Dick said angrily. "I pumped Réal's brain dry and learned a few more details. He went back to Mestre the day Elvira disappeared. From what he could discover, no young lady traveling alone left Mestre at the time Elvira *should* have left to reach her hotel in time to see Pronto that evening. There were two English couples, middle-aged folks, and there was one young gentleman traveling alone. Why didn't Nick see her enter the hotel when she arrived?"

"It's what she did between leaving and returning that's really important," Deirdre pointed out.

"What she did was see Claude, who hastened off to visit Styger. Then Styger left his hired house, to be gone for two days. And in two days, Elvira is to marry Pronto. Hmm." He sat thinking about this for a moment.

"If she's going to marry Pronto, then perhaps she went to tell Claude—as she said she was telling Robert Blackwell."

"You don't tell your husband you're marrying another man."

"You're only guessing she's married to Claude. Perhaps it's Lucy that's married to him."

"Why would Elvira have to tell the Jalberts she was marrying Pronto then? It's none of their business. It doesn't

144

make sense—it's too complicated. Solutions are usually simple, once you get on the right track."

Belami sunk his hand in his fist and frowned. "All the ladies in this case are too complicated to suit me. Elvira laughing up her sleeve at me, Carlotta playing off her stunts and smirking till I can hardly keep my hands off her throat. And I sit here like an idiot, waiting for them to call the tune. We don't have a clue what's going on, that's the trouble. Nothing makes any sense. Elvira doesn't care two straws for Pronto. She's just after his blunt. We can't let Pronto marry that creature. The stomach turns to think of having her always around us in the future, bear-leading him. She's taken control of his passport; after the wedding, she's to handle his money. I shouldn't be a bit surprised if the whole ménage moves in with him. They're planning to accompany him on the treacle moon at least."

This speech inevitably called up a memory of the duchess and turned them both frigid. "I told him he was mad to even consider it," Belami added firmly.

Deirdre pokered up and said, "If there's nothing more to be done tonight, then I shall retire. Good night, Belami." She rose and strode to the door.

Belami was after her in a flash. He grabbed her wrist and swung her around to face him. "Running away doesn't solve anything."

"It solves the problem of being alone with you."

A satirical smile curved his lips. "Being alone with me is a problem? Now, why is that, I wonder? Could it be you don't trust yourself, Miss Gower?"

"It's you I don't trust."

"Wise girl. I wouldn't want to disappoint you."

She looked into his dark eyes that stared at her with a penetrating gaze. There was some enchantment in him. She felt her resolve weaken. His arms went around her, pulling her against him. "You know you love me, and I love you," he said in a husky voice. "Marry me."

The breath caught in her throat as his head descended,

till his lips were just brushing hers. His lips firmed in a ruthless kiss that set her head reeling. But reeling amidst the pleasanter thoughts of seeing Italy with Dick was the tawdry wedding of Pronto and Elvira in a cheap hotel. She didn't want her wedding to be like that. And, of course, there was the duchess to be talked around. Dick's arms tightened till she felt suffocated. She pushed him away and stood panting.

"No," she said. "Not here. Not at the Léon Bianco."

"We can use this palazzo."

"No!"

She saw Dick's passion darken to impatience. "You name the place then. You won't find a city with more churches per square foot than Venice. I don't care where, but I care when. I'm tired of waiting."

"No, Dick. We must rescue Pronto first."

Belami felt guilty at what his passion had led him to suggest. "You're right. Business before pleasure. But after we've settled this business, Deirdre—"

"I haven't definitely said yes."

"You said not here—that implies."

"That implies uncertainty," she pointed out, and before he could say more, she walked away.

Dick stood at the bottom of the stairs, watching as she went up. She turned around at the top and looked at him. Not a smile, or a wave, just a look. Rather a doubtful look actually. He should have pressed his advantage. But first he should save Pronto.

He walked slowly back to the saloon, poured a glass of wine, and thought about Pronto. Was Deirdre right in thinking it was Lucy who was married to Claude Jalbert? Claude Jalbert—he wished he knew the man, then he might have an idea which sort of lady he would have chosen. But then you could never tell. Who would ever have thought Pronto would fall in love with that beautiful Turk, Elvira Sutton? She was already managing him. Once she had him legally shackled, Pronto's life wouldn't be worth one of those counterfeit guineas. Yet if Elvira were single, she would surely get him to the altar. They were halfway there already. There remained only Friday to extricate Pronto from disaster.

And he had no real idea how to set about it. If he could find the dies . . . He'd stick like a burr to Elvira tomorrow. If the dies and money changed hands, he'd be there, ready to pounce. And if they didn't change hands, he'd be waiting at Styger's house near Mira the next day. By hook or crook he'd halt the wedding. And probably lose Pronto's friendship one way or the other. At least Deirdre was beginning to thaw.

Chapter Thirteen

The Sutton party arrived a little late for their visit to the palazzo the next afternoon, but with an acceptable excuse. "We received a note from Cerboni just as we were leaving and had to stop by his shop," Mrs. Sutton explained.

"Not buying more jewelry for those daughters of yours, Mrs. Sutton?" the duchess asked. If "Dear Maggie" was surprised to hear herself addressed so formally, she didn't betray it.

"Only the pearl we have been trying to find for Lucy," Mrs. Sutton assured her grace. "One turned up in Padua, and Cerboni sent me word at the hotel. We went down immediately and arranged to purchase it. He will set it in gold, to match Elvira's."

"I hope he isn't charging some outlandish sum?"

Mrs. Sutton flushed and admitted it had not come cheap.

"Three thousand," Pronto said. "Told her it was steep."

The duchess just shook her head. "Here I thought you were mad to pay a thousand for Elvira's."

"I shall see the pearl first and decide whether it is of the same high quality as Elvira's," Mrs. Sutton explained. "We hadn't thought it would be possible to find one at all."

"Did you choose the diamond necklace yet?" Deirdre asked.

"I have chosen it," Elvira answered. "The price is still to be settled. If Cerboni remains unreasonable, I shall try another shop." .

The old conte was merry as a grig to have such a surfeit of pretty young ladies around him. His watery smile wandered from one youthful face to another, finally settling on Elvira. "Diamonds, they would suit you, signorina," he told her, bowing with great ceremony from his bath chair.

Belami kept his eyes open but could detect no secret looks between Carlotta and Elvira except a shared smile at the conte's drooling behavior.

After a glass of wine, the contessa arranged for a tour of the palazzo. "You especially will be interested in the art, Miss Sutton," she said. "We have mostly frescoes and some rather interesting statuary in the garden."

Lucy and Pronto also rose for the tour. "You will not be interested in that, Mrs. Sutton," the duchess informed the other guest. "You and I shall stay here by the fireside with the conte and have a good cose. One misses half the advantage of foreign travel if she cannot see how the natives live. Why don't we offer Mrs. Sutton some of your excellent wine, Conte?"

"Yes, yes. It is right here," the conte said. Then he turned to Elvira. "Hurry back, my dear," he called.

Belami had no intention of letting Elvira and Carlotta out of his sight, so he and Deirdre also joined the group. It was a good chance to examine the palazzo for likely hiding spots as well. There were so many of them that he felt quite despondent. After an hour's stroll admiring the fading art works, the group returned to the saloon. Nothing of the least interest had happened.

"Are you all set for our masquerade ball?" the duchess inquired when they returned.

"We have been so busy we haven't arranged our costumes yet," Mrs. Sutton admitted. "Mr. Pilgrim tells us there is a shop in the Merceria that has all manner of outfit for hire.''

"Why, there's no need to lay down your blunt. The conte has a room full of old clothes. I'm sure the contessa would be delighted to let the youngsters root around and find something,'' the duchess said.

Carlotta led the young ladies off to try their luck amidst the decaying silks and laces from the past. Lucy found a gold brocade court gown cut daringly low in front and wanted to try it on. When she came from behind the screen to get help with the back fasteners, the gown was seen to be much too low in front and too long. Her feet got caught under the hem at every step.

"That gown would fit you better, Miss Sutton,'' the contessa suggested, measuring Elvira's size and height.

Elvira just shook her head. "No, I mean to go as the Queen of Sheba.''

"What will you wear?'' Carlotta asked. "I confess I wouldn't have a notion what would be suitable.''

"Something very rich and splendid,'' Elvira said vaguely.

Lucy, busily pawing through racks of gowns, exclaimed. "Oh, look, Elvira! This would just suit you. A blue shot silk, with gold ribbons and a sort of shawl thing, all beaded.''

Elvira lifted the gown from the rack and observed it. Carlotta said, "That should fit you, Miss Sutton. I put it on once and it was to large for me. Try it.''

Elvira carried the gown behind the screen. When Deirdre saw Carlotta following her on the pretext of helping her with the gown, she went, too. It might be a ruse for them to have some private talk. "Good gracious, I don't want an audience while I undress!'' Elvira laughed. "Modesty forbids. Lucy! You come and help me.''

Carlotta looked amazed at this blushing speech. "My dear, we are not voyeurs!'' she said haughtily. On this speech she strode from behind the screen, with Deirdre behind her.

There was some girlish giggling behind the screen, and in a few moments Elvira came out, looking regal in the silk gown, with the shawl modestly drawn across her shoulders and hiding her chest. Carlotta regarded her critically. "Take off the shawl," she suggested.

"The fit isn't very good," Elvira said, and went back to remove the gown.

Carlotta watched her as she left. She shrugged her shoulders. "What she didn't want us to see was her large waist," she said in a low voice to Deirdre. "She couldn't get the gown done up at the back. My waist is eighteen inches," she added, spanning it with her own hands. She looked through the racks for a larger gown, but nothing met Elvira's favor.

"I shan't take up any more of your time," Elvira said. "Tomorrow we shall go to the Merceria and choose something, Lucy. I would like to see the statuary in the garden before dinner. May we go outside and wander around, Contessa?"

The contessa was quite satisfied for the guests to entertain themselves. She and Deirdre returned to the saloon for a glass of wine. Belami looked alert when they entered. Deirdre shook her head. Nothing interesting occurred over tea either, except that the conte was so enraptured with Elvira that he didn't watch what he was about and drooled down his shirt front. Pronto became a bit miffed at the old fellow's way of staring at his fiancée.

"Miss Sutton is marrying me the day after tomorrow," he told the conte, rather sternly.

"You are a fortunate man, sir. She is uncommonly pretty. You will have trouble with that one. I like a lady who gives me plenty of trouble. That's why I married my Carlotta," he said fondly.

Pronto sat, trying to figure out whether he'd been complimented or insulted. "Miss Sutton is a very nice girl."

The conte nudged his elbow into Pronto's and smiled wickedly. "They all fool us that way at the beginning. Nice girl—ha, there is no such a thing. And if there were, we ought to have a law against it. I have been to your England. And France. Ladies are the same the world over. All trouble. Love is flame for a year, then ashes for thirty. But that one year makes it all worthwhile." He smiled at Carlotta.

After the party was over and the guests had gone home, Belami found himself wondering why Carlotta had invited them. She hadn't been alone with any of the Suttons for a moment. She hadn't even tried to get any of them alone. Certainly no exchange, even of information or a note, had occurred. It seemed a pointless visit, and Carlotta wasn't a lady who engaged in pointless doings.

The contessa had invited her houseguests to attend the opera that evening along with some other friends. Belami was interested to hear the music and see how an opera was carried out in a foreign country. He thought the music might have been good, had he been allowed to hear it. The Venetians, he learned, went to an opera or a play to flirt and talk. Even the talk was no more than gossip—whose wife had a new *cavalier servente*, who was enceinte, and who was the probable father. He received many interested smiles and more than one invitation to call, always on married ladies. The ladies, it seemed, weren't allowed to flirt or take a lover till they had secured their reputation with a marriage first. Like England in that respect.

He felt he was wasting his time. He had only one more day—tomorrow—to save Pronto. Why was Elvira marrying Pronto? Was it for his money? Maybe she didn't intend to marry him at all. He'd given her a valuable diamond ring. With luck, that was all she was after. He sat staring at the stage, not hearing a sound. Styger returned tomorrow. The wedding was the next day. His head buzzed with questions. Was it the plan for the whole lot of them to disappear Friday night? If so, Carlotta's having stolen the

152

dies might throw a spanner into things. They wouldn't want to leave without the dies. Where was Styger, and what was he doing? And where was Claude? Why had Elvira made that flying trip to see them? If she wasn't Claude's wife, then it hadn't been an amorous rendezvous. Had she gone to get money—counterfeit money—to buy Lucy's pearl and the diamond necklace? Odd that a duplicate of that rare pearl had turned up so quickly and so conveniently in Padua. A jolt of excitement shot through him. Deirdre, sitting beside him, could feel his body jerk. She looked and recognized the smile of success on Belami's face. His eyes sparkled in a certain way. "Shall we go out for a glass of wine?" he asked.

"It isn't intermission," she whispered back.

"The whole performance is an intermission."

He rose and led Deirdre out of the box. "What is it? What have you deduced?" she asked eagerly.

He got two glasses of wine and they went to a quiet corner to talk. "I think I've just been struck with inspiration," he said. "Listen carefully, and stop me if I go astray. We have the Suttons buying for one thousand English pounds a valuable pearl that is reportedly unique. We have Elvira making an inexplicable dash to Claude Jalbert, who that same day visits Styger. Next, Styger takes a short trip. And suddenly another pearl is found, the asking price shot up to three thousand pounds. What do you figure that jeweler in Padua paid for this second pearl?"

"About twenty-five hundred, I should think. He'd want to make some profit."

"Of course. And if the owner paid one thousand, he makes fifteen hundred profit. Have you seen Elvira wear the pearl since they bought it?"

"No, she's waiting till Lucy gets hers."

"The hell she is. There's only one pearl. They bought it for a thousand in Venice, had Cerboni send out an urgent message looking for another. Meanwhile Elvira took the pearl to Claude. Styger ripped off the gold cap and sold

153

the original for twenty-five hundred to a jeweler in Padua, who was convinced he could sell it to Cerboni at a profit. The Suttons make a cool fifteen hundred without even breaking the law.''

''But when they pay three thousand for it, they lose their profit,'' Deirdre pointed out.

''They don't intend to buy it. They'll discover some flaw, or Lucy will decide she wants something else, and Cerboni will be stuck with it.''

''Good gracious! Surely it would be illegal.''

''I think not. *Caveat emptor* applies to the jewelers here. If the Suttons don't like the pearl, they don't have to buy it. They only asked Cerboni to try to find them one. They didn't sign a contract to buy it.''

''I never heard of anything so wicked in my life.''

''And you the duchess of Charney's niece!'' Belami laughed. ''Of course I have no proof of any of this, but it explains the seemingly inexplicable behavior of several of our suspects. I told you it would be all quite simple once we had doped it out.''

''It enlarges our circle of suspects. Mrs. Sutton must be in on it.''

''She's fallen under suspicion before now. I never could credit that a nabob was traveling like a pauper. Furthermore, the whole nabob story was a hoax. She must know one of her daughters is married to Claude. She's going along with the whole game—in it up to her prissy lips and gray hair. In fact—'' Belami put down his wine and began pacing the hall, with Deirdre beside him.

''What?'' she asked excitedly.

''I wish that demmed tenor would stop squawling. I can't think. Deirdre, let's leave.''

''I can't. My aunt—''

''We'll go outside at least.'' He took her hand and they went out into the cool night, where they continued pacing up and down in front of the opera hall.

''We know the Jalbert gang consists of an older man

154

and woman, Mr. and Mrs. Jalbert. Maybe Mrs. Sutton *is* Mrs. Jalbert. She had the newspaper I gave him when he was calling himself Styger. I thought Elvira had got it from Claude.''

''But their passports—''

''Thieves clever enough to counterfeit coins could forge passports or buy forgeries, or steal them for that matter. Then one of the girls could be Claude's wife.''

''But that leaves us with an extra girl, and lacking Claude,'' Deirdre pointed out.

''I'm trying to account for that discrepancy. The group obviously broke up to make their escape easier. Police in various countries were looking for an old couple and a young couple. I imagine that's why Mrs. Sutton was so agreeable to sharing a carriage with your aunt for the trip. The customs people wouldn't expect a duchess to be traveling with common criminals. And it's why I didn't get my note in Paris. Elvira didn't want me sleuthing after them. You see how it's all falling into place?''

''I still don't see where Claude is hiding himself.''

''He and Styger separated in case one of them is caught. That leaves the other free to look after the ladies. Claude's wife must have a sister. That accounts for the extra girl.''

''I'm sure the girls really are sisters. They're very close,'' Deirdre told him. ''Elvira's kind to Lucy, though she used to become impatient with her from time to time. Occasionally during our trip Elvira wanted to be alone with me to discuss men and things, and Lucy would take a pet. Just the way sisters do, you know.''

''I can buy that. They must be sisters, but if Lucy's the married one, she wouldn't have to be excluded from your risqué conversations, would she? Fancy you talking broad. I can't picture it. But I can picture Elvira,'' he added, his voice thinning.

''That's true. Elvira *did* seem the more experienced one. I hope she is married. Then she can't plan to actually marry Pronto. She's just using him.''

"She's taken control of his passport. It would come in handy if they plan to shear off."

"I almost hope they do," Deirdre said.

"In one more day, we'll know. God, Pronto will be brokenhearted. We'll have to be kind to him."

"Do you think they really plan to buy that diamond necklace for Elvira?"

"Of course they do, about ten minutes before they run away. The second pearl, I noticed, was to have some work done on it before the purchase. They don't have to buy it yet. They duck out and leave it behind, along with their counterfeit money, while they run off with a genuine diamond necklace and about fifteen hundred profit from the pearl stunt."

Deirdre sorted all this underhanded business out in her head and sighed. "It's hard to conceive of so much deceit. Only you could figure it out, Belami."

"Thank you—I think."

"What are you going to do to stop them?"

"They haven't done anything illegal in Venice yet. They've just set the wheels in motion. Till they actually spend the counterfeit money, all I could do would be report them to Hoppner and let the English officials take over. You know my opinion of officialdom. I'd rather handle it myself."

"You'll warn Cerboni at least?"

"He thinks I'm a lunatic since their first batch of money proved genuine. That's why Elvira wanted me there, of course. They won't buy the diamonds till they're ready to leave. Cerboni will eventually discover the coin is counterfeit, but by then they'll be several cities away. Maybe even out of the country. That's why she stole my counterfeit guinea, by God! So Cerboni wouldn't have it to compare with the false coins they plan to dump on him. I wonder if they have the counterfeit money in hand yet. Elvira might have brought it back with her. No one saw her enter. On the other hand, ten thousand or so in gold would be too heavy for a woman to handle. I imagine Styger-Jalbert or Claude will bring it to Venice. Réal will be on his tail."

"So we can do nothing but wait," Deirdre said.

"Waiting's the hardest part. I mean to see Pronto tomorrow and try to prepare him for the disappointment."

"Don't say too much. He tells Elvira everything—you know Pronto. Discretion was never his long suit."

Belami turned and gave her a flashing smile. "Nor mine. I'd best return you to your aunt. I wouldn't want to increase her disgust of me just when I'm trying to reingratiate myself. She accidentally smiled at me during dinner."

"She complained of gas while we were dressing. And furthermore, I haven't said yes."

"So there," he said, and laughed. "One thing at a time."

It certainly wasn't a smile that Charney turned on Belami when they entered the box. Her face looked like the death mask of some ancient martyr. "What, you didn't bring any wine back for the rest of us? I made sure that's why you were leaving or I wouldn't have let Deirdre go. Bring us some wine, Belami."

In his eagerness to please, Belami hopped up. The duchess turned her charms on the conte. "It will not be nearly so good as your excellent stuff, Conte. I think if I have it taken to a ship and sent directly home by water, it will make the trip without harm. It is not worthwhile shipping two hogsheads. Let us make it four—and be sure to send me a bill," she added.

Carlotta stared coolly across the box. "Why not pay before you leave us, Duchessa?"

Charney bared her teeth. "Of course! What was I thinking of?"

"I can't imagine," Carlotta replied.

Belami got a glimmering of what might please the old lady and winked at Deirdre, who pokered up and ignored him.

Chapter Fourteen

Belami was at the Léon Bianco at ten the next morning, fully expecting to find his friend in bed. He was surprised to see Pronto not only up and dressed but pacing the lobby. Pronto's haggard appearance suggested that he had either drunk too much the night before or not slept enough. He was no insomniac; he'd been known to fall asleep on his way to bed.

"I take it you were celebrating last night?" he said.

"If you can call it a celebration with Mrs. Sutton and Lucy dogging our every step," Pronto grumbled. "Mean to say, engaged after all. Not as though I was a demmed seven-day beau. Getting a bit peeved with them all, Dick. As bad as Charney."

"Let's eat. You'll feel better," Belami suggested.

They ordered beefsteak and ale, but Pronto just sat staring at his plate. "My last breakfast as a bachelor," he said wistfully. "Tomorrow I'll be Mr. Pilgrim."

"Are things not going well with you and Elvira?"

"How can they? We're never alone for two minutes. And even when we are—not that I mean to say Elvira's a cold woman," he added hastily.

This surprised Belami. He had suspected Elvira of many things, but never of prudishness or a lack of ardor. If anything, he feared she had more experience than a gentleman could want in his wife. "A little shy, is she?" he asked.

158

"Not shy exactly," Pronto said, chasing a piece of beef around the plate with his fork. "Not shy of speaking her mind or of meeting strangers. It's only when we're alone. Tell me, Dick, does Deirdre let you—you know . . ."

Belami looked at his friend's worried face and frowned. "I'm not sure what you're getting at. Deirdre isn't fast, and I wouldn't want her to be. I hope you haven't been—"

"No, no! Nothing like that. I only meant a bit of a cuddle. Well, I know Deirdre does, for I saw you at Fernvale last winter. Close as inkle-weavers. Elvira don't let me do it. Kiss her, except once on the fingers and once on the elbow. Accident. I was aiming for her jaw. She lifted her arm so fast I was knocked galley west. Did get a lick at her elbow though," he added, with some trace of satisfaction.

Belami was relieved to hear this tale. At least Elvira wasn't using her wiles to con Pronto into a hasty marriage. "Perhaps she's just shy of intimacy. Deirdre used to be at first. You'll have to be gentle, persuasive. Don't go leaping at her the minute you're alone."

Pronto squinted suspiciously. "Who told you?"

"Nobody."

"Not my fault there was a moon," Pronto said. "I only ever have a minute. Have to leap if I want to get at her at all. I'm a bit of a passionate fellow, Dick. Might not think it to look at me, but when I'm with Elvira . . ." He speared the piece of beef and gazed at it with fond desire. Belami wasn't sure whether it was the beef or an image of Elvira that brought that mooning look to Pronto's face.

"That's probably the trouble. You have to do a deal of talking first with carefully raised ladies, Pronto."

"I'm not much of a hand at oiling around the ladies. I hear the native lads saying *'Che bella!'* Seems to go down pretty well. I never knew I could speak Italian till I tried. What else should I say?"

"I suggest you work your speech into a well-rounded

159

paragraph. You remember from your grammar lessons—you need a topic sentence. *'Che bella'* is fine for an introduction. A foreign language lends a touch of romance. Then you proceed coherently, starting with her hair and working your way down, compliment by compliment. You could stroke her hair gently as you tell her it's like a raven's wing, or black velvet, or whatever. Jewels make an acceptable simile for the eyes.''

Pronto listened earnestly. "Blue eyes," he urged. "Have to be sapphires.''

"Flowers are good, too. Cornflower or delphinium.''

"Think I ought to jot this down," Pronto decided, and pulled out a patent pen to write on the back of the menu. "Topic—*che bella*. Hair: raven's wing; eyes: sapphire. What's next? Lips.''

"Rosebuds are the usual comparison. Or cherries.''

Pronto scribbled away. "Or apples," he added. "By jingo, we've left off her nose, Dick. There's a hard one. Elvira has a generous nose, but shapely. Can't use a cucumber or carrot.''

"In my experience, noses defy comparison. A nose is a nose," Belami decided. "But the ears provide excellent flirtation. You might just lean forward and breathe heavily into her ear as you compare it to a rosebud.''

Pronto examined his list. "We've got rosebuds for the lips. How about a snail for the ears? The way it sort of curves in on itself . . .''

Belami's lips moved unsteadily. "Let's make it a seashell," he suggested. "And don't forget the breathing. Now for the skin.''

"I know that one. Alabaster. Elvira's skin is hard as a rock. I mean the flesh under it is. She exercises. Been missing her mount here in Venice. I have been myself.''

"The compliments should be accompanied by some tentative caressing as you go along," Belami pointed out. "I mentioned stroking the hair. From there you let your hand glide slowly to the throat, then along the shoulders.

160

From there it's an easy slide to her waist. But don't leap. You want a smooth, flowing performance, like a zephyr rippling a pond, and culminating in a kiss."

"Right, I've got it. *Che bella*. Hair, eyes, ears—blow in 'em—lips, zephyr, pounce—but smoothly."

"It works for me."

"You got Deirdre back, did you?"

"I was speaking more generally. What are you doing today, Pronto?"

"Having the barber come for a haircut. Getting my jacket pressed. Hiring costumes for the contessa's ball. Buying Elvira a wedding present. She's spotted a little emerald brooch at Speccio's jewelry shop. We was there yesterday morning with her mama, picking out a diamond necklace. Cerboni ain't being reasonable about his set."

Belami came to rigid attention. "Have they bought the necklace already?"

"No. We ain't leaving for a few days after the wedding. I talked Elvira into leaving the mother and Lucy behind. Had the deuce of a time finding the guide, but a *polizio* put me on to him. We're sliding off to Rome for a week, just the two of us. By then Elvira will decide which diamonds she wants. No hurry."

"Will they pay cash, as they did for the pearl?" Belami asked nonchalantly.

"Mrs. Sutton's arranging something with the bank."

Pronto finally got a piece of the beef into his mouth, and while he chewed, Belami pondered. If Mrs. Sutton was arranging payment through her bank, it didn't look as though she meant to pay in counterfeit cash. And if they weren't even buying it from Cerboni, then the original purchase of the pearl hadn't been to establish their bona fides. He was still surprised at Elvira's reluctance to use her considerable wiles on Pronto, too. His impression from Deirdre was that Elvira was a shade fast, but apparently it was just talk. Was it possible the ladies were innocent and he had imagined this whole plot?

"You're sure you want to go through with this wedding, Pronto? We could arrange some excuse if—"

"Of course I'm sure. I love Elvira. It's that seminary at Bath that did the mischief. That or her papa, the cleric. I'll talk her around now that I've got my list. I'll have her alone after the wedding if not before. Tomorrow night, Dick. I get edgy as a broody hen looking forward to it."

Pronto had to meet the ladies at eleven o'clock. Belami took his leave at five minutes to. The lesson in lovemaking had fired him with a desire to see Deirdre. She was in the garden sketching a statue of Apollo when he got back to the palazzo. In a simple blue gown and round bonnet to protect her face from the sun, she looked quaintly attractive. To Belami, she appeared irresistible. He pushed his way through the tangled bush and joined her.

"I've just been talking to Pronto," he said.

Deirdre's stiff face gave no indication that she was delighted to see him. "Did you manage to talk some sense into him?" she asked.

"No, I'm more confused than ever," he said, and told her their conversation, including Elvira's shyness, but curtailing his tactics to seduce a timid maiden.

"What a plumper!" Deirdre said angrily. "She's an experienced flirt. She used to climb out a window at the seminary and meet some man, a dancing teacher. From what she said, I didn't gather she was exactly shy. She conned him into an offer of marriage, only she didn't go through with it when she learned he only made two hundred guineas a year."

"Then why is she being so standoffish with Pronto? She's agreed to marry him. She must like him."

"She likes his money. There—I'm so angry I've spoiled my drawing," she said, and set down her charcoal.

"Now I don't believe anything Pronto told me. He very nearly had me convinced I was mistaken. Whatever Elvira's up to, I can't make heads or tails of it. I hope to God she's married to Claude and leaves Pronto standing at the

162

altar. Only there isn't any altar at the hotel. All the wedding plans are extremely shabby. I don't think she intends to go through with the wedding at all. It's dust in our eyes to fleece poor Pronto and convince us she's not Claude's wife.''

"What are you going to do about it?" Deirdre asked.

"I'm going to join Réal at Mira. We're breaking into Styger's house to look for clues—anything that can tie him to the Suttons. If Styger returns while we're there I'll beat the truth out of him. It would help if you'd watch Carlotta and take a look around for the dies.''

"I'm going shopping with her this afternoon to buy a wedding present for Pronto. What are you giving him?''

"I forgot all about it," Belami confessed.

"I thought Elvira might like something artistic. A bulky gift would be a nuisance while traveling.''

"I want to give Pronto something special. He's the best friend I ever had—the best male friend, I mean," he added, with a soft smile. "I've had the good fortune to know a lady who outshines all other acquaintances.''

He reached for Deirdre's hands, but she pulled away. "Fancy your being able to remember one lady above the hordes.''

Belami willed down the urge to violence and reverted to business. "I want to get Pronto a personal gift. I'll go to a jewelry store and have something engraved. It's strange we should be so sad at his marriage, isn't it? I never thought he'd beat us to the altar.''

"He wouldn't have to be a racehorse to accomplish that!''

"Nor even a turtle. I often despaired that he'd ever find anyone, and now that he has, I feel as though I'm going to his funeral instead of his wedding.''

Deirdre had expected more persistence from Belami and was annoyed with him. "I don't know why you're wasting time here. Why don't you go to Mira right away? Once he's involved with those horrid people he'll end up their dupe, taking the blame for all their crimes. I'm going to the palazzo and search the place from top to bottom."

"What are we missing, Deirdre? Why did Carlotta invite the Suttons here yesterday? She didn't do anything but give Elvira a tour of the palazzo, and the Suttons could have seen that at the masquerade party." Belami looked toward the stone palazzo, his eyes narrowed against the sun. He paused a moment, then continued. "If she's trying to sell them the dies, she could hardly carry them with her in a small evening reticule to the ball. They'd have to meet in some quiet corner of the palazzo. Elvira's now familiar with the layout here. All Carlotta would have to say is 'Meet me in my room,' or 'Meet me in the garden,' and Elvira would know exactly where to go."

"That must be why she invited them."

"What they'll use to buy the dies back is the money from selling the pearl. And either Claude or his father has that money. They may keep in touch by mail, but they won't risk money in the post. One of them will have to bring it."

"Nick's watching the hotel. He'll know if the Suttons have a male visitor," Deirdre pointed out.

"He'll know that, but he won't know if Claude just registers under an assumed name and arranges the meeting quietly abovestairs. None of us has ever seen Claude. I wish to God I knew what he looks like."

"It would all make more sense if we had a young man and woman staying with Mrs. Sutton, instead of two girls. Then we'd know where everyone was."

"Claude's probably out arranging more pranks. The pearl stunt could be pulled several times, using any more or less rare jewel. It wouldn't even be reported to the police, as it bypasses the law. I'd best go now, so the gondola will be back in time for your shopping. Wish me luck."

"The very best luck," she said.

"I didn't mean in *words*," Belami countered, and lifted

his hand to stroke her hair. His careful instructions to Pronto were forgotten. Deirdre looked enchanting in the dappled sunlight. He pulled her into his arms rather roughly, and she repulsed him with even greater vigor. The strength of her protests caused his hot blood to simmer, but his speech was of an arctic temperature, uttered with a disdainful sneer. "Am I still under a cloud because I paid Carlotta to interpret for me, or have I committed some new indiscretion?"

"You've had plenty of time for new indiscretions since then. Naturally one assumes Lord Belami has taken advantage of every opportunity."

"Naturally! If you knew the opportunities I've turned down for you, Deirdre!"

"Spare me the list!" she said loftily, and walked away.

Belami watched as she strode angrily back to the palazzo, her hips swinging quite as delightfully as Carlotta's. That touch of the temptress in Deirdre always surprised him.

Deirdre had time for a quick search of the music room, where Carlotta had spent some time displaying the painted organ screen yesterday and Elvira had shown some interest in it. Was this where the assignation would take place tomorrow night? It was convenient to the ballroom, yet discreetly situated around a corner where privacy would be assured. She searched the room thoroughly, but if this were the spot, Carlotta had not yet hidden the dies there.

Belami hopped into the gondola at once for the trip to Mira. When he was about to enter the Mestre Canal, he spotted Réal coming toward him in another boat. The boats drew alongside and Réal leaped like a goat across the water, very nearly upsetting both gondolas. Belami knew by the fierce face of his worker that something was wrong.

"The bird, he is flied," Réal announced. "When I get to Mira this morning, there is men coming out of the Styger house. I speak with Marie next door, and hear the house is for renting to a family from Austria. Mr. Vonheffner and his wife, fat, red of face, with the eyes bulging out of the faces. I make the inquiries for Styger. He is returning last night and giving back the keys. He at once runs away, very much excited.''

"He wouldn't be pleased to learn his dies were missing."

"*C'est vrai*, he is complaining of thievery," Réal assured his master, with much Gallic flailing of arms. "He goes away from the neighborhood and no one has the senses to follow him. I wanted to stay last night. You tell me no, Styger isn't coming back yet. You need me, to stand all night in front of the Léon Bianco, with no one coming in for me to follow."

"Sit down before you knock us both into the canal," Belami said, and pushed Réal onto the seat. "I should have known when the pearl turned up yesterday that Styger had arranged his deal faster than he anticipated. Of course he darted straight back to Mira. But he didn't go to the Léon Bianco or Nick would have seen him. He must be at some other hotel in Venice. They'll all meet to talk over these new developments. We've got to get back to Venice, Réal."

Réal knew his duty. He stood up and snatched the pole from the gondolier to pole them back at a pace that left him gasping. He went directly to the Saint Mark landing. "I will be finding this Styger and following him," he said calmly to Belami. "Where will I go to tell you?"

"I'll be back at the palazzo soon. I have to go shopping."

"Shopping!" Réal's beady black eyes were full of wrath. "Very good. Very excellent. You will do the shopping for jackets while Italy burns. Me, I suggest it is a fiddle you should purchase, Signor Nero."

"Pronto don't fiddle. I rather think a set of wine goblets in silver would be well used. We're going to speak to Nick first, however."

They went to the Léon Bianco, where Nick reported

Pronto was out with the ladies. No one had called on the Suttons.

"Stay on guard," Belami ordered.

"Happy shoppings, melord," Réal said, with an insolent stare that showed the master his opinion of this activity. Réal writhed to consider the possibility that Nick might succeed. Yet to search over a hundred islands with several hundred inns and hotels for two English tourists, possibly not traveling together, was obviously the heavier job. And to make it really interesting, these foolish Italians spoke neither French nor English.

Belami selected his wedding gift with care. He chose six silver wine goblets, each embellished with clusters of grapes around the cup. What should he have engraved on them? "To the Pilgrims from Belami, with love. Venice, 1817." A time and place that would live long in his memory as one of the saddest and most frustrating periods of his life. The jeweler agreed to begin the work immediately. He could deliver them to the palazzo that evening. Belami wanted to hand the gift to Pronto himself and make some speech. Then he returned to the palazzo, to await word from his helpers.

Lunch was over, and Deirdre and Carlotta were preparing for their shopping trip. Charney decided to go with them, which left Belami alone with the old conte. It was a fairly tedious afternoon, but the conte's rambling conversation left half of Dick's mind free to plan. He also arranged to purchase the duchess's "gift" of four hogsheads of wine at a highly inflated price. "But don't tell her yet," he said.

"Indeed no. If I tell her she may have four, she'll want six."

The presence of the servants made any serious search for the dies impossible. Carlotta's woman never left the contessa's room, which was a pretty good indication where they were. On three different occasions Belami made an excuse to pass the door. Always the woman was there by

167

the window, sewing. The crafty look on her face was as good as an admission. At five o'clock the ladies returned from their shopping trip. Shortly after dinner the jeweler came with Belami's gift. The goblets were engraved, and resting in a black leather presentation case lined with blue velvet.

"Very impressive, Belami," the duchess said. "Why, you should want to impress Miss Sutton is beyond me. That knickknack Deirdre bought is plenty good enough."

"It's a genuine antique statuette!" Deirdre pointed out. "I thought the nymph very pretty, didn't you, Belami?"

That careless "Belami" stung, but Dick was determined to be polite. He thought the statuette an inferior imitation and wondered how much Carlotta had made for taking Deirdre to that particular dealer. "Very nice. They'll love it," he said.

"As Miss Sutton didn't see fit to invite me to the wedding, I see no reason to send a gift," the duchess said. "A very shabby affair, if you want my opinion."

"It's a family wedding," Deirdre explained. "Belami and I are witnesses. That's the only reason we're going."

"You'll have an opportunity to offer your good wishes at the masquerade party," Carlotta reminded the duchess.

"They'll need more than good wishes to make anything of this match. Pilgrim is insane, to marry a woman he knows nothing of. She might be anyone. A lightskirt or a thief for all we know. Or even an actress," she added, with a condemning glance at Carlotta.

"At least she knows how to *act* like a lady. I like her enormously." Carlotta smiled.

With great forbearance, the duchess did not say "birds of a feather," but her glare certainly implied it. At ten-thirty the duchess retired. The conte had left the party earlier. Carlotta sat below with Belami and Deirdre, making private conversation impossible. "Guy tells me you bought the duchessa some wine," Carlotta mentioned. "You are generous."

Deirdre cast an embarrassed eye on her suitor, but she was flattered. Why had he done it but to put her aunt in a good mood when he approached her? Whatever their former relationship, she could see Dick and Carlotta were no longer friendly.

Dick just glanced at Deirdre. It was to Carlotta that he spoke. "I can be as generous as anyone. I'm willing to pay for what I want. What I want very much at the moment is to prevent my friend from marrying Miss Sutton. Anything you could do to help me in that way would be appreciated."

"I don't see how I can help," Carlotta answered.

"Any evidence of their counterfeiting, for instance, would be generously rewarded. Counterfeit coins, the dies they used . . ." Carlotta patted her curls and just looked back at him. "*Very* generously rewarded," he added. She didn't even ask how generously. "Say, a thousand guineas," Dick tempted.

Carlotta smiled then, a genuine smile. He thought he had gotten through to her, but her next move disillusioned him. She opened her beautiful lips and laughed. "A thousand guineas! You don't value your friend very highly!"

"The Jalberts won't give you as much," he warned.

"Then I shall have to persuade them," she answered cryptically. "That should be amusing!"

"I shouldn't think old Jalbert your type. It must be Claude you plan to seduce," Belami ventured.

She stared at him. "Seduction wasn't what I had in mind. Of course I haven't met Claude. Perhaps he'll come to my ball. Some uninvited always do sneak into a masquerade party. I shall be on the alert for him." Carlotta rose and straightened her gown. "And now I'll leave you two alone. I know it's not necessary to caution you to behave, Belami."

When she had gone, Belami moved closer to Deirdre on the sofa. Her gesture of moving away was only a token. Their shoulders brushed. "She didn't even ask how much

169

I was willing to give or try to up the price. I wonder what she has in mind,'' Belami said. He raised his arm and placed it along the sofa back, not yet touching Deirdre, but at the ready.

"She plans to keep the dies and use them herself."

His arm nudged lower, the hand just touching her shoulder. "It's a big undertaking. You need a smelter and trained men. That can't be it. The Jalberts could make a new set of dies for a thousand pounds, I should think."

"We'll just have to follow her at the masquerade party and see what she does."

"It's Pronto I'm worried about." Memories of their old friend kept Deirdre from bolting when Dick's fingers began stroking her raven hair. "Once he's married to Elvira, he'll be strongly inclined to protect her. Carlotta must plan to bleed him dry."

"I was never so frustrated in my life."

"It's only one more day." Belami consoled her with a squeeze on the shoulder. "We can't do anything more about it tonight."

This being the case, he settled down to follow his other project in good earnest. He put an arm around Deirdre. She allowed it to remain. He could feel the stiffness ease from her body. "Did I ever tell you your eyes, when you're angry, are like a stormy sky?"

"Several times," she answered, but it was a playful reply. In fact, it was a downright encouraging reply. "And how would you describe Carlotta's eyes?"

"Does Carlotta have eyes? I never noticed."

A gurgle of laughter caught in her throat. It brought out the dimples at the corner of her lips. Dick's head had just begun to lower when the telltale tapping of Charney's cane told him his nemesis approached. When Charney entered, she saw her niece and Belami sitting a foot apart, with Pronto's silver goblets between them. This ploy didn't fool her for an instant.

"I'd like you to come upstairs and read to me, Deirdre," she announced. With a sapient eye at the rake, she added, "I see the contessa's light is still burning. If you want someone to talk to, no doubt she is waiting to oblige you."

"Thank you, your grace," Belami replied blandly. "But Deirdre has already assuaged my appetite for conversation."

On this cryptic speech, he bowed and left.

Chapter Fifteen

Réal had no success in finding Styger, and Nick had nothing new to report from the inn. Belami and Deirdre left for the wedding the next morning carrying their gifts. They sat gazing across the canal, wrapped in a pall of silence, thinking of the past and the future. Things would never be the same again. Pronto was an inconvenient friend, but his heart was always in the right place. It was true he misunderstood things and leaped with unparalleled agility to all the wrong conclusions. He never could keep his mouth shut and had pitched Belami into more scrapes than he liked to consider. If there were a message to be delivered, Pronto was sure to see it went astray. If there were a quarry to be followed, you could always count on Pronto to lose him. And when speed was of the essence, that was bound to be the time Pronto got drunk, or fell asleep, or in love.

"I was hoping we'd get word the wedding was called off," Deirdre said, and sighed wearily.

"So was I. It might happen yet." He hoped Pronto would be waiting at the landing, ringing his hands, and saying Elvira had changed her mind, or left Venice. But no one awaited them.

"Try to smile," Belami urged Deirdre when they entered the Léon Bianco. They went, wearing smiles that smacked of rictus, to the private parlor that had been fixed up with flowers and candles. The minister, a Reverend Hackwell from Bath, was there with Pronto. They set their gifts on a table and went to speak to the bridegroom, all freshly shaven and shorn for the occasion, and looking like a stranger.

"This is the big day," Belami said heartily. "I wish you all the best." He reached to shake his old friend's hand.

Looking at them, Deirdre saw a film of moisture in Pronto's eyes. She blinked away a tear and offered her best wishes, too. "I hope you'll be very, very happy," she said in a trembling voice, and kissed Pronto on the cheek.

"A fellow never had such good friends," Pronto said, and sniffed into a handkerchief. "I see you brought presents and all, like a real wedding. Thank you. I'll let Elvira open them. She likes presents."

Dick and Deirdre exchanged a speaking glance. Pronto handed Belami the ring. "You give me this when the minister starts the bit about 'with this ring, I thee wed.' Do I look all right, Dick? The dashed barber skinned me like a rat. Cut my hair so that it don't wave as it ought. My hair was always my best feature." He patted it nervously.

"You look fine," Deirdre assured him, though she secretly agreed the barber had destroyed his hair. It was strange the Suttons weren't here yet. It was only minutes till the ceremony should begin.

"Where is Elvira?" Belami asked, glancing at his watch.

"Here the Suttons are now," Deirdre exclaimed as the door opened. She and Dick looked resignedly at each other. There was now no hope that the wedding wouldn't take place.

They all turned to view the bride. Elvira looked enchanting, as usual. She wore no trace of nervousness or indecision as her moment drew near, but her usual calm air of self-possession. She strode forward, smiling, to greet the party. Her dark hair was mostly concealed under a

173

band of flowers, but that was the only indication that she was the bride, other than the nosegay of pink rosebuds and babies' breath she carried. Her gown was one often seen before—a pretty blue—though Pronto said she was having a new gown made. There were some general greetings and comments on the flowers and candles.

"You look lovely, Elvira," Deirdre said. "And you, too, Lucy." Lucy wore a rose gown and looked more nervous than the bride.

Mrs. Sutton was pale and distracted. "We might as well get on with it," she suggested.

"Ready when you are," Pronto agreed, and wiped his moist hands on the sides of his trousers. "We'd best go and stand together. Oh, we are standing together."

They arranged themselves before Reverend Hackwell, who stood with his open book to read the service. Pronto appeared a comic figure beside his statuesque bride. Elvira's shoulder rode a few inches higher than the groom's. Dick ranged himself beside Pronto, angled to see them both, and Deirdre took up a similar position on the other side, with Mrs. Sutton and Lucy standing off to the left. As the fateful words began, Belami felt overcome with sadness.

"We are gathered together before God," the minister began.

But in Belami's mind, they were no longer together, Pronto and he. Pronto was leaving him, and he felt as though he were losing a part of himself. Pronto was about to become the lifelong partner of this woman beside him. This woman who hadn't even the grace to blush or to buy a new gown for her wedding day. Elvira stood like an odalisque, her set jaw showing nothing but satisfaction. Belami fingered the ring in his hand. It slid up his little finger as he played with it. It was loose there, so he palmed it again. He didn't want to drop the ring in midservice as Pronto could be relied on to do if—*when*—he and Deirdre got married. Even a shabby wedding was a solemn occasion, one bound to bring memories of the past and hopes for the future in its wake. Belami looked at Deirdre and wished with all his heart that they were the bridal couple. He caught her eye, and they exchanged a long, meaningful look.

He glanced at Pronto, who was clenching and unclenching his lips and taking little darting peeps at his bride. Elvira never once glanced at him. She kept her head high, looking straight ahead. What was she thinking? There, she was looking at Lucy now. A slight smile trembled on her lips then, as they exchanged one brief look. Lucy had a tear in her eye. Did she feel as sad to lose Elvira as he felt to lose Pronto? The sisters were obviously very close.

Dick stood alert, ready to prompt his friend if Pronto forgot his lines. "I, Ernest Rodney Pelham Pilgrim, do solemnly swear . . ." He was afraid Pronto would trip over that long name. Strange to think of old Pronto having such an impressive array of names. How had he come to be called Pronto?

It was Elvira's turn to speak. Dick listened to learn her full name. "I, Elvira Sutton, do solemnly swear . . ." It was odd she only had the one name. A wistful smile lifted Dick's lips. "Odd"—that was Pronto's clue that something was suspicious. But there was really nothing suspicious in a girl having only one Christian name.

He became aware that Pronto was reaching for the ring and handed it to him. He turned his gaze to Elvira as Pronto pushed the ring over her finger. Large as it was, it was a little tight. Pronto muttered as he rammed it home. Belami found himself wondering if Pronto had had any luck in trying his list of endearments on her. Elvira's hair really was as black as a raven's wing. It looked lovely against her flower band and pale face. The ears were not precisely seashells—a generous ear on her. And a generous nose, too, a handsome nose it would be called if it graced a gentleman's face. Dick noticed a little nick on the side of Elvira's jaw, nearly invisible. She'd covered it with powder. Pronto must have got at her last night after all. The girl was lucky she wasn't maimed. Now how had Pronto done that—it looked like a scratch from his fingernails.

And suddenly the ceremony was over. The minister was closing up his book. Pronto, blushing like a blue cow, pulled Elvira into his arms for the traditional kiss. Elvira, shy or aloof, turned her head slightly aside so that the kiss only grazed her cheek.

"Your turn, Dick," Pronto said. "This is the only chance you'll have to kiss my bride. And don't make it long either."

Belami smiled and inclined his head for the token gesture. He felt Elvira's body stiffen. Again she turned her head aside so that he only nipped the corner of her chin. She was more demonstrative with her mother and the ladies. They were allowed to embrace her.

"Well, it's done," Pronto exclaimed with satisfaction. "Now it's time for the *vino* and *viando*." He turned to Dick and muttered, "Don't make a day of it. We only have this afternoon to—you know—consummation devoutly to be wished and all that." Belami bit back a smile. It seemed almost fitting that Pronto should unwittingly have referred to Hamlet's suicide soliloquoy in his choice of quotation. "Going to the masquerade party tonight. Haven't told Elvira yet that I ain't going to be her slave."

"Don't worry, she can't back out of it now. And I shan't linger long. Good luck with the consummation."

Pronto yanked at his shirt collar. "I'll need it. I'll tell you, Dick, your list of compliments ain't worth a tinker's curse. I made no progress at all last night. Thought she was going to land me a facer when I tried to get at her."

"I think you did land her one," Dick joked.

"No such a thing. Never got within ame's ace of a kiss."

They joined the minister to sign the wedding certificate. "A nice little ceremony." Reverend Hackwell smiled and left.

The remaining party moved toward the door, the ladies first. At the dining parlor, Elvira held the door for them.

"Let me do that, my dear," Pronto said, and leaped forward, jostling his bride.

"Watch what you're about!" Elvira exclaimed angrily.

Really, the woman was a confirmed shrew. The wedding not five minutes old, and already she was acting like a harpy.

"Sorry, my love," he muttered.

Bearing Pronto's request in mind, Belami didn't linger over dinner. No one seemed very hungry. Pronto in particular didn't eat a bite, though he had several glasses of wine. When dinner was over, Dick rose and made a short speech, praising the bride and informing the Suttons that they were indeed fortunate to have gained Pronto as a member of their family. They all clapped lightly, and it was Pronto's turn to praise his bride.

He rose on unsteady limbs and cleared his throat. "*Prego,* everybody. I never was much in the speechmaking line," he said, and pulled from his pocket a piece of paper. "Ladies and gentlemen: *Che bella.* Hair: raven's wing. No, dash it, that ain't it. Ah, here we are," he exclaimed, and read his short speech, written with much soul-searching and uncertainty.

Elvira gazed at her plate and did finally blush then, when her bridegroom hovered from compliment to compliment, comparing her to the sun and the moon, the lilies of the valley and Eclipse, the first Derby winner. "Eclipses them all. Even Eclipse," he finished, and lifted his glass in unsteady fingers.

As soon as the last toast was drunk and Pronto sat down again, he cast a commanding look at Dick. "Daresay you and Deirdre want to run along now. Thankee kindly for coming. Oh, they've left us presents in the other room, Elvira. Your mama can take them up to our room. No, *her* room. We shan't want to be disturbed."

Elvira turned a demure face to him. "You are rushing

177

our guests, Pronto, my dear. There is still plenty of wine," she pointed out.

"We'll take it upstairs," he said, and grabbed a bottle.

"I want another glass of wine now, dear," she insisted.

"Oh. Well, if you feel you need a little encouragement, I daresay it don't matter whether we have it here or there," Pronto agreed, and filled her glass to the brim.

She took a suspiciously long time over it. "Drink up, my pet. We haven't got all day," he urged once or twice.

"We have the rest of our lives, dear," Elvira told him.

Pronto smiled blissfully. "She's right, you know." But as he glanced at his watch, he saw he had only a few hours till it would be time to dress for the masquerade ball. "Don't hurry your last drink," he added, with emphasis on the "last."

With this subtle hint, Belami set down his glass. "We have to be going now. Good luck, Pronto, and to you, Mrs. Pilgrim, every happiness for the future."

"We'll see you tonight," Deirdre added.

When they left, Elvira was just filling her mother's and sister's glasses once again. Pronto frowned, wondering just how firm a bridegroom ought to be. Didn't want her disguised—on the other hand, to play the heavy wouldn't put her in a loving mood. To solve this problem, he poured himself another glass of wine.

Before leaving, Belami stopped to speak to Nick, who was sitting in the hotel lobby. "Did anything interesting happen while we were busy?" he inquired hopefully. Nick shook his head. "I'll be at the palazzo if they turn up."

"Why do I feel I've just attended a wake?" Deirdre said as they went to the gondola.

"I felt like bawling," Dick admitted.

"It's enough to turn a man against marriage."

"Only against marrying Elvira Sutton. Elvira Pilgrim now. I've failed Pronto. He may never speak to me again when I have to turn her in."

"She didn't even buy a new gown. At least you can stop

178

wondering whether she's married to Claude. He would never sit still for her marrying someone else.''

"Much he'd have to say about it if she treats him as she treats Pronto. We know who'll wear the breeches in this marriage.''

"I shouldn't be surprised if she buys herself a curled beaver and cane, and even takes up shaving,'' Deirdre said.

She suddenly realized she was walking alone. Dick had stopped dead in his tracks. "What is it?'' she asked. Belami looked as though he had just been struck by lightning. "She already has a razor,'' he said. His voice was light, questioning.

"I know. Come on, Dick. I have to try my costume gown on. Haskins is hemming it for me.''

Belami was so excited he didn't seem to notice he had ceased being Belami. "Wait, just a minute,'' he said, and began slowly pacing the landing. "I'm either insane or inspired. Let me think.'' After a few laps he said, "I've got to go back to the hotel, Deirdre. Will you come with me?''

"Oh, very well.''

He walked so quickly she had to run to keep up with him. He went directly to his valet. "The night Elvira got into the hotel without being seen, Nick, you mentioned a young man coming in. He didn't register, you said—just went upstairs. Can you describe him to me?''

Nick wrinkled his face and described him. "He was a good-looking youngster. Smallish but well-set-up. Black hair. Wearing a blue jacket with brass buttons.''

"An English jacket, would you say?''

"I'd go a step further. It was the work of Stultz. The young lad was a strutter—you know the sort.''

"Was he carrying anything?''

"He had a small case with him, an overnight bag.''

"But he didn't check in?''

"No, I fancied he must be joining his wife here, or a lightskirt. We get a bit of that."

"I'll bet there was some of it that night. Have you seen him around since?"

"Not before nor since. Is it important?"

"It's crucial."

"Should I follow him if he shows?"

"He won't show. At least I don't think . . . But if he does, stop him. Stop him dead."

"That I will, sir."

"Thank you, Nick." With a broad smile he turned to Deirdre. "Let's go, my dear. We want to prepare for the ball."

"What was all that about?" she demanded. "Was the man Claude?"

"Of course it was. I should have seen it days ago."

"But Claude was described as fair-complexioned. I assumed he had fair hair."

"So did I. He must have dyed it. If I'm wrong, I'll look a flaming fool, so I shan't reveal my suspicions. But I think—yes, I really fear Pronto has just committed a gross indiscretion."

"We both know it. Why should that set you to grinning?"

"It's you who should be grinning. You were right—it *is* Lucy Claude's married to."

"Then that means Elvira was single all along."

"Not necessarily," he replied, but his laughing eye told her there was some joke in the air. "I only said she wasn't married to Claude."

"Then who was she married to? I wish you would not be so provoking, Dick. I know you've deduced something important."

"Not deduced. I wish it were that certain. My conclusion is based on ratiocination. But if I'm right, I know how to rescue Pronto. Mind you, he may already have rescued himself before the masquerade ball, but somehow

180

I think not. Elvira will keep him in line. She'll get him drunk or she'll have a maidenly fit of the megrims.''

"Why are we walking so fast?" she complained, as she ran along to keep up with him.

"Time flies, and so must we." He looked down at Deirdre, his eyes glistening with excitement. "Did you call me Dick?"

"Certainly not."

He laughed and drew her arm through his. "I wasn't that preoccupied. It slipped out unawares. Forward wench!''

"I could call you plenty worse!"

"And shall, no doubt, after we're shackled. But, pray, don't become an Elvira on me."

Why this should set Dick chuckling was a mystery. Deirdre only smiled. She knew she and Dick were engaged again without quite knowing how she knew. She even hoped that at some future date they might actually get married.

Chapter Sixteen

"Yes, I know it's inconvenient and inconsiderate and intolerable of me to ask," Belami admitted, "but will you do it, Deirdre?"

Deirdre liked her shepherdess gown very much. With the aid of starch, iron, and new ribbons, Haskins had worked wonders in reviving it. The stiff, full skirt, nipped in at the waist, looked very well on her.

"But I don't want to wear a domino," she objected. "I've gone to a deal of trouble to arrange this outfit. And the guests will be arriving any moment." It was just after dinner that they met in a quiet corner of the contessa's saloon to make plans for the masquerade party.

"You can wear your gown till everyone has seen you. In fact you must wear it till you've been identified. I only want you to change when I give the signal. I've put the domino under the sofa Charney is sitting on."

They both looked across the room where her grace sat in state, her head rigged out in a hideous construction of egret feathers and her gaunt body draped in what looked like a black shroud. In her hand she held a half mask on a long handle.

"You'll have to tell me why, Dick."

"I'll need some help keeping track of all our suspects. I fancy the whole Jalbert gang will be here. I sent Réal over to the hotel with Nick, but he'll give me a hand when he returns.''

"What's Réal doing at the hotel?''

"He'll search the Suttons' rooms after they leave. We'll welcome them all when they arrive, and let them see what we're wearing. I fancy they'll dance and party in a normal way for an hour or so to allay my fears. Then one of them will slip out to exchange money for the dies Carlotta has. Before that time, we must be wearing new disguises so we can keep close watch on them without arousing their curiosity. My disguise will be the gondolier's outfit from Carlotta's collection.''

"You hope to catch them in the act of exchanging?''

"Precisely. I want to catch them before they buy the diamond necklace. Pronto said next week—on Monday, late in the afternoon, I should think, just before Cerboni closes up shop. They'll leave the city immediately, before he discovers he's been paid in counterfeit money.''

"Elvira mentioned some other shop.''

"Only to make Cerboni eager for their business. They'll deal with Cerboni. He's convinced they're wealthy customers.''

"Then how will you get the phony money? Wouldn't it be wiser to wait till they try to buy the diamonds?''

"Elvira might leave on the honeymoon before the purchase is made. We can't let her escape. She's the ringleader.''

"Surely Claude and Styger . . .''

He didn't contradict her, but his tight little smile was a tacit denial. Deirdre was usually more eager to assist Belami than this interview would suggest. What had put her in a pelter was that Dick had spent a good part of the afternoon with Carlotta. "You didn't have any luck trying to buy the dies from Carlotta?'' she asked, as this was his alleged reason for seeking the siren's company.

"No luck. I upped the ante to twenty-five hundred English pounds, and still she didn't budge an inch. She wasn't

183

even tempted. They can't possibly pay her more than that, not in real money. She wouldn't be fool enough to accept counterfeit."

Carlotta suddenly rose from the sofa and motioned for a footman to push her husband into the entrance hall. It was time for the dancing to begin. Carlotta was a vision of loveliness in a perfectly modern black silk gown, cut very low to show an expanse of white bosom. Her hair was a tousle of black curls, in which a red silk rose nestled. At her throat she wore a lavish necklace of Strass glass, which closely resembled the Ginnasi diamonds. Even the duchess wasn't sure they were fakes.

"Carlotta will wear a domino and mask later, when she goes to make the trade," Belami said.

"Is there anyone in particular I should watch?"

"I plan to watch Elvira. Why don't you take Carlotta?"

Deirdre was happy to learn Dick hadn't chosen Carlotta as his quarry. She felt he was safer following his best friend's new bride. Carlotta would open the dancing. The dinner guests surged into the ballroom where the musicians were scraping their bows and glancing at their music.

The dilapidated ballroom looked elegant at night with the chandeliers burning. The guests' gay costumes added a festive note. There were ladies wearing high white wigs and panniered gowns from the court of Louis Quatorze. There were Italian noblemen of yore, harlequins and columbines, dairy maids and half-a-dozen various Borgias, and of course an inordinate number of unimaginative gentlemen in dominoes of all hues.

Deirdre hoped to have the opening waltz with Dick, but as in England, the first piece was a minuet. To further rob her of pleasure, the contessa claimed Belami as her partner. Deirdre was presented to an Italian nobleman who didn't know a word of English, though he spoke fluent Italian, with both hands.

The guests were arriving, each being announced in

184

whatever guise he had chosen to wear, to conceal his or her identity. Part of the enjoyment of a masquerade was trying to guess the guests' true identity. Deirdre watched closely, listening for the words "The Queen of Sheba" and whatever consort Pronto provided her. The announcement came just as the minuet finished. Deirdre glanced to the raised entrance and recognized the newlyweds at once. Elvira's costume was in no way authentic, but it was lavish and beautiful. She was wrapped in bands of various-colored silk to suggest the opulence of King Solomon's court. But what caught Deirdre's eye at once was the necklace she wore. It was the diamonds from Cerboni's shop. She hardly glanced at Pronto except to notice his eyes were as red as a ferret's. He tagged behind in a sheet, a white wig and beard, and carrying a shepherd's crooked staff. Just who this conglomeration of pieces represented she couldn't imagine, unless it was Father Time with his scythe changed to a staff.

She caught Belami's eye and together they went to greet the new arrivals. "Did you see Elvira's diamonds?" she asked.

"See them? You could hear them a mile away. They don't add authenticity to her outfit. I wonder why she wore them?"

Deirdre stared at his obtuseness. "Any lady would wear a new set of diamonds, Dick."

They hastened forward to greet the Pilgrims and the Suttons, who were following close behind. Deirdre wanted to be aware of how all their quarries looked and noted that Mrs. Sutton wore an antique embroidered gown from early Italy, predominantly gold, with a green feathered mask. Lucy was more simply attired in a pretty peasant girl's dress, with a white blouse and flowered skirt. The kerchief covering her hair should make her easy to follow. Deirdre hadn't noticed anything similar at the ball.

"Who are you supposed to be, Pronto?" Belami asked.

"King Solomon. Supposed to be wise—why I wore the

185

white hair and beard.'' Why a king noted for his displays of wealth was wearing a bed sheet wasn't mentioned.

"He refused to come as my slave." Elvira pouted.

"But it is supposed to be a masquerade party, Mrs. Pilgrim," Belami replied archly.

Elvira slanted a knowing smile at him. "Touché."

"That's the new set of diamonds you're wearing, is it?" Elvira fingered them covetously. "Mama gave them to me today—a surprise wedding present."

"I doubt a queen from the tenth century B.C. wore anything so modern, but they are lovely. They suit you."

"I didn't like to leave them at the hotel."

Belami became aware that Pronto was signaling him behind Elvira's back and attempted to gain some privacy. "Will you promise me the next dance, Mrs. Pilgrim?" he asked. "I know this jealous husband of yours will claim the first."

"It will be a pleasure," Elvira agreed. Then she put her white fingers on Pronto's arm and led him away, before any privacy was gained.

It was arranged that Belami would stand up with Lucy, but first the newcomers wanted to stroll around the hall and see the costumes. It left Dick a moment with Deirdre. "She's outwitted us again," he said, not without admiration. "By God, she's up to anything. She must have had her mother slip down to Cerboni's late this afternoon."

"I wonder how she paid for them."

"They must have met up with Styger somewhere. He didn't go to their hotel or I'd know. They can't plan to stick around Venice for long. Cerboni knows by now that the money is fake. He'll be at the hotel waiting for them— which means they've checked out already. They plan to leave tonight." His eyes sparkled with excitement. Deirdre felt a frisson scuttle up her own spine.

"But she just got married!"

"What a devilishly cunning trick to lull our suspicions. I wish Réal would get here. He won't be far behind them,"

Belami continued. "Unless he's following their woman. She must be in charge of harboring their luggage and having some means of escape ready. With so many gondolas at the landing, no one would notice another."

"You think they're all gathering here?"

"Birds usually flock before they migrate. They're somewhere nearby. Styger might be posing as their gondolier. He could be at the dock right now. I'm going to scout around."

"What about watching Elvira? And you're supposed to have the next dance with Lucy," Deirdre reminded him.

"You watch Elvira for me. Nothing should happen yet. I'll get the musicians to delay the music a few moments. I'll be back in time to keep my date with Lucy."

Deirdre was nervous with so many suspects to keep an eye on. Her job was made easier when Carlotta joined the new arrivals. Deirdre hastened forward to hear if Carlotta said anything that would indicate a place of rendezvous. The conversation could hardly have been more innocent. Carlotta complimented the ladies on their costumes, and especially Elvira on her new diamonds. The ladies complimented the contessa on her ball, then Carlotta passed along to speak to some other guests.

"Where do they keep the *vino* and *aperitivos*?" Pronto asked Deirdre.

She told him, and he went off with the ladies. Deirdre stationed herself at the door to keep an eye on the refreshment parlor and the front entrance for Dick's return. He was back in five minutes. "Styger's not there," he told her. "I quizzed the gondoliers. The party came in a hired boat, which left."

"At least we know the ladies came alone."

"We don't know that Styger isn't here already, in one of those black dominoes that litter the room. If you see a domino approach any of the ladies, try to get close enough to hear if the man speaks English. There aren't many *Inglese* here, which will be a clue it's Styger. I've left word

187

at the dock to be called if he comes. Where are all our quarries?"

"Pronto took them for a glass of wine."

When the music started, Belami sought out Lucy. Pronto was dancing with his bride, which left only Carlotta for Deirdre to worry about. She was happy to see Mrs. Sutton take a seat beside the duchess of Charney along the wall. The old conte was with them, clapping more or less in time to the music and ogling all the ladies.

The evening proceeded calmly for an hour. After a few dances, Elvira professed herself tired and went to sit with her mother. The conte soon got her onto a chair beside him to flirt with her. Lucy was standing up with a harlequin who spoke Italian, and Carlotta was dancing with one of her dinner guests, a certain Marchese Laderchi, whose only crime was that he was her lover.

Belami took advantage of the lull to have a private word with Pronto. He knew by the disgruntled frown on his friend that the marriage thus far wasn't to his liking.

"How did the afternoon go, Pronto?" he asked, with a smile that told Pronto he was referring to conjugal intimacies.

"Molto malo." Pronto scowled. "And don't bother telling me to stroke her hair and tell her her ears are like snails, for it don't work."

"No contact at all?" Belami asked.

"My own fault, I daresay," Pronto admitted. "It's the wine that did me in. Thought I might oil the wheels by getting her disguised. Not actually foxed, you know, but a trifle disguised to get down her guard. That woman can hold her wine, Dick. A regular Dane. She drank me under the table. I woke up at seven o'clock with a splitting headache and an empty bed."

"Elvira meanwhile received the diamonds from her mother?"

"Must have. She was already changed into her Queen of Sheba outfit when I woke up. Didn't cut up stiff about

188

me not being a slave though. Got to give her credit for that. I told her how it would be messy for after the ball. Mean to say, shoe blacking and white sheets, to say nothing of Elvira herself.''

"I'm surprised at you, Pronto. I've seen you start on a third bottle without keeling over.''

"Only had one bottle. One to myself, I mean. Elvira had one, too. The Italian wines are potent—or maybe it was your silver bumpers. Very nice, by the by. Appreciate it.''

"Glad you like them,'' Dick said, but his mind was elsewhere. Elvira must have laced Pronto's wine with laudanum.

There was no longer any doubt that the Jalbert gang were gathering, poised for flight. They were here for the sole purpose of getting their dies back from Carlotta. If it hadn't been for that, Belami didn't think they would have actually gone through with the wedding. Elvira's not having a new gown tended to confirm it. She had actually said she was ordering one. It was all smoke and mirrors, to conceal the truth.

And Carlotta—what was she up to, that she'd refused an offer of twenty-five hundred in genuine money for the dies? What did she hope to weasel out of the Jalberts? He looked to Elvira and was struck by the light of her diamond necklace. That was it. Carlotta thought she could hold them to ransom for the diamonds. And if the necklace hadn't been purchased yet, no doubt she would have held on to the dies till it was. She was a leap ahead of him all the way. But Carlotta was outmatched if she thought she could bring Elvira to heel. Surely the contessa wouldn't leave herself outnumbered in the final confrontation. What allies had she brought in?

"What ails you, Dick?'' Pronto asked, bringing Belami back to attention.

"I'm just wondering what I can do to help you.''

189

"Don't worry. I'll help myself. I'm her legal husband now. I'll have my pound of flesh."

From Hamlet to Shylock—another fine misplaced quotation. An odd coincidence he should choose *The Merchant of Venice*, considering Portia's disguise. He wondered if Pronto had begun to suspect his bride was not the shy maiden she seemed to be. The body has its own wisdom, folks said.

"There's Réal beckoning you from the doorway," Pronto pointed out. "Got on a domino. Was he invited to the party?"

"Anyone can crash a masquerade. That's what makes them so interesting."

"That's true. I'd swear I saw a *polizia* here a minute ago. Recognized his ugly phiz—the one I had a word with when I was trying to find the guide for the Suttons while me and Elvira go to Rome. Going to show her the catacombs, Dick. Maybe we'll even tootle on to Paris, if she shows a taste for bones."

"A policeman?" Dick asked.

"Yes—fellow had the gall to strut right up to the contessa and talk to her, too. Bold as brass."

"I see." Trust Carlotta—she had her allies on hand for the job. She would enjoy the irony of using lawmen to help her break the law. He could almost see the expression on her face when she confronted Elvira. "If you think you can get away with it, think again. I have half a dozen of Venice's stoutest constables standing on guard in the hallway. You won't leave the palazzo unless you do as I say." She'd be lucky if Elvira didn't put a knife through her ribs. She couldn't know the whole truth about Elvira.

Pronto straggled off, and Belami went to speak to his groom, who was puffed with importance. "What's afoot at the hotel?" he asked.

"The Sutton party, they are still registered as guests," Réal told him, then watched with infinite satisfaction as his master's brow creased in eagerness—an eagerness that

190

only he could abate. "When I am knocking at their doors many times, however, there is no answers. I take the precaution to open the doors with my *passepartout*. No ones is there. The female servant, she is gone, leaving much of confusion behind. Also leaving behind a rope tied at the window, how she is leaving without paying *l'addition*."

"Excellent!" Belami exclaimed. "Just as I thought."

Réal felt a twinge of annoyance that his marvelous news should have been foreseen. "Some of the clothing of Miss Sutton, they are *chez* Monsieur Pilgrim. This also I checked, not using the *passepartout*, but speaking with his valet." This was a task invented by Réal himself. He slid a sharp glance to Belami, hoping to read astonished gratification on his face but finding only a pensive look.

"Mrs. Pilgrim will leave them behind. She'll have no further use for them."

"Only the one blue dress is all the trousseau she has brang to him. What else she wears was still with her mother. Many of these items are gone away," he pointed out.

Belami considered this a moment. "Perhaps she plans to be Miss Sutton again, or Miss Somebody Else. Did you go over the Suttons' apartment closely?"

"With the fine-tooth comb. This I find under the table," he said, and produced his *coup de grâce*. It was a wrinkled receipt from Cerboni to Mrs. Sutton for a diamond necklace, priced at nine thousand guineas, paid for in English gold coins. Réal stood with bated breath, expecting to see his master break into shouts of delight.

Belami just glanced at it. "Nine thousand, eh? That must be all the counterfeit money they had. I wondered at Elvira bothering to haggle the man down. Well done, Réal," he added, but it wasn't said in the proper tone. Réal had failed to astound, and dissatisfaction coiled like a snake in his breast.

"Now what jobs I am to do?" he asked, hoping to pull victory from the ashes yet.

Belami touched his finger to chin while he conjectured what had to be done. "Elvira's wearing the diamond necklace. I begin to see all my planning and arranging of second disguises was unnecessary. Carlotta can't demand the necklace till Elvira's leaving, or we'd notice it was missing. What we do, Réal, is circulate, keeping an eye on Elvira and Contessa Ginnasi. When Elvira starts making noises about leaving, we can't lose sight of them. The exchange won't take a minute."

"This is true." Réal nodded, but he saw no way to distinguish himself in the business. "I shall keep my eyes very much busy," he decided, and stationed himself at the door, arms crossed, to guard the suspects.

The dance finished and Lucy went to sit with her mother and Elvira. Within thirty seconds, Deirdre strolled along beside them. Belami caught her eye, and she joined him. He hastily explained his deductions. "It may happen sooner than you think," she said. "Pronto's been nagging Elvira to go home. She mentioned a moment ago that she has a headache, but she just wanted to lie down for a half hour. The conte offered to send for a headache powder. She said she'd wait a moment. I noticed she kept glancing toward Carlotta."

"Then they're getting ready for the swap. We should soon see Carlotta speak to a couple of gentlemen in black dominoes—she's brought in some police. They'll be kept beyond range of her voice, but close enough that she can call for help if needed. Trust me."

They scanned the floor for Carlotta. She looked around and spoke to one man wearing a black domino. The man walked away rather quickly and spoke to another. Carlotta watched them, then strolled nonchalantly toward the conte, who was sitting with the duchess and all the Suttons. She smiled and chatted a moment with her husband, then turned to Elvira. Elvira touched her hand to her head. Carlotta said something, then Elvira rose and left the room.

Carlotta remained, chatting to her conte. "She's not going!" Deirdre exclaimed.

"Patience, my dear. They don't want to make it obvious." A guest came along and asked Carlotta for the next dance. She rose, and they began walking to the floor. "You must be wrong, Dick," Deirdre said.

Just as the sets were beginning to form, Carlotta spoke to her partner and walked away, out the door after Elvira.

"I knew it," Dick said softly. The tight knot in his stomach eased to satisfaction.

Deirdre felt as though a herd of wild horses had invaded her insides. She looked toward Dick, a frightened shadow in her eyes. He smiled with infinite satisfaction. "This is it!" he said softly.

Chapter Seventeen

By the time Belami and Deirdre got to the doorway, Carlotta and Elvira had disappeared, but Réal stood bristling with eagerness.

"Which way did they go?" Belami demanded.

Réal pointed down the hall, to the left. "They went in at the third door."

"The music room," Deirdre said.

"You stay here and don't let anyone else join us," Belami said, and began hastening toward the door. He saw a pair of black dominoes loitering at the other end of the hall.

Réal stood like a pointer dog, rigidly alert, staring after his master. He didn't see Pronto coming from the ballroom. Deirdre saw him and was filled with apprehension.

"*Bonsoiro*, Deirdre," he said. "We didn't have our dance yet. Afraid I'll have to disappoint you tonight. I'm taking Elvira home to—heh, heh. Bit of a headache actually. No offense, m'dear. She said to meet her here in half an hour."

"She's—she's upstairs," Deirdre lied quickly. "She's only been gone a moment, Pronto. You're early."

"This ain't the time to be late. Hope the headache powder works. I'll just go and get the other ladies' wraps. The Suttons have decided to come home with us."

Deirdre scrambled in her mind to detain him a moment.

194

"How will you get home? You dismissed your boat, I think?"

"No problem. Carlotta offered the use of hers. Stands to reason she won't need it. She's already home. *'Scusomoi.* I'd best get those wraps."

"There's no hurry," Deirdre said. "The other ladies aren't here yet. I haven't had an opportunity to congratulate you, Pronto."

"Course you have. Wished me happy a dozen times."

"I mean on your costume," she invented. "So clever. Where did you get it?"

"Off the bed. Cut a hole in the sheet, you see, and just slid it over my head. Got the wig and beard at the costume shop where Elvira got her outfit. Now I really must—"

Deirdre reached for his arm to detain him. As she glanced down the hall, she saw Dick stood at the doorway, listening. The two policemen were watching him closely, but their orders were apparently not to move unless the contessa called them.

"You haven't complimented me on my outfit," she said, smiling to distract him.

"Very nice. Very nice. And now I—"

"It's a shepherdess costume," she said, turning him from the doorway by a gentle pressure on his arm. "I'm the one who should be carrying the crook. Did King Solomon use a crook?"

"Ain't a crook. It's a staff. All old gaffers use 'em. Charney does. Solomon did, I daresay."

Her delaying devices began to wear thin. "It's a very nice staff," she said.

Pronto shook his head sadly. "I know I used to roll my eyes at you when you and Dick was on the outs, Deirdre, but it's too late for us now. You must remember I'm a married man now. Elvira's waiting for me. She'd have my head on a pole if she caught me flirting with you."

"She's not waiting for you. She's lying down with a headache. Half an hour, she said."

195

"In sickness and in health. You heard the vows. A husband's place is by his wife's side. Just let go of my arm."
He firmly removed her fingers and began walking down the hall. Deirdre looked helplessly, then began to follow him.

"She's upstairs," she said.

"I'm going to say good night to Dick. See him down the hall there."

While this was going forth, Belami stood with his ear to the door, listening. The door was not on the catch. He could see a line of light coming from the room and hear quite well.

"Here's the money," Elvira said. "Where are the dies?"

"I'll examine the money first," Carlotta answered. "I wouldn't want any of your homemade efforts, Mrs. Pilgrim."

"It's legitimate Italian paper money," Elvira said.

"So I see, but it's not very much money, is it?"

"It's worth a thousand pounds, the price agreed on."

"That was several days ago. I've been offered more than twice that amount since then. Lord Belami was exceedingly eager to get hold of this evidence. The penalty for counterfeiting is harsh in England. Hanging, I believe," she taunted.

"It's all I have."

"I'm not difficult to deal with. I'll take legal tender. Say—your new necklace?"

Belami heard a sharp intake of breath from Elvira. He pushed the door open a small crack, fearing Carlotta might find her life threatened. But Elvira was just looking, with a cold, angry face, as Carlotta spoke on. "It's that or I turn you over to the police, Mrs. Pilgrim. Right here, in public, at my ball. I always take the precaution of having a few policemen attend to protect my guests' jewelry. The men are within shouting distance. Come now, my dear, don't sulk. You'll have your dies back and can make up a new batch of money."

"You daren't call the police," Elvira said. "I'll tell them you stole my dies."

"Are you sure you want to publicly claim possession of counterfeiting equipment? And who do you think the police will protect? A counterfeiter, a foreigner in the country, or the Contessa Ginnasi—and Lord Belami and the duchess of Charney?"

Belami couldn't see much—just a line of Carlotta's back behind the organ screen. He heard a rustle, then a short shriek. He saw Carlotta move violently and pushed open the door. Elvira had one hand on Carlotta's shoulder, the other hand was raised, as if to strike her. Something glittered in Elvira's raised hand. In an instant he saw it was a small dagger and realized that swooshing sound had been caused by Elvira's pulling the dagger from the folds of her gown.

There was a sudden convergence of people at the open doorway. The Italian police heard the scream and came running. Pronto heard it and pelted forward, Deirdre fast behind him. Réal wasn't about to be left out of such excitement and elbowed them all aside, as he couldn't see over their shoulders. He had a prime view of his master performing an act as heinous as murder. Belami raised his closed fist and lashed out to strike a crushing blow on the jaw of a very beautiful lady, who was the bride of his best friend. Elvira went reeling against the organ. *"Sacrebleu. Il est complètement fou!"* Réal gasped.

Pronto stared, speechless. He felt he had fallen into a nightmare. This couldn't be happening. Dick punching a lady—*his* lady! Even as he watched, Dick leaned over her inert form and began pulling her from the floor, looking as though he meant to land her another facer. Pronto raised his staff and brought it down with all his force on Belami's skull. A ringing, hollow sound filled the room and Belami fell on top of Elvira. Pronto knew perfectly well he'd killed his best friend. He was surprised to hear Dick's head was hollow. He was sure it would be full of brains. He was relieved to remember it was all just a nightmare.

Deirdre screamed like a banshee. She couldn't believe Dick had struck a lady either, but of greater horror was that Pronto had possibly rendered Dick a moonling for life. She wrenched the staff from Pronto but hadn't the strength to lift it. Her arms had turned to string—limp, useless. Carlotta surveyed the debacle and emitted a low, gurgling laugh.

She took the two policemen by the arms and pushed them out the door, speaking in Italian. "This is a purely domestic squabble. I shan't be requiring your services at the moment. Do go and have a glass of wine. No, on second thought, go and keep an eye on the English ladies, Mrs. Sutton and her daughter. Don't let them leave." Then she closed the door.

Réal observed the scene and saw a way to polish his tarnished reputation. Monsieur Pilgrim had spoken of using the contessa's gondola, but the master thought otherwise. There might be an enemy gondola at the landing, ready to carry the miscreants off. If this was the case, Nick, the *vaurien*, had not discovered it. He went hurrying off to the dock.

Belami was the first to recover. He shook his head and stared up into the petrified face of Pronto Pilgrim. A pair of blue eyes stared back of him, full of outraged accusation. "Pronto, it's not what you think," he said.

"I ain't blind. I know what I saw. You'll be hearing from my second, sir." He elbowed Belami aside and lifted Elvira's head tenderly into his arms. "Wine—somebody bring wine," he ordered. No one moved.

"That's Claude Jalbert," Belami said, pointing at the body in Pronto's arms.

Pronto shook his head and looked at Deirdre. "I've addled his brains with that blow."

Deirdre looked uncertainly from Elvira to Dick. Was

198

Dick deranged? She went and studied Elvira's still face. In repose, and lying down, the jaw assumed a larger proportion than before. The nose appeared more masculine from this position.

"It's true," Dick assured them all.

It was Carlotta who kept her head. "That should be easy enough to verify," she said, and bent over Elvira's inert form to begin unfastening the bosom of her gown. Pronto pushed her aside roughly. His hands were stroking Elvira's black hair. He slid a look to where Carlotta had loosened the gown and noticed something amiss. Carlotta's lovely bosoms had gone awry. One had fallen down under her armpit, the other had moved to the middle of her chest. "Egad! There's something havey-cavey going on here."

Elvira opened her eyes and let off a string of curses in a guttural voice never heard to utter from her lips before. Pronto was thrown aside, where he stumbled to his feet, frowning in consternation beneath his wig, which was sliding to one side. Claude leaped to his feet and grabbed Pronto in front of him. The dagger was still in his hand. He pushed the point of it against Pronto's neck. "One move and I kill this bastard," he growled. "I've been wanting to long enough."

Deirdre felt Belami's fingers reach surreptitiously for hers. He removed the crook from her hand, and in an instant it flashed in the air, the hook catching on Claude's wrist and jerking it violently. The dagger fell, and before it reached the floor, Belami was on top of Claude, his fingers around his throat. She was convinced now that Elvira was Claude, but some sense of horror lingered to see Dick fighting with what still looked like a lady.

"Someone stop him!" Carlotta shrieked. "I don't want a murder at my ball!"

Deirdre pulled Belami up from the floor, where Claude now lay motionless. Carlotta bent over, her back carefully angled to hide what she was up to, while she pretended to be reviving him. While the others argued amongst them-

199

selves, Carlotta carefully removed the diamonds from Claude's neck. She put them in her reticule and pulled Claude's shawl up around his throat to conceal the loss. In the excitement of the moment, no one was likely to notice.

Réal was the first one to come to the door. He looked around and announced, "I have the Styger tied up. Nick, blind h'as well as stupid, let him land at the dock. He is easily fooled, that one. Styger is wearing the Italian gondolier's hat and coat. Poof!" he said with disdain, to show his opinion of such a paltry attempt at disguise. "I ask Styger what time it is, and he say *in English* he don't know. I dunk him quick into the water, hit him with the oar, and bind him up in the boat."

"Excellent work, Réal," Belami complimented.

"You want I should call the policemans now?"

"Yes, if you please," Carlotta said. "I want this rubbish removed from my home as quickly as possible. Tell them to take Mrs. Sutton and Miss Lucy out with them. I shall fetch some wine. I'm sure we're all faint from excitement." She took her reticule with her and tossed the diamonds into a large urn that stood in the hallway, before returning with the wine. Réal, walking silently behind her, watched this move. His heart fluttered with a nearly unbearable excitement. He called the police. One officer had taken the Sutton ladies into custody. Réal directed him to take them outside and wait. Before rejoining the gathering, Réal retrieved the diamonds and put them in his pocket.

When Carlotta returned with the wine, Claude began to revive and made a gargling sound, clutching at his throat and pointing to her.

"Shouldn't he be bound and gagged?" Carlotta suggested. She handed Pronto the wine tray and undertook to perform the chore herself, using a scarf for the hands. But even before they were secure, she tightly tied her handkerchief around Claude's mouth to prevent his complaining about losing the necklace. Pronto poured himself a stout restorative and gulped. Thank God it was only a nightmare, but Elvira looked very real, lying there on the floor with her eyes bulging in vexation, as though she were trying to tell him something. Wanting a glass of wine, very likely. No point wasting wine on a nightmare. He poured himself another glass and drank thirstily. It was beginning to be borne in on him that if this wasn't a nightmare, he was in a bit of an embarrassing situation.

"There's a set of counterfeit dies here somewhere that we'll need for evidence," Belami said to the policemen, and began looking around for them. They had fallen to the floor. He explained briefly who the prisoners were, and that they should be kept under close guard. "I'll go down to the station in the morning and clear up any details," he said. "You'll want to get in touch with Cerboni, the jeweler from the Merceria, and keep the counterfeit money he has for evidence as well. We'll contact Hoppner, the British consul. He'll arrange safe passage to England for the Jalberts."

The prisoner was led out the door. Carlotta drew a contented sigh. "I must return to my party. The conte will be wondering what has happened to me. So kind of you to confine this little tempest to a teapot, Belami. Why, it's enough to ruin a lady's reputation, inviting a parcel of thieves to her party." She laughed gaily and returned to the ball.

Pronto poured his third glass of wine and cast a woebegone eye on Belami. Dick knew his friend was about to become thoroughly disguised. It seemed the best occupation for him, till he could invent a story to cover Pronto's shame.

"A nightmare," Pronto mumbled, and staggered to a chair.

"The nightmare's over, Pronto," Deirdre said gently.

Pronto grabbed her hand. "Sorry if I was brusque to you before, Deirdre. A very nice outfit you're wearing. You're right about the shepherd's staff. You can have it."

His wig suddenly felt very warm. It made his head itchy, too. He pulled it off and tossed it to the floor. What remained of his luxuriant brown hair was all tousled. With his eyes beginning to shut, he looked remarkably like a bedlamite in his white sheet and beard.

"Why don't you take Pronto up to bed, Réal?" Belami suggested. "You can put him in my room. I'll get Carlotta to give me another room tonight."

It proved to be a job for more than one man, so Belami went with them. Deirdre stayed alone in the room, thinking over the night's activities. Like Dick, she too was busy inventing a story to help mitigate Pronto's embarrassment. Yet she was happy to learn Pronto wasn't really married to Elvira Sutton, né Claude Jalbert. How had Dick figured it out? She blushed to remember the many intimate conversations she had enjoyed with Claude when he was being Elvira. Claude must be married to Lucy—which would explain Lucy's sulky behavior when Elvira spent too much time with herself. She went scrupulously over their friendship, and while there was much to embarrass her, she had not been compromised.

It was a quarter of an hour before Belami returned to Deirdre. "Is he all right?" was her first question.

"He's a million miles from all right, and will be worse tomorrow when he discovers his dilemma is not a nightmare."

"You'll have to think of something to help him, Dick."

"I'll work on it tonight. God, I'm glad it's over. When I hit Claude and he crumpled over like a reed, I had the terrible feeling he really was a woman. He's very slight in build, of course, which is the only reason he could carry off this masquerade. Slight, and fair in complexion. That black hair is dyed, I think. The newspapers said fair—and those delicate, fair-haired men have very little in the way of a beard. The truth didn't hit me till this afternoon at the wedding, when I saw that nick on his jaw, just where the razor often catches. Then I began remembering other

202

things." He smiled and shook his head. "Did you know the Queen of Sheba had hairy legs?"

"What?"

"She had; it's mentioned in the Koran. And Pronto said that Elvira had hairy legs. Suspiciously smooth arms though. I expect she—he shaved them."

"Carlotta noticed his waist was large, when we were trying on costumes. And Elvira would only let Lucy help her undress. That's why they were giggling behind the screen."

"There were dozens of little clues. I noticed at the wedding that her ring was enormous. I remember Elvira hopping to open a door for the ladies, like a regular gentleman. And, of course, most telling of all, she had no use for me," he added quizzingly, "nor I for her, if it comes to that."

Deirdre patted her hair and smiled. "True. Elvira was particularly fond of me, ac-tually."

"I assume he behaved himself, or you would have twigged to it that Elvira was no lady?"

"What I am wondering is how Pronto didn't realize it."

"He never got anywhere near her. She dosed him with laudanum this afternoon after the wedding."

"I mean all the time he was courting her."

"He said she was shy, but the way he described, it sounded more like frigid to me. He did no more than pat her here and there. Why do I keep calling Claude her, I wonder? I remember he also said her muscle tone was very firm. There were dozens of clues staring us in the face. I took the notion she was Claude's wife, and thinking I had plumbed her secret, I looked no further."

Deirdre nodded. "We were always wondering where Claude was through all this business. Now we know."

"If we had caught on to that, the explanation would have been really simple, as true solutions usually are. You said yourself it would make more sense if it were Claude and Lucy with Mrs. Sutton, instead of Elvira and Lucy. It explains how he got back into the Léon Bianco without being recognized the day he went off to Mira. He went to the inn and changed into his male's outfit. It was a young man who called on Styger at Mira and later returned to the hotel in Venice."

"Then he knew he was being followed?"

"He might have spotted Réal or Nick lingering around the hotel. He knew I suspected him of being involved with the Jalberts in any case. So he changed his sex to make following his movements more difficult when he went to Styger. Réal even mentioned finding a razor in the ladies' rooms—not in the box of paints, but by the water pitcher. And I, like a fool, only thought Claude had been visiting."

"It's odd that Claude went so far as to actually marry Pronto." Deirdre frowned. "I mean I can understand letting him court her—No, I can't though."

"At the risk of tooting my own horn, that may have had something to do with me. As long ago as in Paris, Elvira knew I was suspicious. She could learn though Pronto what I was up to. And, of course, the great romance brought some pretty baubles her way—the diamond ring, the emerald brooch, the passport. I think the Jalberts intended to shear off before Saturday, but when Carlotta got hold of their dies, she was calling the tune. The wedding was arranged, and to cancel it would have caused suspicion. Pronto kept urging the wedding forward. Besides, I think Claude wanted to make Pronto look a perfect fool. He must have been pushed to the edge of fury by Pronto hanging on to him like a leech. It was a fiendish revenge."

"Poor Pronto won't be able to hold up his head if this story gets out."

"It won't," Dick said firmly. "No one knows but us and Carlotta."

"He'll blab it himself," Deirdre pointed out. "What we should do is convince him it never happened. He half thinks it was all a nightmare." She noticed Belami wasn't listening to her. He sat, staring into a corner with a frown on his brow.

"What is it?" she asked.

"Carlotta. Did you notice how broadly she was smiling when the Jalberts were dragged away? Why should she have been so happy? I wager she pocketed the thousand pounds Claude was supposed to be paying her for the dies. That was their agreed price."

He rose and began looking around the floor for the money. "This is where they were talking. She took the money from him—I seem to remember seeing the envelope fall when Claude drew the knife on her. Ah, here it is!" he said, and lifted the envelope from the floor. The bills were still stuffed inside.

"She was just laughing to discover Elvira was a man."

"No reason that should set her to grinning. She was happy, Deirdre. She was radiant. The diamonds!"

"There's no way she could have gotten them. We were all in the room, watching her."

"Not very closely. Didn't you notice how Claude was gagging, trying to tell us something. I'm going to the police headquarters and make sure they got the diamonds."

He opened the door and nearly fell over Réal, who had been listening at the keyhole. "Réal, you can go for me. You overheard what we were saying?" he asked, which brought Réal to bristling indignation.

"I am just this instant arriving!" Réal insisted.

"From where?"

Réal wished to prolong his glory. "From deep thinkings," he announced, and tapped his forehead. "I am wondering if you remembered to give to the police the diamond necklace which Madame Pilgrim was not wearing when she is taken away."

"He wasn't wearing it?" Belami asked. "Are you sure?"

"But yes. When I come back from capturing Styger all by myself, I see at once the necklace is not on the neck as it was when I leave. You do not notice this?'' Réal asked, with a condescending look. ''Lord Belami, who is the great investigator of crimes doesn't notice the diamond necklace is missing?''

''By God, no. Carlotta!'' He glanced at Réal. Seeing the flush of victory on that saturnine face, he held out his hand.

With a dismissing shrug, Réal dropped the puddle of diamonds into it. ''Lucky it is one of us keeps the eyes open.''

''Where'd you get it?'' Belami asked, but he asked in the beloved tone of admiration used by one expert to another.

''From the jug in the hallway where the contessa conceals it when she goes off for wine, which she do not drink after getting it. I noticed this, me.''

Deirdre felt Dick was not being sufficiently effusive and said, ''Réal, you're a wonder! I wager Cerboni will offer a reward for the diamonds' recovery.''

Praise was all the reward Réal wanted. He looked hopefully to his master. ''Good work, Réal. What would we do without you?'' Belami said, and clapped him on the shoulder.

Réal smiled modestly. ''All in the day's work,'' he said, with a nonchalant toss of his shoulders.

It was well the door was open and Réal was there to play propriety when the duchess of Charney came storming in. She glared first at Belami, then her niece. ''I hear some very strange rumors running around the ball,'' she announced. ''I daresay you are at the bottom of them, Belami. What's afoot? The Suttons have left, and someone said Pilgrim was taken to bed drunk. A fine thing, and this his wedding night.''

''It's true there was a little altercation,'' Belami said discreetly. ''Something to do with the Suttons having paid for Elvira's necklace with counterfeit money. In fact, the Suttons are the Jalbert gang.''

206

"What the devil is the Jalbert gang?" she demanded. So he told her. She listened with varying emotions, not least amongst them regret that she might have got hold of some of that counterfeit money herself had she had her wits about her. There was much in his story to please her, as it gave her a whole battery of reasons to deride this handsome young jackanapes and send him packing.

"Fine work. You knew all along the Suttons are thieving criminals and hadn't the decency to tell us. You let Deirdre and myself be exposed to them. We might have been robbed or killed in our beds."

"The Jalberts are counterfeiters, not murderers. And if you will recall, your grace, all I did was to arrange a carriage for them. It is yourself who befriended them."

As this was true, the duchess turned to another imagined victim. "And you set young Pilgrim on to them to find them out," she charged. "A fine way to treat a friend. The man will look an utter jackass when word gets about you married him off to a man. That was doing it a deal too brown, sir."

"It wasn't like that," Deirdre objected.

She was hard pressed to account for the little smile that lit Dick's eyes. "More or less like that, but Pronto quite insisted on involving himself."

"Dick! Pronto didn't—"

"Of course he didn't want to do it," Charney interjected. "You may have such mawworms as Pilgrim and the contessa dancing to your tune, Belami, but I take leave to tell you I am not one of your puppets. Dinner is being served, Deirdre. Come along. I have found an extremely eligible partner for you. A marchese, very old Italian family, the Laderchis. The conte recommends him highly. He is a good friend of the Ginnasis."

"Yes, you run along, Deirdre," Belami said. She tossed a pout over her shoulder as she left. "I have to take these diamonds to the police station. I'll see you tomorrow morning."

207

Belami did as he said. As Réal sped him across the canal, Belami was deep in thought. Rescuing Pronto from disgrace was the more exigent matter. And as soon as he'd done that, he'd think of some way to beguile that old Tartar, Charney.

Chapter Eighteen

It was late the next morning when the duchess came tottering along the hall from her bedchamber to the staircase. She leaned on Deirdre's arm, wondering why the chit was suddenly stepping up the pace. She could hear nothing yet, but was familiar with Deirdre's stunt of trying to rush her out of the way of any interesting doings, particularly when they involved Belami. What caused Miss Gower's haste was a view of the contessa storming into a bedchamber. It was an unused room so far as her grace knew, for while she seldom missed a beat, she was unaware that Dick had switched rooms the night before.

As they passed the door, however, Charney heard that dulcet voice she knew and loathed. "Good morning, Carlotta," Belami said. The duchess gave up any pretense of doing anything but eavesdropping. Had her spine been less rachitic, she would have leaned over and put her ear to the door. Failing this flexibility, she shuffled closer and listened, motioning Deirdre to silence with a bat of her hand. Deirdre was of two minds. She was nearly as eager to overhear the conversation as to prevent her aunt from doing so.

"Where is it?" they heard the contessa demand imperiously. This was neither the tone nor the speech Charney expected, but she listened avidly.

Deirdre knew Dick was enjoying himself when he answered in his affected drawl. She could see in her mind's eye the lift of his brow, the flash of amusement in his dark eyes. "Are you referring to the money Claude left behind for the dies or to the diamond necklace?"

Neither of the listening ladies was familiar with gutter Italian, but they realized from the contessa's voice that she was extremely irritated. "I'm referring to my necklace."

"The pretty Strass glass beads you wore last night, Carlotta, or the diamond necklace you purloined?"

"I knew it!" Charney grinned. "The strumpet has stolen the conte's diamonds!"

"It's bought and paid for," Carlotta replied.

"Paid for with counterfeit coin, and even that not paid by you. What makes you think you should have it?"

"Because I was the only one who had the wits to make off with it."

"Another adage blown to bits," Belami drawled. "There is no honor amongst thieves after all."

"I have as much right to it as you. Where did you hide it?" Carlotta demanded.

"I hid it at the police station last night. Cerboni came down and collected it. If you have your heart set on stealing it, you'll have to break into his shop. That should pose no problem to one of your talents, Contessa."

"Get out of my house. Get out this instant, and take that gaggle of noble geese with you!"

"Our rent is paid till the end of the month," Belami reminded her.

"Rent?" the duchess demanded. She spoke to Deirdre, but her voice was rather carrying. Deirdre tried to pull her aunt away. "Do you mean to tell me the jackanapes has paid for our rack and manger, and here I have been making myself a servant to that bath-chair antique of a conte?"

"Shh, they'll hear you, Auntie," Deirdre said.

The duchess put her ear to the door to hear the contessa's reply. "You've got the money Claude gave me for the dies. Let that be your refund. And don't think to apply to

210

Guy for permission to stay. I pay the bills in this mausoleum. What I say goes. And I say I want you out of my house today.''

There was a patter of footfalls indicating that Carlotta was approaching the door. Deirdre hastily pulled her aunt toward the staircase, narrowly avoiding collision as the contessa came pelting out. ''That goes for you, too, your grace,'' Carlotta snipped.

Charney shook her head sadly. ''I recognized that one for a trollop the minute I laid eyes on her. Common as clay. Come along, Deirdre, I shall have my gruel, as it's bought and paid for. Were you aware Belami was footing the bill for us here?''

Deirdre knew her aunt's dislike of what she called ''betrayal'' and claimed ignorance. ''I had no idea. So generous of him.''

''Hmph. I'm surprised he hasn't thrown it in our faces before now. No doubt he'll present me with a bill when he learns his ruse didn't work, and he has not got my permission to court you.'' This last was said with a commanding glare.

''He hasn't been courting me.''

''Some gentlemen don't know when a treasure is staring them in the face. He'd rather carry on with that thieving baggage. What's all this about her trying to steal Elvira's necklace?''

While the duchess ate her gruel, Deirdre gave her a brief account of the affair of the necklace. Charney listened with some interest, but her mind began wandering off to other matters. It would be a touch uncomfortable continuing on here with Carlotta in the boughs. She could always threaten to tell the conte his wife had stolen the Ginnasi diamonds, but the conte had an inexplicable fondness for his trollop, and might not be so severe as she could wish. Feelers had been put out to friends and relatives of the conte, but no offers had been received yet to visit other noble Italian homes at no cost. Having come this far, her grace was not averse to seeing more of Italy. Rome, for instance, ought to be worth a look. One could obviously disparage the papists more expertly if she had been to Rome and seen their depravity with her own eyes.

"Where does Belami go from here?" she asked Deirdre.

"I expect he'll go to Ravenna next, then down the peninsula south to Naples. He has friends all along the way who will be waiting to receive him," she added cunningly.

With very little knowledge of geography, Charney said, "Then we shall go to Rome to avoid him. I'll speak to the conte after breakfast and get letters of introduction along our way."

As soon as the duchess had finished eating, she went in search of the conte. Deirdre was about to go upstairs when she heard Belami's voice approaching the breakfast room. Looking up, she saw Dick and a very chastened Pronto enter. She looked to Dick, hoping for a clue as to how she should behave.

"Good morning," she said.

Behind Pronto's back, Dick winked. She understood from this that he had conjured up some face-saving device for his friend and waited eagerly to discover what it could be.

Pronto sat down and said, "G'day, Deirdre. I expect you're surprised to see me and Dick still alive. About the duel—called it off. Heat of the moment, lost my head. Apologized."

"I'm so glad," Deirdre said. "Do you want some coffee?"

"Hit the spot," Pronto agreed, and passed his cup.

She saw Dick preparing a speech and listened to learn what tack she should take. "We've just been going over the case," Belami began. "Pronto certainly excelled himself this time." Deirdre stared, astonished that Dick should state his friend's folly so bluntly. "Yes indeed, we would never have solved this one without his help."

212

"Of course," Deirdre said in relieved confusion.

"His pretending to be taken in by Claude's disguise was a master stroke. Why, for a few days there, he even fooled me."

"Me, too," Pronto admitted.

"Of course he knew all along, but I think you might have told me in so many words, Pronto. I didn't pick up on your clues about his hairy ankles and hard muscles. Pronto used the ploy of pretending to be in love with Elvira to work his way into her confidence," he explained to Deirdre.

"It made it easier to follow her, too," she added, getting into the swing of it.

"And left me free to follow other clues," Belami said.

"I ain't quite sure yet why I went ahead and married her," Pronto admitted, and looked hopefully to hear an explanation of this piece of ingenuity.

"You couldn't let Claude realize you were on to him," Belami explained. "You had to lull his suspicions so he wouldn't take fright and escape before we sprung the trap."

Pronto cast a wary eye at Deirdre to see how this went down with an unbiased audience. He saw only admiring acceptance and felt encouraged. "I did it all without even knowing I was doing it. Dick explained it to me this morning."

Belami rushed to his assistance. "At a deeper level, of course, he knew perfectly well Elvira was a man. He even compared her to Portia, in *The Merchant of Venice*. You remember how she posed as a judge. Strange how the mind works, is it not?"

"Incredible," Pronto agreed.

Deirdre bit back a smile, and finally had to resort to her coffee cup when she caught Dick's fiercely condemning eye. Belami continued to elaborate on his theme. "Pronto was always careful to include the mother and Lucy on his expeditions. His deeper mind had a secret *tendre* for Lucy,

I believe. Remember at Paris, Pronto, you were quite taken with her, and remarked a few times that Elvira was too bold to suit you—too mannish is what you meant. That long ago you sensed she wasn't a real woman, and knew you were safe to associate with her, without falling into parson's mousetrap. Once you realized this, you asked yourself, why not pretend to love her, and see what you could discover?''

"Rhymes," Pronto said. "Love her—discover. You didn't realize you was doing it. Deeper mind at work."

"I always felt I had the heart of a poet," Belami admitted modestly.

"This certainly proves I have the heart of an investigator. Getting on with the job the whole time," Pronto said, shaking his head at his cleverness.

Before they got into any deeper water, Belami decided it was time to widen the topic of conversation. "You and I both coming to Italy is another example of the deeper mind at work," he began, turning his attention to Deirdre. "Both denying we came because we were to have had our honeymoon here. Something in our deeper minds and hearts drew us hither."

"Same with me and Elvira." Pronto nodded. "Hither and thither, both drawn to Venice. One thing does bother me though, Dick," he said. Belami moved uncomfortably in his seat, wondering what new leaps of imagination would be called for. "About that marriage—am I married to Claude? Thing is—he's married already. Bigamist."

Belami breathed a sigh of relief. "No such a thing. If Claude were a woman, which of course you knew all along he was not, then *he* would be a bigamist."

"She," Pronto corrected. "If he was Elvira, he'd be a she. Married to Lucy. There's odd twists in that lad."

"If Pronto were a woman, is what you meant," Deirdre said.

"Precisely," Belami agreed. "In any case, it is the person who has two spouses who is the bigamist, not the two partners. Your marriage is null and void. It never existed."

"Never was consummated either," Pronto assured him. "Never came anywhere near it. The deeper mind at work, and that strong Italian wine. All the same, Dick—you, too, Deirdre, I'd appreciate it if you didn't tell anyone at home about the wedding. Some folks wouldn't realize about my deeper mind. Think I was a bit of a dupe."

"Your ingenuity ought to be shouted from the rooftops, Pronto," Dick said, "but if you are so self-effacing you want to keep it secret, it's fine with me."

"I shan't breathe a word," Deirdre added.

"I hope Charney keeps her mouth shut," Pronto muttered. "Where's she off to next, Deirdre?"

"Rome." Deirdre looked hopefully to Belami. "Where are you two going? We heard Carlotta telling you to get out of the Palazzo Ginnasi."

"Rome is certainly on my itinerary," Belami said. "What sort of mood is Charney in this morning?"

"Foul," Deirdre replied, "and her mood will only deteriorate when she's put to the expense of hiring a carriage and paying hotel bills. I hope she doesn't decide to go home."

"Rome, eh?" Pronto asked. "Been wanting to get into the catacombs. Hear they're all the crack."

The duchess, passing by the door, saw her niece in conversation with two of the worst rattles ever to have come out of England and went to her rescue. She was in a wretched mood. The contessa had been busy turning the conte against her, with the result that her letters of introduction to potential hosts were limited to one, and he an old hermit who lived in a shack. That bit of spite was certainly the contessa's doings, which was not to say the letter wouldn't be used, and the shack, too, if it had more than one room.

The duchess went storming in. "I am amazed to see Mr. Pilgrim is still speaking to you, after the way you have

215

used him in this affair, Belami," she began. "Making him marry that wretched counterfeiter person."

"No such a thing," Pronto bristled. "All my own idea. I did it to trap the Jalberts."

Belami rose politely to his feet and offered the duchess a chair. She never could resist food or drink. The coffee still looked potable, and she accepted a cup from Deirdre.

"The credit for solving this case is entirely Pronto's," Belami said. "We were just discussing the continuing of our trip, your grace. It seems the contessa has houseguests arriving soon—today, in fact—and would appreciate it if we could see our way clear to leaving immediately."

"Hmph, houseguests, is it?" She admired a gentleman with polish, and it was well done of Belami to try to wrap the affair up in clean linen. "It's no bother to me. The stench of these canals is enough to turn a person's stomach. We are only too happy to escape."

"I shall be leaving early this afternoon," Belami continued. "The Marchese Benzoni has been importuning me to visit him. You are, perhaps, familiar with the marchese's estate, his Villa Benzoni? A marvelous example of Palladio's work—one of the show places of Italy, situated high in the Alban Hills, overlooking the sea from the western limits of his estate, and down on Rome from the north. A monstrous place—one needs a guide to tour it."

"How many rooms?" the duchess asked.

"I meant a guide is needed to tour the entire estate. The villa has only eighty or ninety rooms, I believe," Belami answered with a show of indifference. "The fountains alone are worth the trip—set in a vast parkland, with old Roman statuary. You really ought to arrange a tour of the place while you are at Rome, your grace. I hope you are able to find accommodations on such short notice. The vineyards are of particular note. The red wine especially is considered nonpareil," he added.

The duchess's mouth fairly watered at this description. She was torn between jealousy and hope. "You are for-

216

unate you had time to plan your trip well in advance. Deirdre and I dashed off in such a pelter I hadn't time to write to anyone.''

"Deeper mind," Pronto said obliquely. "You had nothing to say about it, your grace."

"What rubbish is this?" she asked.

Belami flew in to divert disaster. "I really ought to go and make arrangements for transportation to visit the marchese. Good horses are difficult to come by in Italy."

"Impossible," Pronto mumbled.

"We'll want a team of four, and a well-sprung traveling carriage," Belami tempted. "The trip will be expensive," he added mischievously, "but then the marchese will not hear of my undertaking any expense once I am with him. No doubt he will insist on putting his house in Rome at our disposal as well, Pronto. We shall want to spend considerable time in the city, admiring the architecture and statues."

It was too much to be borne. The duchess rose to her feet. "Come along, Deirdre. We must oversee Haskins's packing or there won't be a gown fit to be worn without pressing."

Deirdre rose and gave a hopeful smile to Dick. Before her aunt reached the bottom of the staircase, almost before they were out the door, the duchess stopped.

"This Marchese Benzoni fellow sounds extremely eligible," she said.

"Yes." Deirdre didn't mention the marchese was a seventy-year-old widower with children older than herself.

"Eighty or ninety rooms, and a house in Rome besides."

"And a vineyard."

"I shall have my four hogsheads from this curst spot shipped directly home. No point taking them to Rome with us. A good thing I settled it before the contessa turned her husband against us. The old fool refuses to believe she's stolen his necklace. I have been thinking, Deirdre,

217

how unpleasant it will be for us to travel to Rome without any male escorts.''

"We'll have to hire a guide, along with the carriage and team," Deirdre said slyly.

"I see no reason why Belami's servants should travel with him while we joggle along alone. There will be room in his carriage for the four of us—Pilgrim, himself, and us."

"He didn't invite us, Auntie."

"Have you lost the use of your wits? Get in there and conciliate him. Not too conciliating, mind! Don't let the wretched fellow get the notion I give the match my approval, for I don't, which is not to say his escort to Rome is worse than nothing. At least he speaks English, which is more than can be said for that moonling, Pilgrim."

"It would be nice if the marchese invited us to stay at his villa," Deirdre mentioned.

"He can hardly do less when we land at the door with Belami. We shall be utterly rolled up from the trip—anyone with a shred of human kindness in his veins would ask us to remain. I intend to arrive in a fit of vapors."

Deirdre bit her lip to hold in the shout of glee that rose up in her throat. "Shall I go back and be nice to Belami?"

"You'd best do it. He'll have to arrange carriages for our servants while he's at the travel office. And Deirdre—"

"Yes, Auntie?"

"Make sure you get your wedding gift back from Pilgrim. The little statue will make a suitable gift to Benzoni when we leave, in two or three months. A pity Belami had his goblets engraved or he could use his as well. He never uses his head. But then he is so rich it hardly matters."

"Yes, extremely eligible," Deirdre agreed blandly.

Charney's eyes narrowed to slits. Why must the world be so contrary? Why couldn't the decent boys be wealthy? "Go on, minx, before they get away."

The duchess's pace as she went to her room was hardly slower than Deirdre's dart back to the morning parlor. She

218

opened the door and flew in. "It worked! We're going with you, Dick!" She laughed and ran into his arms.

As Dick whirled her in the air, Pronto took a close look at her ankles. Not a hair to be seen, but he'd advise Dick to check her out and make sure she was a real girl before he married her. He felt a pinching ache in his heart to see the joy of the young lovers and rose to leave them some privacy.

"I'll be waiting in the gondola, Dick," he said. It must have been his deeper mind speaking. He didn't even know he was going to say that. Curst rum thing, the mind, knowing all along his Elvira was a man, when he hadn't a notion. Wouldn't do to admit it though. Might give folks some peculiar ideas.

When they were alone, Dick returned Deirdre's feet to the floor. "What did Charney say?"

"She said I was not to be too conciliating. We're not home free yet."

"Out of the woods is good enough for me." He folded her in his arms for a fierce kiss. Deirdre forgot her aunt's injunction in the fever of the moment. She became so conciliating that her mind reeled off to a bright future, which might really come after all.

After a long kiss, Belami released her. "I felt lost without you, darling. You know there was nothing between Carlotta and me. There was never anyone but you, from the moment I met you."

"I'll try not to be so jealous from now on."

"No, be jealous. It's flattering. I was jealous as Othello when I learned Elvira was a man. But don't be jealous if you catch me buttering up Charney. I must turn her up sweet—very soon. If my threadbare charms fail to persuade her, we'll count on Benzoni's wine and free lodgings to bring her around. Thank God for avarice."

"That sounds horrid, Dick!"

"It is. I'm a horrid man," he warned her with a perfectly charming smile, and pulled her into his arms to prove it.

219